D1009581

"I need a wife ... *wife. Will you marry me?"*

Ben needed a pretend wife, and he'd asked her. The pain was overwhelming. All the loneliness of the past three years, the secrets she had to hide, swept over her. Not daring to look at him, Janie turned and tried to hurry back into the kitchen.

But Ben moved more quickly than she'd expected. He grabbed her hand and pulled her into a chair next to him. Her body remembered his touch, and his heat seemed to flow around her, warming her in places she hadn't even realized were cold.

"Give me a chance to explain. I owe you that much, at least."

"You owe me nothing, Ben. I thought we'd already agreed on that."

"I wasn't talking about what happened that night. I meant I owed you an explanation now. You're my only hope of getting Rafael's adoption approved. If I marry anyone else, no one's going to buy it. Our 'nonromance' has taken on too much of a life."

All the memories of that one night came roaring back. Why did Ben have to offer her the one thing that she wanted in all the world, the one thing she couldn't have?

Dear Reader,

You'll be glad the kids are going back to school, leaving you time to read every one of this month's fabulous Silhouette Intimate Moments novels. And you'll want to start with *One Moment Past Midnight*, by multiaward-winning Emilie Richards. You'll be on the edge of your seat as Hannah Blackstone and her gorgeous neighbor, Quinn McDermott, go in search of Hannah's kidnapped daughter.

Elizabeth August makes a welcome return with *Logan's Bride*, a cop-meets-cop romance to make your heart beat just a little faster. With *The Marriage Protection Program*, Margaret Watson completes her CAMERON, UTAH miniseries, and a memorable finale it is. Historical author Lyn Stone has written her first contemporary romance, *Beauty and the Badge*, and you'll be glad to know she intends to keep setting stories in the present day. *Remembering Jake* is a twisty story of secrets and hidden identities from talented Cheryl Biggs. And finally, welcome Bonnie K. Winn, with *The Hijacked Wife*, a FAMILIES ARE FOREVER title.

And once you've finished these terrific novels, mark October on your calendar, because next month Rachel Lee is back, with the next installment of her top-selling CONARD COUNTY miniseries.

Enjoy!

Leslie Wainger

Leslie Wainger
Executive Senior Editor

Please address questions and book requests to:
Silhouette Reader Service
U.S.: 3010 Walden Ave., P.O. Box 1325, Buffalo, NY 14269
Canadian: P.O. Box 609, Fort Erie, Ont. L2A 5X3

THE MARRIAGE PROTECTION PROGRAM

MARGARET WATSON

INTIMATE MOMENTS®

Published by Silhouette Books

America's Publisher of Contemporary Romance

If you purchased this book without a cover you should be aware
that this book is stolen property. It was reported as "unsold and
destroyed" to the publisher, and neither the author nor the
publisher has received any payment for this "stripped book."

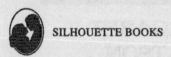

SILHOUETTE BOOKS

ISBN 0-373-07951-6

THE MARRIAGE PROTECTION PROGRAM

Copyright © 1999 by Margaret Watson

All rights reserved. Except for use in any review, the reproduction
or utilization of this work in whole or in part in any form by any
electronic, mechanical or other means, now known or hereafter
invented, including xerography, photocopying and recording, or in
any information storage or retrieval system, is forbidden without
the written permission of the editorial office, Silhouette Books,
300 East 42nd Street, New York, NY 10017 U.S.A.

All characters in this book have no existence outside the imagination of
the author and have no relation whatsoever to anyone bearing the same
name or names. They are not even distantly inspired by any individual
known or unknown to the author, and all incidents are pure invention.

This edition published by arrangement with Harlequin Books S.A.

® and TM are trademarks of Harlequin Books S.A., used under license.
Trademarks indicated with ® are registered in the United States Patent
and Trademark Office, the Canadian Trade Marks Office and in other
countries.

Visit us at www.romance.net

Printed in U.S.A.

Books by Margaret Watson

Silhouette Intimate Moments

An Innocent Man #636
An Honorable Man #708
To Save His Child #750
The Dark Side of the Moon #779
*Rodeo Man #873
*For the Children #886
*Cowboy with a Badge #904
*The Fugitive Bride #920
*The Marriage Protection Program #951

*Cameron, Utah

MARGARET WATSON

From the time she learned to read, Margaret could usually be found with her nose in a book. Her lifelong passion for reading led to her interest in writing, and now she's happily writing exactly the kind of stories she likes to read. Margaret is a veterinarian who lives in the Chicago suburbs with her husband and their three daughters. In her spare time she enjoys in-line skating, birdwatching and spending time with her family. Readers can write to Margaret at P.O. Box 2333, Naperville, IL 60567-2333.

For Chelsea. Your kindness, your loving heart and
your generosity of spirit are the joy of my life.
I am so proud of you. I love you.

Chapter 1

He was still there.

Janie Murphy looked out of the kitchen of Heaven on Seventh and saw that Deputy Sheriff Ben Jackson was the last person left in her restaurant. Even Mandy, her waitress, had gone home.

And Ben didn't look like he was in any hurry to leave.

She'd have to face him sometime, Janie told herself, and wiped suddenly damp hands on her dress. It might as well be now. At least there was no one else in the restaurant to hear them.

Fixing what she hoped was a pleasant, impersonal smile on her face, she pushed through the swinging door and grabbed a pot of coffee. "Do you need a refill?" she asked, standing at a careful distance from his table. The memories of what had happened the last time she got too close to Ben Jackson were still far too vivid.

Ben studied her, his dark eyes unreadable. "I've had about as much coffee tonight as one man can hold," he finally said.

She set the coffee down and turned back to him. "Then can I get you your check?" She tried not to sound too eager.

He shook his head. "I need to talk to you, Janie." He took a deep breath. Almost, she thought, as if he was bracing himself. "It's important."

Her heart skipped once, then began pounding in her chest. How many times had she imagined this scene? And how many times had she told herself that it wasn't possible?

"What can I do for you?" Her voice was polite, and she struggled to suppress all emotion.

He stared at her, holding her gaze with his own, as if he was gathering his words. There was at least three feet between them, including the table. But awareness of him rippled over her skin and hummed along her nerves. He surrounded her, his scent filling her head, and she throbbed as if she were standing next to an electrical current.

It happened every time she got too close to Ben. It was why she stayed so far away from him.

"I need a wife, Janie," he said abruptly, his voice harsh. "A temporary wife. Will you marry me?"

"What?" She grabbed the edge of the table to steady herself as she stared back at him. "What did you say?"

"I said I needed a wife, and I asked you if you'd marry me."

Anger stirred, and she welcomed it. "Is this supposed to be a joke?"

His eyes darkened. "I wish it was." He sighed. "I'm sorry, Janie, for springing it on you this way."

"Then why did you?" she asked, her voice fierce.

For the first time, she saw a flash of humor in his eyes. "I figured if I didn't get right to the point, you wouldn't stick around long enough to hear me out."

He needed a pretend wife. And he'd asked her.

The pain was overwhelming. It engulfed her, pounding at her with its unleashed fury. All the loneliness of the past three years, the secrets she had to hide, the essential unfairness of the events that had changed her life, swept over her. She opened her mouth to say something, but no sound came out. A huge lump lodged in her throat and threatened to grow. She couldn't, wouldn't break down in front of him. Not daring to look at him, she turned and tried to hurry back into the kitchen. She had to get away.

But Ben moved more quickly than she'd expected. He grabbed her hand and pulled her into a chair next to him, but he didn't let her go. Her hand trembled in his. Even after five months, her body remembered his touch. His hand was hard and calloused on hers, and his heat seemed to flow around her, warming her in places that she hadn't even realized were cold.

She stared at his hand, seeing his tanned skin dark against her paleness, seeing his long, narrow fingers circling her fingers easily. The treacherous memories swamped her, and waves of sensation crashed over her. She knew she had to move away, but for just a moment, she allowed herself to feel the pleasure, allowed herself to enjoy his touch.

As if he felt the same current as she did, his hand dropped away suddenly and he eased away from her. When he let her go, the emptiness inside her yawned wide again.

"At least hear me out, Janie. Give me a chance to explain. I owe you that much, at least."

She looked at him steadily, determined he wouldn't see the pain in her heart. "You owe me nothing, Ben. I thought we'd already agreed on that."

A dull red colored his cheeks. "I wasn't talking about what happened that night. I meant I owed you an explanation after asking you to marry me like that."

"I misunderstood," she muttered, cursing the color that rose in her own cheeks. She'd assumed that he'd forgotten all about that stolen night so long ago.

The silence throbbed with unasked and unanswered questions. Finally, Ben said, "Do you want to stay here?"

"No one will interrupt us."

Ben hesitated, then glanced at the windows in the front of the restaurant. "That's fine with me."

Janie followed the direction of his gaze, and realized that the darkness outside and the lights inside illuminated them to anyone passing by. For the first time since she'd started talking to Ben, she remembered why she didn't like standing in front of lighted windows. And was appalled that she'd been able to forget for so long.

"Maybe we'd better go somewhere else."

"Fine with me." Ben pushed away from the table, and waited while Janie turned off the lights in the restaurant. Before stepping out the door, she let her gaze drift over the shadows that lined the street. It was a ritual she had performed every night for the past three years, even though nothing had happened since she'd been in Cameron. But still she checked every night.

As she pulled the door shut behind her and locked the door, Ben put his hand on her arm again. And again she froze, unable to block out the sensations crashing through her. Before she could move away, he slipped her key chain out of her hand and stared down at it.

"What are you doing with pepper spray?" he asked, his voice hard. "You've been here long enough to know you won't need it in Cameron."

She grabbed the key chain out of his hand and dropped it in her pocket. "Old habits, I guess." She tried to keep her voice light, but wasn't sure she succeeded. "They're hard to break sometimes."

She wasn't sure if her trembling was because of his

touch, or the fact that he'd noticed the pepper spray. Afraid that the evening was getting out of control, she turned and started walking down the street.

"Do you want to come to my house, Janie, or shall we go to yours? It's up to you."

Neither, she wanted to shout. She didn't want to spend any time with Ben. She didn't want to listen to the reason for his outrageous question. She wanted only to get away from him and the painful memories his closeness aroused.

When she didn't answer, he slowed, then stopped and turned to face her. "Or maybe you'd like to go sit in the park."

For a moment, his face was filled with raw need and the memories of that night. His dark eyes flashed at her with desire barely held in check. *I was wrong,* was all she could think as she stared back at him. He hadn't forgotten anything. The memory still burned as bright in Ben as it did in her.

But she'd had five months of practice at ignoring the need that rose up inside her. "All right," she said abruptly, willing to do almost anything to break the spell that had her feet rooted to the pavement. "You can come to my house." Nothing could induce her to step foot into his house. She had worked too hard to suppress the memories of the one time she had been there.

"Thank you."

She didn't want to stand on the street, staring at him, for any longer than necessary. She needed to be in her own house, needed the reminders of what was at stake if she allowed herself to give in to her emotions.

Her house was only a few blocks from the restaurant, and she turned and began to walk again. Ben laid a hand on her arm, and she froze. Against her will, her nerves quivered and longing rose up deep inside her. It had been so long. And she was so lonely.

And she would stay that way. She stepped back, and his hand dropped away.

"I have my truck. Do you want a ride back to your house?"

The fear came rushing back then, all the lessons she'd been taught and all the warnings she'd received. *"Don't ever get into a car with anyone, even someone you think you know."*

"No thanks." She turned and started walking toward her house. "I spend too long inside the restaurant all day," she said lightly. "I enjoy walking, especially when the evening is as soft as this one."

He walked along with her, and after a moment, he said, equally lightly, "Now there's an expression I haven't heard about Utah. I didn't think anything about this state was soft."

"It may be a hard land, but the people have soft hearts," she said, watching the street in front of her rather than looking at him.

"You're right, but I didn't think you'd noticed."

Even without looking at him, she knew he'd moved closer to her. "What do you mean?" she asked, edging away.

"You're a figure of mystery in Cameron," he said. His voice was light and teasing on the surface, but she heard the questions underneath. "No one knows you very well, and you don't seem to have a lot of friends."

There was one night when you knew me very well. She couldn't suppress the thought, or the panic that stirred inside her at his words. He shouldn't have been able to read her so easily. *The best defense is a good offense.* "I could say the same thing about you."

"My job keeps me busy." There was no inflection in his voice.

"So does mine." She swallowed. "When would I have time for a social life?"

"I guess we're in the same boat, then," he said, and she felt the jaws of a trap easing closed around her. He'd deliberately steered the conversation in this direction. Now they were allies, she thought uneasily, two people with something in common. *But not marriage. Never that.*

They had nothing in common, she told herself firmly, in spite of that one magical night. That one mistake, she corrected harshly. And that's the way it had to stay.

As they turned the corner onto her street, she automatically dipped her hand into the pocket of her loose dress and let her fingers curl around the tube on the key chain. The streetlights showed the street to be deserted, but she didn't care. She wasn't alone tonight, but that didn't make any difference. She was prepared for anything.

Ben slowed as they approached her house and looked it over carefully. For a moment, suspicion flared in her mind. But then he said, "One of the deputies drives down your street about this time every night. We know you're walking home by yourself."

"Thank you," she managed to say, hoping that he couldn't hear the remains of the fear and suspicion in her voice. "That's very thoughtful of you."

He shrugged. "Dev takes his job as sheriff seriously. And so do I."

It was comforting to know that someone had been watching out for her at night. It didn't change a thing, but she felt another surge of affection for Cameron. In the beginning, she'd never imagined she'd think of the town as her home. Now, even though she knew she might have to leave again, she felt like she belonged here.

She stepped into the front yard, opening the gate and listening with satisfaction to the loud squeal of its rusty hinges. She smiled to herself. It was a small thing, but an effective early warning system.

"Maybe you should oil that gate," Ben said. "It's pretty loud."

She shrugged. "It doesn't bother me."

"What about your neighbors?"

"They haven't complained."

He looked around her yard, and she wondered if he noticed how bleak it was, how empty. She felt a small stab in her heart every time she looked at it. The barrenness was an affront to her gardener's soul, but bushes and plants were potential hiding places. She'd ruthlessly removed every living thing from her yard before she'd moved in, and she'd resisted the need to plant more. In her mind's eye she saw perennials blooming, bushes outlining the house and annual flowers creating a lush frame for her small property. But they remained in her mind's eye only.

Unlocking the door, she kept the key chain and the spray in her hand as she moved into the house. All the lights inside were lit, and she waited for Ben before locking the door behind him. If he noticed the heavy-duty security locks, he didn't say anything.

"Come on in. Would you like something to drink? Iced tea or a soft drink?"

"Tea, if you have some made."

She led him into the living room, grimacing at the social charade. Some things couldn't be forgotten, she supposed, and manners were one of them. "I'll be right back," she murmured.

She left him standing in the middle of the room, looking around, and she wondered what he was thinking. The room was plainly furnished, with no family pictures on the wall, no mementos on the bookshelf, nothing personal anywhere. It was a room without a soul and she hated it with a passion, but it was the way she had to live.

Her hands shook as she poured the tea into two glasses, then arranged some homemade chocolate chip cookies on a plate. Even her house seemed to be aware of Ben's presence in the other room. The old frame structure suddenly felt like it was suffused with life, holding its breath and waiting for something to happen.

Mimi, her calico cat, wrapped herself around her ankles and chirped at her. She reached down and scratched her ear, whispering, "All right, Mimi. I haven't forgotten. I'll get your dinner."

She quickly fed the cat, then washed her hands and lifted the tray. Taking a deep breath, she closed her eyes. She could do this. She could listen to Ben's explanation, then tell him that what he asked was impossible and usher him out of her house and out of her head.

She had no choice.

As she walked into the living room, her skin prickled with awareness. He sat in one of her chairs, his stillness a direct contrast to the alert watchfulness of his eyes. His dark eyes had been cataloging the room, but he looked at her and stood as soon as she entered the room.

"Sit down, Ben." She set the tray on the table next to him and arranged herself on the couch, as far away from him as she could get. "Why don't you just tell me why you asked me...your question."

"You don't mince your words, do you?" One side of his mouth quirked up in a small smile.

"No. I've learned it's a waste of time." She sat on the edge of the couch and prepared to harden her heart to his request.

Ben stared at her for a moment, then set his glass down on the table with a snap. "It's about Rafael."

She shot up from the chair. "What's wrong with him? What happened?"

"Nothing is wrong, Janie." He stared at her with dark

eyes, and she couldn't read his expression. "At least not physically. Rafael is fine."

"What is it, then?" She sat back down slowly, watching Ben. Rafael was one of the children Shea McAllister had smuggled into the country from the small South American country of San Rafael. She had reunited the others with their families, but Rafael didn't have any family in this country. Ben had found Rafael in the mountains after he'd run away, and she knew that he had developed a bond with the boy. Just as she knew that his search for the boy had evoked painful memories that had led to their night together. She tried to banish any thought of that night from her mind. Clearly, what Ben was asking had nothing to do with the night of passion they had shared.

"Rafael and I...get along. He likes living with me."

Janie continued to watch Ben. Although his eyes softened, his voice was full of pain. "That's wonderful, Ben. I suspect you're just what Rafael needs."

"I want to adopt him." His stark words echoed in the silence of the house.

Janie swallowed. "And you need a wife to do that."

"You catch on quickly."

Janie steeled herself to ignore the spark of appreciation in Ben's eyes, ignore the warmth that bloomed there. It wasn't for her, she told herself. It was merely because she'd grasped the situation right away and understood his dilemma.

And she could be no part of it.

Pain and anguish crashed over her again. If she were living a normal life, if she could have allowed herself to be attracted to Ben, would this moment be different? Would his proposal be the culmination of a courtship? Would it have been real?

It didn't matter, she reminded herself. This was her life, normal or not, and what Ben asked was impossible. It would have been impossible even if she wanted to agree. Which she didn't, she told herself.

"I'm sorry, Ben, but I can't do it."

He waved his hand at her. "I didn't think you'd agree right away. At least hear me out, Janie. I'm sorry I had to spring this on you, but I'm desperate. You're my only hope of getting Rafael's adoption approved."

He moved over and sat next to her on the couch. Before she could move away, he slid her hand between his, holding her lightly. It was a comforting gesture, nothing more, but her entire being was focused on the touch of his hands. She could barely concentrate on his voice. Finally she drew her hand away and curled it into a fist in her lap.

He didn't seem to notice. "The whole situation with Rafael has gotten too much publicity in the last few months. The damned reporters have been swarming all over Cameron." He scowled and stood up to pace around the room again, and she drew in a wobbly breath. "Everyone knows about him now, about how he lied to Shea's courier about his family so he could get out of San Rafael. The adoption agency has couples calling from all over the country who want to adopt him." He scowled again. "Hell, Shea and Jesse even wanted to adopt him. But he wants to stay with me. The problem is, the social worker assigned to him told me that I have as much chance as a snowball in hell of having my adoption approved. What judge is going to let a single man adopt him when there are couples waiting in line?"

"You've built a relationship with him," she said, watching him pace. Her mouth felt stiff and her voice sounded unfamiliar. Her heart ached for him, for his situation, but she refused to think about what he'd asked her. "You're the one spending time with him. He's living with you, for heaven's sake. Doesn't that count for anything?"

"Apparently not. They're not going to dispute my temporary custody because they know I'd raise a hell of a stink. Rafael has just begun to come out of his shell and trust me. They don't want the kind of publicity that moving him would cause. But permanent adoption is another matter. Rafael has become high profile, and that means that everything has to be perfect. If he was just another lost kid, they'd be glad to let me adopt him. He's eight years old, and he suffered a lot in San Rafael. Most people want perfect babies, not troubled children. But now Rafael is a celebrity. No social service agency is going to take a chance on giving him to a single father with the whole country watching.''

"If you marry now, won't the judge realize you did it only to get custody of him?'' She had to concentrate on the practical, the details. It's what she had become good at, these last three years. There was no room for emotion in her life anymore, no room for feelings.

He stopped pacing and came over to sit next to her again. His dark gaze bored into hers with an intensity that made her heart begin to pound again. She wanted to move away, but forced herself to remain motionless. "Not if I marry you, Janie.''

She heard the reluctance in his voice, and although her heart twisted painfully, her mind told her to rejoice. He didn't want to marry her, not really. He was only concerned with Rafael. Forcing herself to try and think logically, she asked, "Why me? There are other single women in town around my age.''

"Not many. And most of them already have children. I don't want to involve any other children. I don't want to take a chance on hurting a child.'' He spoke too quickly, and didn't quite meet her eyes.

"I can name several women who are single with no children. Have you already asked them?''

He didn't answer for a long time. Finally he looked

directly at her and slowly shook his head. "It has to be you, Janie."

"Why me?" she whispered. Emotions churned through her in a chaotic swirl. Fear, disappointment, curiosity and pain chased themselves through her mind. And underlying all of them, a deep, insidious pleasure.

He closed his eyes and took a deep breath. When he opened his eyes again, he stared at her steadily. "I suppose because of what happened. We made a mistake, Janie, one that I've regretted bitterly, but everyone in Cameron must suspect what happened."

He swallowed, and she watched the ripple of muscles in his neck. "We've avoided each other since, but that hasn't stopped the people in Cameron. In fact, it's just made things worse. Hell, the gossip mill has been in overdrive ever since that night. There are too many people with too much time on their hands around here, and 'Ben and Janie's non-romance' has taken on a life of its own."

He still watched her steadily, and she tried to hide the pain that engulfed her. He was right, of course. What had happened between them had been a mistake, a huge one. She'd known that from the beginning. But hearing him say so in such blunt, brutal terms made something shrivel up and die inside her.

"We both know that there's nothing to the gossip, but no one wants to believe that." He took a deep breath. "I need to make it plain to you that the last thing I want in this life is a wife. But now I have no choice. If I need a wife to adopt Rafael, I'll get married. And too many people in this town have been talking about us, even though we've been avoiding each other. If I marry anyone else, no one's going to buy it. Hell, I don't know if the child welfare authorities will buy it, anyway. But you're my only chance."

His face hardened. "Do you have any idea what Rafael has gone through?"

She shook her head.

"Neither do I. He won't talk about it. But it was bad enough to force an eight-year-old boy to run from his country, to try and get as far away as possible." He glared at her. "Do you know that Rafael isn't even his real name?"

"No, I didn't know that," she whispered.

His eyes turned to flat, opaque stones. "No one knows what his real name is. He wouldn't tell the courier, or Shea, or even me. The courier named him Rafael, after the country. He's too scared to tell anyone his real name. So I don't care if you think what I'm doing is unethical. Someone has to save that boy. And right now, it looks as if that person is me. I'll do whatever it takes."

He paused, and his eyes glittered at her. "And if it took doing something that was illegal, I'd do that, too. I just wouldn't involve anyone else."

"Surely the judge will understand that," she said, and she heard the desperation in her voice. "I can't believe they'd take him away from you, if he's already attached to you."

He gave a derisive snort. "Don't you read the papers? Every day there's another couple holding a press conference, saying what good parents they'd make for Rafael. Parents who could give him what I can't, who could give him every material advantage. Families where he'd have a mother and a father. There's not a judge in this country who would turn them down and give him to me, a single father."

"You don't know that. There must be judges who could see what you can give him."

"I'm not willing to take that chance," he said flatly. "I can't gamble with Rafael's future."

She stared at him for a moment, then looked down at her hands. "I'm sorry, Ben. I can't do it. I can't marry you, even for Rafael's sake."

"Don't say that yet, Janie." He came over and sat beside her, but he didn't touch her again. "I know you have no reason to help me out with this. It sounds like there's nothing in it for you. But I'll give you whatever you want. Just name it, and it's yours."

She couldn't bear to meet his eyes. He couldn't give her the only thing she wanted—a normal life, and he'd already told her he couldn't give her a normal relationship. And even if he could, she couldn't allow herself to take it. "I'm sorry. But there's nothing that I want."

"Is it money?" he asked. "Is that what you need?"

At that she looked up at him, fury crackling through her. "Is that why you think I said no? Do you think I'd risk a child's future for money? Is that the kind of person you think I am?"

"I have no idea what kind of person you are," he said quietly. "I haven't wanted to find out. That's why I don't know what to offer you. I'm sorry if I've offended you, but right now, I only care about Rafael."

Her anger dissipated without a trace, leaving only an aching loneliness behind. How could she fault Ben for wanting to protect a child?

A fist grabbed her heart and squeezed and Janie fought against the lump that swelled in her throat. "I'm sorry, Ben. I wish I could help you, but I can't."

"At least tell me why." He ran his hand through his hair again, and one silky black lock fell over his forehead. "You owe me that, at least."

She closed her eyes, reluctant to look at his pain, and unwilling to let him see hers. "I can't."

She didn't open her eyes, but she felt him staring down at her. "I can't accept that answer, Janie. I'm sorry, but

I'll be back. Just remember, time is running short. I have to get married soon, or Rafael will be lost.''

He let himself out of the house. Janie stood on trembling legs and walked to the door, securing the locks. Then she leaned against the wall and let the pain wash over her.

Why did Ben have to ask her to marry him? All the memories from that one night came roaring back, memories she'd tried every day to forget. The images danced in front of her, taunting her with their impossibility. Why did Ben have to offer her the one thing that she wanted in all the world, the one thing that she couldn't have?

Chapter 2

Ben took a firm hold on Rafael's hand and looked around the park. People were milling everywhere, setting up blankets and opening picnic baskets, and he felt the tension running through the boy.

"It's okay, Rafael," he murmured. "I know it seems like a lot of people, but just about everyone in Cameron comes to the town picnic. It's the last big party before school starts." He paused. "Are you looking forward to starting school?"

The boy gave a small nod. "Yes."

His English was almost perfect, and Ben knew he had to have learned it in San Rafael. But Rafael wouldn't talk about anything connected with his former home.

"What do you say we pick out a spot for our picnic?" Ben asked, turning to look at the child.

Rafael stared back at him with solemn, dark eyes. "All right."

"Where do you want to sit?"

Rafael looked around, then pointed to a spot near a tree. "There."

A family with three boys had set up their picnic not far away, and Ben wondered if that was why Rafael had picked the spot. He hoped so. He wanted to see Rafael playing and having fun with other kids his age.

As he laid a blanket on the ground and opened the picnic basket, he saw Rafael watching the three boys. After a moment, he walked over to the boy's father. "Hey, Tom, how's it going?"

Tom Jessup, one of the local ranchers, turned and saw Ben and smiled. They talked for a moment, then Ben said quietly, "Would you mind if I introduced Rafael to your boys?"

Tom look startled. "Of course not." He looked over to where his kids were chasing each other and yelled, "Come over here, guys."

The Jessup boys galloped toward their father, and Tom smiled at them. "There's someone I'd like you to meet," he said.

Ben looked over at Rafael, who was watching him with unreadable eyes. "Come on over, Rafael."

The boy approached slowly, watching the three Jessup boys. One of them was older, and one was barely more than a toddler. But the middle boy looked about the same age as Rafael.

"Rafael, these are the Jessup boys." Ben casually laid his arm across Rafael's shoulder. "That's TJ, Stevie and Chuck. Boys, this is Rafael."

TJ, the oldest Jessup boy, grinned and said, "Hi, Rafael. You want to play a Power Rangers game with us?"

Rafael looked up at Ben, his eyes hopeful. Ben's heart moved inside his chest, urging him to scoop the boy up and fold his arms around him, but instead he squeezed his shoulder and said, "That's fine with me, Rafe. Go ahead. I'll be right here."

Rafael watched him for a second, then turned and stepped toward the Jessup boys. They immediately took off, running and yelling, and after only a moment's hesitation, Rafael followed them.

Ben leaned against the tree, watching Rafael run and play. Right now, he looked like a normal boy, a child with nothing more to worry about than the game he was playing. A fierce determination burned inside Ben. He would make sure that *this* boy was always safe.

A movement caught his attention behind the boys, and he saw that Janie Murphy had arrived at the picnic. Even in a crowd, he always seemed to notice her. His heart sped up as he watched her move through the crowd, just as it did every time he saw Janie. And he ignored it, just as he always did.

Three of the teenage boys from the town followed her, hauling large containers that he knew contained beverages for the picnic. Janie always supplied beverages for the town picnic, and as Ben watched, the teens set the containers on a large table.

They wandered off, and Janie fussed with the stacks of cups for a moment. Then she shoved her hands into the pockets of the loose dress she wore, and turned to survey the crowds.

Even from across the park, Ben felt her tension vibrating in the air. She scanned the crowd continuously, watching everyone around her. He'd bet anything that her hands hidden in her pockets were clenched into fists. Several people came up to speak to her, and she smiled and answered them, but her air of watchfulness never relaxed.

Janie was a mystery. She always had been, but after that one night, she'd been a puzzle that Ben went out of his way to avoid. She'd touched a part of him that he wanted to keep buried, and he'd been determined not to let it happen again.

Now things had changed. He glanced over at Rafael, but the boy was still playing with the Jessup kids. Janie had refused his proposal, but as far as he was concerned, the siege had just begun. He hadn't been too shocked that she'd refused his request the other night, but he had been surprised that she wouldn't give him a reason.

And he'd been stunned at the pain in her eyes, pain that she'd done her best to hide. What she hadn't known was that Ben was a master at hiding pain. He'd done it so often that he had no trouble spotting it in someone else.

Pushing away from the tree, he sauntered over to Tom Jessup. "Would you keep an eye on Rafael for a few minutes, Tom? I need to talk to someone."

"Sure thing."

Ben gave the rancher a casual wave as he headed toward Janie. Her red-gold hair was loose around her shoulders today, curling around her face, and the subtle breeze that blew through the park molded her dress to her slight frame. His throat tightened at the sight of the curves she usually kept hidden behind shapeless clothes, and his heart began to pound. Every inch of her body was imprinted on his memory.

It didn't matter. His body might react at the sight of Janie, but he wasn't interested in her for any reason other than a marriage of convenience. For Rafael's sake. In order to keep Rafael, he had to convince her to marry him. But that was as far as his interest went.

His body called him a liar, but he put the mocking voice out of his mind. Ignoring his hormones was a matter of self-control. Asking Janie to marry him had been the logical choice. It had nothing to do with the way she made him feel.

"Hello, Janie," he said, stopping in front of her.

She jerked once, in surprise, then managed to hide her reaction. "Hi, Ben." Her dark blue eyes lingered on him for a moment, then she looked away.

"Are you looking for someone?" he asked.

Her gaze flew back to him. "No. Why do you ask?"

"You've been scanning the crowd ever since you got here."

If he hadn't been watching her carefully, he wouldn't have noticed her tense even more. "How do you know that?"

"It's my job to notice all kinds of things," he said, trying to keep his voice light.

She shrugged and forced a smile. "I was just trying to figure out if I brought enough iced tea and lemonade."

"Looks good to me," he said, glancing at the huge yellow containers. "Did you bring a picnic with you?"

"No. I have a lot to do at the restaurant today."

"Isn't Heaven on Seventh closed because of the picnic?"

"Yes." She gave him a level look. "That means I can get through a lot of paperwork."

"Why don't you at least stay and have something to eat? I brought enough food to feed an army."

"Thanks, but I need to get back to the restaurant."

He moved closer, ignoring the fireworks exploding inside him as her scent surrounded him. "Running away, Janie?"

She held her ground, although he saw her eyes darken. "What would I be running away from?"

"I haven't forgotten what I asked you the other night."

She swallowed once but didn't let her gaze drop. "I have. There's nothing to run away from. I already told you, the answer is no."

"Then come and have lunch with me. Enjoy the picnic and the games." He gave her a bland gaze. "You're as much a part of Cameron as anyone else. If you don't have anything to run away from, stay and prove it.''

He saw all her emotions chasing themselves across her face. She wanted to tell him to go to hell, but she didn't want him to think she was afraid to stay and face him. Finally she gave a curt nod. ''All right. I'll have something to eat with you.''

''Great. Our stuff is over there.'' He pointed to the tree. ''Rafael is playing with the Jessup boys.''

He touched her arm to guide her toward his picnic spot, and felt the current jump between them. He also felt her flinch, and wondered if it was because she felt the connection, too. Dropping his hand to his side, he deliberately moved a step away from her. He might want her help with Rafael, but he had no intention of playing with fire.

She sat down on the blanket with him, but edged as far away from him as she could. ''What do you have in there?''

For a while, neither of them spoke as they ate cold chicken and potato salad. Most of the people who walked by his blanket gave them a considering look, but Ben pretended not to notice. Janie continued to scan the picnic area, and again he wondered why.

She wouldn't tell him. He knew her well enough to realize that. He'd just have to bide his time. Sooner or later, he'd figure it out.

''Hey, Ben. How're you doing, Janie?'' His boss, Devlin McAllister, dropped down on his blanket and pulled his wife, Carly, down with him.

''Hi, Dev. Carly.'' He watched as Dev reached for his wife and twined their fingers together. He couldn't help the sharp stab of envy and loneliness. Since they'd gotten married the previous winter, the sheriff and his wife had been deliriously happy. No one could miss the glow that surrounded them.

His marriage had never been like that.

They talked for a few minutes, the conversation casual, but Ben didn't miss the sharp look that Dev had given him when he spotted Janie sharing his picnic.

After Dev and Carly had sauntered away, Janie said, "You asked me to share your picnic deliberately, didn't you?"

"What are you talking about?"

"I saw that look the sheriff gave you." She tossed her fork onto the picnic basket. "And all the other people who have been staring at us. It just took me a while to put everything together."

Janie jumped to her feet, poised to flee. He uncoiled himself to stand next to her. He touched her elbow again, ignoring the heat that flashed between them. "I need your help, Janie."

Her eyes sparked and she opened her mouth to answer him, but before she could speak, Rafael appeared at his side. Janie abruptly closed her mouth.

"Can we eat now, Ben?"

"Of course, Rafe." He settled his hands on the boy's shoulders and turned him to face Janie. "Do you know Ms. Murphy? She owns the restaurant in town, Heaven on Seventh."

Rafael nodded once. "She has pretty hair. I saw her when we went there to eat."

Janie looked down at the boy, and the anger in her eyes melted away. "Hi, Rafael. It looked like you were having a good time with the Jessup boys."

He nodded once, shyly. "They have to eat now. But we're going to play again later."

"What were you playing?" Janie squatted down in front of Rafael, so their eyes were level. "It looked like fun."

"We were playing a Power Rangers game. They're the good guys. They fight the bad guys, and they always win.

Stevie said maybe I could come over to their house sometime and watch the Power Rangers show on TV with
them." He twisted around to face Ben. "Could I?"

"Of course you can. Anytime." Bless the Jessup boys
for making Rafael feel welcome.

"Good."

Ben saw him eyeing the food in the picnic basket, and
he let him go. "Why don't you eat something, Rafe? Then
you can play with Stevie again when he's done with his
lunch."

"Okay."

Janie started to move away, but Ben caught up with her.
"Don't go, please."

"So you can try to pull on my heartstrings a little
more?" She glared at him. "You knew I wouldn't be able
to resist Rafael. That's another reason you forced me to
have lunch with you."

"I don't recall doing any forcing," he said mildly.
"You chose to join me."

"You weaseled your way around my defenses," she
muttered.

"I didn't think you should make any decisions until you
met him," he said. "He needs you, Janie. And so do I."

"I understand what you're trying to do, Ben. Really I
do." Her voice had a desperate tinge to it. "If I was in
your position, I'd probably try to do the same thing. But
you picked the wrong person to help you. I can't marry
you. Not for Rafael, not for any other reason."

Suddenly he wanted to know the truth. He wanted to
know everything about Janie Murphy, and Rafael had
nothing to do with it. He wanted to know what had put
the pain in those dark blue eyes, what had put that wariness
in every line of her body. He'd been aware of her for three
years, ever since she arrived in Cameron, but he didn't
know one thing about her.

Except for the way their bodies fit together.

"I have to go, Ben."

Janie's low voice bit through the sensual haze that surrounded him. He reached out for her, curling his hand around hers. "Stay a while longer," he said, quietly. "Talk to Rafael for a few more minutes. He needs to feel like he's a part of Cameron."

He saw the indecision in her eyes, as well as the understanding. She knew what he was trying to do. She understood that he was trying to bind them together, to make it more difficult for her to say no. Most other people would have walked away.

She looked down at the little boy on the blanket, and her eyes softened. Sitting down beside him, she touched him lightly on his arm. "Tell me what you like about Cameron," she said to Rafael.

Uncomfortable with the sincerity on Janie's face, Ben couldn't watch her as she spoke to Rafael. He was trying to manipulate her, to get her to do something that she clearly didn't want to do, but still she reached out to the child. Watching them together, the red-gold of her hair blowing around Rafael's cap of shining black hair, he felt a burning sensation in his chest. If only things were different, if only he could be a different man, the scene in front of him might be real, instead of a carefully staged fake.

He couldn't afford to think like that. He couldn't afford to have anything take his focus off of Rafael. He especially couldn't afford to look into himself and discover yearnings like that. Because they would never be fulfilled.

"Hi, Ben."

He looked up to see Keara Carmichael, the music teacher at the elementary school, smiling at him. "Hey, Keara."

She nodded at Rafael. "This must be your boy, Rafael."

An odd combination of pleasure and pain prickled at his chest. "That's him. Let me introduce you."

He knelt down and touched Rafael's head. "Here's one of your new teachers, buddy."

The boy immediately swiveled around and stared at Keara. The teacher's kinky, dark blond hair was pulled together at the back of her head, and her eyes were covered by sunglasses. She stuck out her hand and gravely shook Rafael's.

"Hi, Rafael. I'm Ms. Carmichael," she said. "I'm going to be teaching you music. Do you enjoy music?"

Ben saw a light flare in Rafael's eyes, and he nodded shyly. "I want to play the guitar."

Keara smiled at him. "When you're a little older, you can take lessons. But in the meantime, I'm sure you'll enjoy music classes at Cameron Elementary. I'm looking forward to having you in my class."

The music teacher stood up, smiled at Ben and Janie, and drifted away. Janie watched her go. "I didn't know Keara came to the town picnic."

"She's as bad as you," Ben said, watching her disappear. "She doesn't come to any of the town functions, but she always comes to the picnic. She makes it a point to meet all of the new kids in school. She says it makes them feel less intimidated the first week or two if they've already met their teacher."

"Can't you see how much she loves kids?" Janie turned to him. "Ask her. She'd be perfect." It sounded like she was begging.

He had no interest in marrying Keara Carmichael. "It can't be Keara." She had her secrets, too, and Ben knew she would never agree to a marriage of convenience. And he knew why she would never agree. But he didn't say more. Although Ben knew who she really was, he had no intention of discussing Keara with anyone.

"Then pick someone else." She waved her hand at the crowd of people. "Surely there's another woman in Cameron you can ask."

"I told you, it has to be credible. And there's no one else in Cameron who fits that requirement."

"You've hardly spoken to me in the three years I've been here." Her face suffused with color, and Ben knew she was remembering one time when they'd done a hell of a lot more than talk. "How can anyone say you're interested in me?"

He turned to face her, struggling to hide the heat he was afraid she would see in his eyes. "Logic has nothing to do with it, Janie. We've become an interesting story in Cameron, and people will see what they want to see. And right now, watching you sitting here with me at the picnic, everyone is going to be nodding their heads, telling themselves that they'd spotted it a long time ago. And when questioned, half the people in Cameron will be happy to say they knew all along we were going to get married."

"How can you be so cold?" she whispered. "Not only are you using me, you're using yourself and your own emotions. You're twisting them to suit your own purposes."

"I'm doing what I have to do." He gestured to the boy on the blanket, who was now watching the Jessups with longing in his eyes. "He's beginning to make friends. He wants to go to school. He's finally beginning to relax. I can't bear to think about him losing all that. And I'll do anything to prevent it. Anything. If I have to make a fool out of myself, I will. If I have to beg, I will. If I have to hold my most private emotions up for the scrutiny of Cameron, I'll do that, too." He leaned closer to her. "Don't you understand that?"

"I understand that you love him."

He felt his face harden and shuttered his eyes. "I didn't say I loved him. I said that I'd do anything for him."

"Isn't that the same thing?"

"I feel sorry for him. It's not the same thing at all."

Janie watched him for a moment, and he forced himself to look steadily back. But the understanding in her eyes disturbed him, and finally he looked away.

"I'm glad you had lunch with me," he said.

She didn't answer for a moment. When he looked up at her, he saw nothing but compassion in her face. "I need to talk to you, Ben," she said, and he saw that she'd made a decision.

Hope leaped inside him. "Have you changed your mind?"

"No. But I still want to talk to you."

"I'll come over to your house tonight, after Rafael's in bed. I'll have my neighbor watch him again."

"Fine. I'll see you then."

After saying goodbye to Rafael, she walked away without looking back and hurried out of the park. He watched her walk down the street until she turned a corner and disappeared.

Ignoring the loneliness that swept over him, he turned to Rafael. "Are you ready to play some baseball, buddy?"

Janie glanced at the clock, then looked around her house once more, but nothing was out of place. Nothing was ever out of place, she told herself bitterly. This wasn't a home. It was merely a place to stay.

She told herself again that she was making a mistake, that she was taking a chance, but she didn't care. She had to make Ben see that she couldn't marry him. He had to be convinced, so he could find someone else. Because she couldn't bear it if they took Rafael away from him.

It had taken only moments for her to fall in love with

the solemn, shy child. Ben was right. He needed to stay in Cameron, with Ben. She'd seen Rafael beginning to open up at the picnic earlier today, saw the beginning of trust and hope. If they took him away from Ben, she was afraid that his trust would be crushed into nothingness, irretrievably lost.

So she had to tell Ben why she could never marry, not him or anyone else. She had to make him understand, so that he could find someone else while there was still time.

Fear rippled over her at the thought of sharing her story with anyone. But Ben wasn't just anyone, she told herself. Ben could be trusted. She knew that with a certainty she didn't want to examine. He would never betray her, never put her at risk. In spite of all the warnings she'd received, she knew he would guard her secrets.

A part of her argued that she didn't owe Ben anything. But the rest of her knew that if she didn't tell him the truth, he'd continue to pursue her. And she was afraid that she'd be weak enough to give in, weak enough to reach for what she wanted. Like she had done once already. So she'd tell him her story, and send him on his way.

The front gate squeaked, and she instinctively grasped the tube of pepper spray in the pocket of her dress. Then she forced her hand to relax. It was almost certainly Ben. When the doorbell rang, she looked through the peephole, then opened the door to let him in.

The short-sleeved polo shirt he wore emphasized his wiry strength. His upper arms were ropy with muscle, and dark hairs covered his forearms. Forcing herself to look away, she said, "Come in." She nodded to the chair he'd chosen the other night. "I fixed you a glass of tea."

"Efficient, aren't you?"

"I try to be."

He didn't sit down in the chair she'd indicated. Instead, he stared down at her. He wasn't much over six feet tall, but he seemed to tower over her. She drew herself up to her full five feet four inches and stared back.

"What am I doing here, Janie?"

"I need to talk to you."

His eyes lightened. "Have you changed your mind?"

"No, I haven't. But I feel like I owe you an explanation."

"Why? You didn't feel like you owed me any explanations the other night. In fact, I think you implied that you didn't owe me a thing."

"I hadn't seen you with Rafael the other night."

"What difference does that make?"

"You need him, Ben. You need him as much as he needs you. That was very clear this afternoon at the picnic."

"I don't need him." His voice was rough. "He needs me. For some reason, he decided he trusts me. He's bonded to me. And I'm all he has. If they take him away, he may never trust anyone else."

"I agree. And if they take him away from you, you may never recover, either."

"This isn't about me," he said, glaring at her. "This is about Rafael."

"I think it's just as much about you as it is Rafael. And that's why I'm going to tell you why I can't marry you."

"I'll be happy to listen to you tell me why you think you can't marry me. But it won't make me change my mind."

"I think it will." Her voice was quiet, and the anxiety that had been building inside her all day melted away. This was the right thing to do. Ben needed to know, and she could trust him to keep her secret. For the first time in three years she was going to tell someone her story, and she felt nothing but a sense of liberation.

She spread her hands and looked up at him. "Anyone

who's close to me is at risk. I can't take that kind of chance with either you or Rafael.

"I can't marry you, Ben. I can't marry anyone—because at any time, I could be killed."

Chapter 3

"What the hell is that supposed to mean?" Ben's scowl deepened.

"I'm in the witness protection program. I was moved to Cameron to get away from a killer, and I have no guarantee that he won't eventually find me."

She saw the shock bloom in his eyes and was bitterly triumphant. "Now do you understand?"

"I don't understand a thing," he said slowly, the shock in his eyes changing to speculation. "Tell me what's going on."

"It's very simple. The witness protection program of the U.S. Marshals' office changed my identity, gave me a new name and a new background, and moved me to Cameron. They also lent me the money to buy Heaven on Seventh and my house. But they can't guarantee that I'll always be safe. They can't guarantee that the man who tried to kill me won't ever find me." She shrugged and closed her hand on the tube in her pocket. "When it comes to protecting myself every day, I'm on my own."

He reached out a hand, almost involuntarily, it seemed, and touched her cheek. "Poor Janie. How alone you must feel."

His touch burned into her, searing her down to her soul. And because his touch, and his sympathy, moved her more than she wanted to think about, she stepped away. "It's the price I pay for being alive. So all in all, it's a bargain."

"No one in Cameron knows about this." It was a statement, rather than a question.

"You're the first person I've told." She clenched her hands into fists in her pocket. "Aside from the obvious security risks, what if I befriended someone? What if I got close to someone, and the murderer found me? I would be putting that person at risk, also."

"Aren't you exaggerating? What are the chances of someone finding you here? In a small town like this, strangers would be noticed. You should be fairly safe here."

"I'm not safe anywhere," she said, her voice low and passionate. "I've already learned that lesson."

"How would anyone find you in Cameron?"

She saw the sympathy in his eyes and for just a moment, she wanted to lose herself in it. She wanted to believe that he was right, that the killer wouldn't find her in Cameron. Then she shook her head. "He'll find me. Eventually."

"How can you be so sure?"

"I was in a safe house, supposedly secure. Only the Chicago Police Department knew where I was. But he found me. It was only a matter of luck that I wasn't hurt. Then, when I was moved again, he found my sister and her children. My only family. They weren't so lucky. Their house was bombed, and they were burned. They all lived, but they had to be placed in a safe house, also. It was clear that the killer would do anything to draw me out, even hurt the members of my family. Now they're in the witness protection program, too. I don't know where they are, or even if they're alive.''

"What happened, Janie? Why is there a murderer after you?"

"I witnessed a murder in Chicago," she said, and once more, the scene replayed itself in her mind. "It was my boss. He owned a nursery, and I was his landscape designer. It was late at night, and we were in one of the greenhouses, discussing a job we had to do the next day. We heard someone come in, and my boss went to tell them that the nursery was closed. It was dark, and I was standing behind some large plants, so the men didn't see me. But I saw them.

"There were two men. One of them stayed in the shadows, but the other stepped right into the light. The man in the shadows said something to my boss, and then the other man shot him. When Jim fell down, he stood over him and shot him again."

She swallowed hard, remembering the horror of seeing her boss, a man she had always liked and respected, gunned down in front of her. And remembered her own fear. "I knew that if those men found out I was there, they'd kill me, too. So I tried to stay perfectly still, hoping they wouldn't search the greenhouse. The man in the shadows never came any closer, so I didn't see his face. But he told the man with the gun to take Jim's money, to make it look like a robbery. They searched Jim's pockets, then went into the front of the greenhouse. I heard the cash register open, then I heard the front door close. I was afraid to move for a long time."

"What happened then?" Ben took her hand, and she gripped his fingers tightly.

"Jim was dead. He was dead even before the killers left the greenhouse. The police told me that, later. I finally forced myself to move, and called the police." She remembered the sirens, the police officers swarming the scene, the sense of unreality and shock. And the acute sense of separation from everyone else, the sense that she'd changed and would never be the same person. "The police were kind, but they were busy trying to gather evidence. They took my statement and sent me to a police artist to draw a picture of the man I'd seen. To give them credit, they realized that I was in danger, so they hid my identity from the reporters and had someone guarding me."

"Did they catch the man who killed your boss?"

"Yes. Apparently he had a long record. Once the police saw the artist's drawing, they showed me some mug shots and I was able to identify him. But he refused to tell anyone who was with him. He insisted that he was alone, that he only wanted to rob the greenhouse and didn't know anyone would still be there. He stuck to his story all through the trial."

"And you had to testify," Ben said grimly.

"If I hadn't, he probably wouldn't have been convicted." She gave him a humorless smile. "He was a professional, Ben. Clearly it was more than just a robbery, but the police couldn't figure out the motive. And the murderer wouldn't talk. He didn't leave any fingerprints, and they never found the gun he'd used. There was no physical evidence linking him to the murder. I was the only witness."

"Why didn't you tell them to go to hell?" Ben said roughly. "If you hadn't testified, no one would have known your identity. Why put yourself in danger like that?"

"I owed it to my boss. He didn't deserve to die, and I couldn't bear the thought that his murderer would get off scot-free. I wouldn't have been able to look his wife and children in the eye if I had refused to testify."

"So now the other man knows who you are. And he tried to come after you." Ben's voice was grim.

She nodded. "I was in a safe house. They were trying to work on the murderer, do a plea bargain for a lesser sentence if he would give them the name of the other man, but he refused. He probably knew that he'd be killed, too, if he gave up the name. No one was supposed to know where I was, but someone broke into the safe house and tried to kill me. Fortunately, the man who was guarding me was able to stop him, but shortly after that my sister's house was bombed." She stopped, feeling the tears clogging her throat. "I couldn't even go to the hospital to see my sister or my niece and nephew. The police were sure that was what the killer was waiting for."

"So you got a new name and ended up in Cameron."

"Yes."

"I'm sorry, Janie," he said, and then he frowned. "That's not even your name, is it?"

"Yes, it is," she said fiercely. "I'm Janie Murphy now. The person I used to be has ceased to exist."

"You're a brave woman, Janie Murphy." His voice was low, and he reached out to brush a strand of hair away from her face.

"Not that brave," she said, and she detested the quiver in her voice. "My sister and her children were hurt because of me, and I didn't even face them and tell them I was sorry."

She saw his eyes soften, felt his hands reach out for her, and knew she should back away. Knew that the safe thing, the smart thing, would be to avoid his touch. But instead she moved forward to meet him, and when his arms closed around her, she leaned into his strength.

His heart galloped beneath her ear, and his hands were unsteady as he stroked her back. Before she could tell herself to stop, she wrapped her arms around him and moved closer.

His muscles were rock-hard and trembling. She felt his tension, and an answering tension began to build inside her. Her legs weakened and his male scent filled her head. Suddenly there was more than comfort in their embrace. Heat began to build, low in her abdomen, a fire that flickered then grew stronger.

His hands tightened around her, and his touch was no longer impersonal, no longer merely comforting. When he slid his hand up to her head, tangled it in her hair, she felt him shake.

"Janie," he whispered, then closed his eyes. His fingers trailed across her cheek, then down her throat. His hand lingered, as if he savored the texture of her skin, the planes of her face.

He bent his head, touching his forehead to hers, then slowly set her away from him. His hands clung to her shoulders for a moment, then slid down her arms and finally let her go.

She stood in front of him, still too close, aching for him to touch her again. And knew that she was playing with fire.

He moved away first. "I'm glad you told me," he said, his voice raw with emotion. "Thank you for trusting me."

"I do trust you," she replied. "And I wanted you to understand why I couldn't help you."

He lifted his head and watched her steadily. "This doesn't change anything, Janie. Nothing you told me makes any difference. I still want you to marry me."

The pain was almost too much for her to bear. "How can I do that?" she whispered. "If anything happened to you or Rafael, I'd never forgive myself."

The emotion faded from Ben's eyes, replaced by the remote, closed look he usually wore. "Come sit down."

He took her hand and led her to the couch. Once they were seated, he drew his hand away from her.

"Nothing is going to happen to any of us, Janie. No one has to know your secret in order for us to get married. And the chances of that murderer finding you in Cameron are remote. Are you going to live the rest of your life in limbo? Are you never going to relax, never going to get close to anyone? What kind of life is that?"

"It's the kind of life you're offering me," she said quietly. "You're not talking about a real marriage. You're not talking about becoming close, about love. So why should you care whether I live like that alone, or with you?"

"Think of this marriage as a dry run," he said, leaning forward. "While you're helping Rafael, you can get used to life again, used to being around other people."

"So that when our fake marriage ends, I can look for a real husband?"

Pain slashed across his face, pain that he couldn't hide. "Exactly," he said after a moment.

She shook her head. "None of that matters," she said. "If I marry you, I'm putting you and Rafael at risk. I saw what happened to my sister and her children, and I won't be responsible for that happening to anyone else." *Especially someone I care about.*

She didn't say the last words aloud, but they still shocked her. She couldn't allow herself to care about Ben Jackson. She couldn't even allow herself to care about Rafael. It was dangerous, both to them and to her peace of mind. She was better off living in suspended animation, doing her job every day, coming home to her cat and her empty house. If she started to care, if she started to think about what she was missing, she wasn't sure if she could bear it.

He leaned forward, his elbows on his knees. "Then think about it this way. I wanted to know what I could give you to make you agree to marry me, and now I know. I don't for a moment think that Rafael or I will be in any danger, and think of the benefits to you. It would be like a marriage protection program. You'll be much safer living with someone else, especially if that someone is a cop. If anything suspicious happens, if there's anything that doesn't seem right, I'll be there. We have something to offer each other. You'll give me what I need, and I can help you, too.''

"It doesn't work that way, Ben." A sharp stab of regret moved through her, and she realized that she wanted to help him. Wanted to help *Rafael,* she reminded herself firmly. "I would always be afraid for both of you."

"There's no reason, Janie." He moved closer, his face animated in a way she'd never seen. "Why would anyone look for you in Cameron? You had no connection to the town, no reason to come here. Did you?"

She shook her head. "No."

"So why would he come here? Why would anyone even look for you in Utah? Of all the places in the country, there's nothing that would lead him here."

She wanted to believe him, so badly. She wanted to reach out for the lifeline he was offering, grasp the reassurance and hug it to herself. She wanted to be part of the life of this town, make friends here, feel free again.

But she couldn't succumb to the temptation of his words. She couldn't allow herself to take false comfort. "He found me in the safe house," she said, her voice low. "That wasn't supposed to happen. His accomplice was too frightened of this man to save himself by naming him. I'm afraid I'm dealing with a powerful man, someone in authority. Someone who'll find a way to discover where I am." She refused to look at Ben. "I can't marry you," she said. "I can't take that kind of chance."

"I'm as much at risk, then, as you. Don't you think I should have a vote?"

"It's not just you. There's an innocent child involved, too." Her voice cracked with pain. "And don't think that would stop this man. He didn't hesitate to try to kill my sister's children."

"Do you honestly think I would do anything to hurt Rafael?" he demanded. "If I thought there was even the slightest chance he could be hurt, I'd agree with you and say goodbye." His voice softened. "I understand why you've been so careful, so wary." His mouth curled up in a smile that made her chest ache. "I even understand the pepper spray, now. But I don't think you're in any danger here in Cameron. And as long as you stay in Cameron, stay out of the spotlight, why would that change?"

"Marrying you, going to court for Rafael's adoption would put me squarely in the spotlight." She couldn't allow herself to weaken.

"We can arrange it so that it doesn't." He spread his hands. "Who outside of Cameron other than Rafael's social worker would need to know we'd gotten married? The other couples might have gone on television, might have pitched their cases publicly, but we don't have to do that. We'll just be working quietly within the system. And once we're married, we're just another couple trying to adopt Rafael. The couple with the best chance, because he's living with us." He reached out and took her hand. "The only way my adoption of Rafael would cause a stir is if I was unmarried."

His fingers were warm and strong as he held her hand, and she wanted to turn her palm to his, press their hands together and tell him yes. She wanted to tell him that she'd marry him, that she'd agree to a marriage of convenience for Rafael's sake. But her heart knew there were other reasons she wanted to agree, reasons that had nothing to

do with convenience or Rafael. And because she couldn't
trust herself to make the right decision, she gently removed
her hand from his grasp."

"I'm sorry, Ben. I hoped if I told you the truth, you'd
understand why I couldn't marry you. I know you think
I'm being foolish, but my answer is still no."

He stared at her for what seemed like a long time, then
he stood up. "Thank you for trusting me with your secret,
Janie. I won't betray you."

"I know you won't. Please find someone else and get
married. For Rafael's sake."

He smiled at her then, a slow curving of his lips that
held enough heat to melt her bones. "I'm going to get
married, Janie. Never doubt that." He held her gaze for a
moment, then touched her hair with one finger. "I'll see
you at Heaven tomorrow morning."

Janie stared at his back as he walked out of the house.
It took her a moment to remember to lock the door. Then
she went to the window and watched him walk over to the
Blazer he drove. His dark hair gleamed in the light from
the streetlamp, and the muscles in his back rippled beneath
his polo shirt as he climbed into the truck. In another minute his car had turned the corner and he was gone.

Slowly she let out the breath she hadn't realized she'd
been holding. Now Ben knew the truth about her. He knew
why she couldn't marry him. He'd find someone else in
Cameron, another woman who would help him out, help
him save Rafael. And himself.

She should be glad, she told herself as she climbed into
bed. She should be relieved that he would be leaving her
alone, that he would be focusing on someone else.

But as she stared up at the ceiling in her dark bedroom,
all she could think about was the touch of his hand on her
face and the feel of his heart beating against hers, a touch
she'd craved since their night together. All she could re-

member was the regret that had burned in her chest as he'd walked away from her.

Ben paused at the door of Heaven on Seventh several mornings later to look for Janie. It had become a habit of his, although he'd tried to hide it. Now he didn't bother. He wanted everyone in the diner to see him searching for Janie.

She was in the kitchen. He could just see the red-gold crown of her head above the counter. He stood there for a moment, watching her fly around the small kitchen, every move efficient and graceful.

Then he moved over to the corner booth to join Devlin and the other deputies for their morning conference. Janie would come out of the kitchen eventually. This morning, he'd stay until she did.

When there were only two or three other patrons in the restaurant, he rose and made his way over to Janie.

"Morning, Janie."

Her gaze flew up to him, and although she tried to hide it, he saw the momentary pleasure in her eyes. Then they were guarded again.

"Good morning, Ben. What can I do for you?"

"At least you didn't call me 'deputy,'" he said pleasantly. "That's a start."

Her eyes became even more guarded. "Nothing's started. We've already had this discussion, and we ended it."

"I need to talk to you," he said.

"All right." He noticed her wipe her hands down the apron she wore over her dress.

She poured herself a cup of coffee and automatically freshened his, then slid into the booth. When she moved as far away from him as possible, he was both relieved and disappointed.

"I have a problem," he began. "Rafael's caseworker told me that because of all the publicity, the judge wants to move his custody and adoption hearing forward. I have four weeks."

"Four weeks!" The color drained from her face. "That's not fair. That doesn't give you time to prepare anything."

He shrugged. "The judge thinks it's fair. And to be honest, I can see his point. As far as he's concerned, the sooner Rafael has some stability in his life, the better off he'll be. But if I can't stand there as part of a married couple, I won't have much chance of keeping him. Any adoption won't be final for a while, but if I'm not married, I'm not even a candidate."

She leaned forward. "Have you found someone to marry?"

"I've found someone."

"I'm so glad." He thought he saw a trace of sorrow in her eyes, then it was gone. "Who is it?"

He watched her steadily, and suddenly she drew back. "Oh, no, Ben. We've already had this discussion. I thought you understood why I had to say no. I thought you were looking for someone else."

"You're the one who doesn't understand. Don't you see, Janie? If I get married now, the judge and Rafael's caseworker are going to be very suspicious. They're going to think that I got married just to get custody of him. Especially now that the hearing has been moved up. You're the only one I can marry who can deflect that suspicion. You're the only woman I've spent time with recently, the only woman I've been seen with around town. You don't think your neighbors know I've visited your house? Twice? Trust me, the story is all over Cameron. I'm sorry, Janie. I know I'm backing you into a corner, but you have to marry me. Time has run out, and if you say no, I'm going to lose Rafael.''

Her hands were clenched around the coffee cup, and she stared down into its depths as if she could find an answer there. When she looked up, her face was drawn and colorless.

''You can't expect me to make a decision like that right now. At least give me the day to think about it.''

She raised her eyes, and the haunted look in them was almost enough to make him forget the proposal. Almost, but not quite. He was enough of a bastard to return her stare unflinchingly.

''Come to the house tonight,'' she finally said. ''I'll have an answer for you then.''

''I'll be there.'' He wanted to say more, tell her that she wouldn't regret marrying him, assure her that everything would work out, but instead he slid out of the booth. ''I'll see you tonight, Janie,'' he said softly, then walked out of the restaurant.

Janie paced her living room, listening for the sound of Ben's Blazer in the street. Her stomach fluttered, her hands were damp and her heart boomed against her ribs. ''Let's just get this over with,'' she said fiercely to the cat, who sat on the couch and watched her.

Mimi's inscrutable green gaze tracked her as she paced, following her around the room. Finally she threw herself onto a chair. ''What am I going to do, Mimi?''

The cat rose from the couch, stretched, then jumped lightly to the floor. Her tail in the air, she walked out of the room. A few moments later she heard the cat eating. ''I'm afraid that food isn't going to solve this problem,'' she muttered.

Finally she heard the sound of Ben's truck outside her house. Wondering uneasily how she was so certain it was

Ben's, she looked out the window to be certain. When she saw him striding up the walk, her hand tightened on the material.

Deliberately unclenching her fist, she walked to the front door and waited for him to knock. When she opened the door, she hoped her hands weren't shaking and her face was calm.

"Come on in, Ben."

He stood in the hallway, searching her face. Turning abruptly, she led the way into the living room. She had to maintain some distance between them.

"Sit down."

He chose the couch, and she retreated to the chair on the other side of the room. She saw faint amusement flash in his eyes, then he leaned forward.

"What have you decided?"

"You believe in getting right to the point, don't you?"

"We've about discussed this to death." He made an impatient gesture. "Either you're going to marry me, or you're not."

"What will you do if I say no?" she asked.

His face hardened. "Then I'll fight as hard as I can for Rafael. I'll hire the best lawyer I can find, I'll do whatever I have to do. But I'll still lose."

"Why are you so certain of that?"

"Because you're not the only one with a past. I was married before, and if I'm single, I'm sure that'll be an issue. If I'm married, I hope that it won't be."

"What happened?"

His face looked like it had been carved from stone. "It doesn't matter. It's in the past, over and done with. All that matters is your decision."

She closed her eyes, feeling as if she was falling off a

cliff. She didn't know where the bottom was, or if anyone would be there to catch her. Taking a deep breath, she said, "All right. I'll marry you, Ben. And God help all three of us."

Chapter 4

Ben stood in the front of the church, watching Janie waiting at the end of the aisle. She clutched a bouquet of flowers that Carly McAllister had given her, turning them around and around in her hands as she waited for the music to start.

Ben knew very well that Janie felt she was putting him and Rafael in danger, that not only did she have to worry about her own safety, but his and Rafael's, too. And he didn't even want to think about the other things they'd have to worry about, once they were living in the same house.

A familiar flash of heat seared him, but he ignored it. Just as he'd ignored every similar instance of need he'd felt since Janie had come to Cameron.

Every instance but one, he reminded himself.

He shifted at the altar and deliberately looked away from Janie. He couldn't allow himself to think about that night. Not now, not ever again. Janie wasn't marrying him because she was in love with him. And he wasn't marrying her for love, either. They were marrying for the sake of a child.

Rafael stood next to him, scrubbed and polished, wearing his brand new suit and holding the wedding rings. Ben glanced over at him and felt his heart softening, as it always did when he saw Rafael. The boy looked so solemn, so serious.

While he was watching Rafael, the minister stuck his head out of a side door in the sanctuary, looked around, then closed the door again. If he was waiting for more people, Ben thought, he was going to be disappointed. Their wedding was going to be small and intimate.

Their wedding. Panic fluttered over him for a moment, then Devlin laid his hand on his arm.

"You all right, Ben?" he whispered.

Ben took a deep breath and glanced over at his friend. The concern in Devlin's eyes steadied him. "I'm fine. Just a little nervous."

Dev's face relaxed, and he grinned at Ben. "Now there's a surprise. Every groom in the history of mankind has been nervous. Remember how you had to practically hog-tie me to get me to the altar?"

Ben smiled back at his friend. "Yeah, I remember how you fought and kicked to get away from Carly."

Devlin's smile faded. "That was different. We had a lot more time to think about our decision. This *is* awfully sudden. Are you sure you don't want to wait?"

Wait? Ben wanted to laugh, but he didn't dare. It had taken all his and Janie's organizing abilities to pull off a plausible wedding in three days. And it had still been close.

He shook his head. "And give her the chance to change her mind?" he said lightly. "I got her to say yes in a weak moment, and I'm not going to give her any way out."

Dev slapped him on the back. "Everyone in town has been waiting for this day. It's too bad you couldn't wait awhile and make it a real shindig."

Thank goodness for the gossip that would make their wedding seem more real. And thank goodness they had an excuse to avoid a "shindig." Janie would have been horrified by the idea. "We didn't want to prolong things because of Rafael." It was the story he and Janie had agreed upon. "Both Janie and I want him to have time to get to know her before he gets busy with school starting."

"It makes sense, I guess."

"Janie and I know what's best for us. And for Rafael."

Devlin's glance was sober. "I hope so, Ben. For all your sakes."

Just then the door at the side of the sanctuary opened again, and this time the minister emerged, closing the door firmly behind him. The organist started playing the wedding march and Carly, the matron of honor, stepped into the aisle at the back of the church.

As Ben watched her walk toward the front of the church, he remembered the argument he and Janie had had about the wedding. She didn't want to get married in church, and she didn't want anyone else present for the wedding. A quick ceremony in front of a justice of the peace in the county seat was what she'd had in mind.

But he had wanted to get married in Cameron, with at least a few people present. It was for the sake of the social worker who would be closely examining their marriage, he'd told Janie. A church wedding would go a long way to making it seem real.

Now he wished he'd agreed to the quick, emotionless ceremony in an impersonal, sterile office. Watching Carly float down the aisle made him uncomfortable. And the sight of Janie, standing in the back of the church in her borrowed wedding gown, brought bleak pictures to mind, memories he'd tried hard to banish.

Carly reached the front of the church and stepped into her place opposite Devlin, after exchanging a private smile with him. Ben's heart twisted painfully at that smile. He and Janie might be getting married, but he doubted if they would ever exchange that kind of intimate, loving look, the kind that didn't require any words.

And he didn't care, he reminded himself fiercely. He didn't want that kind of intimacy in his life. He didn't want that kind of caring, that kind of love. He didn't ever want to be that close to anyone again.

The music changed and the handful of people in the church stood, turned and looked back to where Janie waited. Ben saw her draw in a deep, trembling breath, then she forced her face into a smile and stepped into the church.

He couldn't take his eyes off her as she walked up the aisle. Shea Coulton had lent Janie the wedding dress she'd worn herself only a few months earlier. It had been her mother's dress, and Ben still remembered the tears that had glittered in Janie's eyes as she'd fingered the delicate material. Today, the satin and lace gleamed in the burnished light of the softly lit church, and Ben allowed his gaze to linger on Janie as she walked toward him.

It was all for show, he tried to tell himself, but his heart beat uncomfortably loud in his chest. Deliberately he tore his gaze away from Janie and looked over at Rafael. The boy had turned around with everyone else, and now he stared at Janie, too. He was doing this for Rafael, Ben told himself. That was the only reason.

Instead of watching Janie approach him, he watched Rafael. He had told Rafael that Janie would be living with them from now on, but the child hadn't shown much reaction. Now Rafael seemed to be as involved in the drama as the rest of the people in the church.

Every groom watched his bride come down the aisle, he reminded himself. Steeling himself to watch Janie approach, he turned back to her. She was close enough now that he could see the panic in her eyes, the belief that she'd made a horrible mistake. And suddenly all his fear disappeared.

They would pull this off. He and Janie could convince the world that they were completely in love and truly married. He was desperate enough, and Janie was strong enough. They would succeed.

When he smiled reassuringly at her, he saw some of her tension dissipate. And when she reached his side and he held out his hand, her fingers barely trembled in his.

They turned together to face the minister. And when he gave them an approving nod, Ben tightened his hold on Janie. He knew what she was giving up to marry him, the chance she thought she was taking. She had done it for Rafael's sake, and because he had backed her into a corner, but he was still very grateful. As the minister read the beautiful language of the marriage ceremony and Ben repeated the vows after him, he made another vow to himself. He promised Janie silently that he would never give her reason to regret her generosity.

"You may kiss your bride."

The minister stepped back, and Ben looked down at Janie. She looked up at him with wary eyes, and he slowly leaned forward to put his hands on her shoulders. He meant to give her a quick brush of a kiss on the lips, no more than minimum contact. No one would fault him for restraint in a church.

But she looked so lost, so sad, that he wrapped his arms around her instead. When he pulled her close, he felt her trembling. And when he bent to kiss her, her scent wrapped itself around his heart and squeezed.

When he touched her lips with his, need that he'd kept under lock and key for five months burst out, heating his blood, raging through his body. He couldn't stop himself from pressing her closer.

Unbidden and unwanted, memories of that night crashed over him like a wave that has been held back for too long. He remembered how she tasted, how she felt, how she gave him back passion for passion, touch for touch. He remembered the fierce desire that had seized both of them, and how it seemed so right at the time.

He also remembered the fear in Janie's face the next morning, and the pain in his own heart. He'd felt more for Janie in that one night than he had for his wife in their entire marriage. He'd done exactly what he'd always promised himself wouldn't happen again, and gotten involved with a woman. And not just an anonymous woman he could walk away from and forget. This was Janie, a woman he would see every day of his life. A woman he'd yearned for since the day she'd arrived in Cameron.

He'd told himself he was relieved when she said that morning she couldn't see him again, couldn't spend any time with him. He'd agreed with her, told her that he didn't have anything to offer her, either. But a tiny part of his heart had shriveled and died as she'd walked away without looking back.

Now when he kissed her, she went rigid with surprise. But then he felt her melt into him. Her hands clutched at his back and her lips opened beneath his. As he tasted the dark pleasure of her mouth, he felt the moment that she surrendered. He savored and swallowed her throaty moan of pleasure, gloried in the way she buckled against him. And allowed himself a moment of undiluted triumph in the knowledge that she was now his.

The thought stopped him cold. Janie was not now, nor would she ever be, his. There was nothing more between them than a marriage of convenience. She was doing him a huge favor, marrying him so he could adopt Rafael. And he, in turn, would try to protect her from whoever wanted to kill her. They had made a bargain, not a marriage.

He ignored the pain in the corner of his heart as he eased away from her. When he looked down into her dark blue eyes, now almost black with desire, he cursed himself for an insensitive fool. After what had happened between them, Janie would undoubtedly make more of his kiss than he'd intended.

But she recovered quickly. Her eyes cooled and she stepped away from him before he could move away from her. The minister said, "May I present Mr. and Mrs. Ben Jackson." She turned too quickly to face the people in the church, and stumbled slightly on the carpet.

He took her hand to steady her, and realized she was still trembling. When he forced himself to look at her face, he saw the sheen of tears in her eyes.

But she didn't let them fall. Janie straightened her spine, and he could almost see her willing herself not to cry. After a moment, she blinked the tears away and her hand steadied in his.

He wanted to bend down and kiss her again, tell her how strong she was and how much he admired her for it. Instead, he pulled her hand through his arm and gently led her down the aisle.

When they reached the back, he swung her around to face him before the other people came to offer their congratulations. "I'm sorry," he said quietly. "I didn't mean to kiss you like that in front of everyone in the church."

"I thought that was precisely what you intended," she answered, her voice cool. "Think of how good it will look on the social worker's report. It certainly makes the wedding seem more authentic.''

''Dammit, Janie, I wouldn't play with you like that.''

''Then what do you call this charade of a wedding?'' Her hand brushed down the dress she wore. ''I'm even wearing Shea's mother's wedding dress, for God's sake. Your kiss was just one more false thing about today.''

Nothing about that kiss had been false, he wanted to tell her, but he pressed his lips together and bit back the words. If his heart occasionally betrayed him, no one else had to know.

Then Carly and Devlin reached them. Dev shook his hand, and Carly hugged him. ''Congratulations,'' they said together, then they reached for Janie. Ben clenched his teeth as Shea approached him, and steeled himself for the day ahead.

Janie wasn't sure how she was going to make it through the rest of the day. She looked around her restaurant, Heaven on Seventh, and wondered wildly when her two waitresses, Mandy and Phyllis, had managed to find the time to decorate the place. They had been at the church for the ceremony, so they must have come over early this morning to mass fresh flowers around the room and hang streamers from the ceiling.

She hadn't wanted to have a reception. A reception implied a celebration of the marriage, something that would be completely false. And now, seeing the familiar faces smiling and talking, she felt a curl of shame about the deceit that she and Ben were perpetuating.

But before she could give in to impulse and run out the door, Melba Corboy came over and touched her arm. The older woman was dressed in what Janie was sure was her best dress, and a smile softened her face.

''You thank that husband of yours for inviting me to

your wedding, Janie," she said. She glanced over her shoulder at the young woman who stood talking to Shea Coulton. "And for inviting Tessa, too. It was kind of him to include her and make her feel like a part of Cameron."

Janie couldn't stop the smile that bloomed as she looked at Melba and Tessa. Ben, she knew, had been particularly protective of Melba ever since someone had broken into her boarding house to harass Carly while she was staying with Melba. Janie knew that he went over to Melba's frequently to check on the older woman. Melba's latest guest was Tessa Shipley. Tessa was a friend of Carly's who had moved to Cameron after ending her abusive marriage, and a close friendship had developed between the quiet young woman and the crusty Melba.

"Ben and I were both happy you could join us, Melba," Janie said. That, at least, was sincere. It was one of the few sincere things about the day. "And I'm glad to get a chance to get to know Tessa."

Melba's eyes softened. "I'm glad she's moved here," she said gruffly. "She's been good for me."

Janie knew it was the closest Melba would come to saying how much she cared about the young woman, and Janie glanced over at Tessa with interest. She was talking to Carly now, waving her hands through the air in delicate, graceful gestures. "It looks like she's describing her latest jewelry design to Carly," Janie said lightly.

Melba shook her head. "That girl needs to think about something besides her work. She needs to get out and meet more people."

"Sometimes focusing on your work is the best way to heal yourself." Janie compressed her lips. She could never tell Melba that she spoke from experience.

"Maybe so." Melba glanced over at Tessa again. "But one of these days, she's going to have to come out of her cocoon."

Janie knew Ben moved beside her before she felt his touch. And when he slipped an arm casually around her shoulders, her heart thumped against her chest almost painfully.

"She'll do it when she's ready, Melba," Ben said in his deep voice. "And in the meantime, you've been dam... darned good to her. That's what she needs."

Janie was surprised to see Melba's cheeks flush pink. "I take care of my guests," she said, and her voice was sharp. It was almost sharp enough to hide the pleasure that flashed in her eyes.

The rare smile that spread across Ben's face made Janie's heart flutter. "That you do, Melba. In fact, you take such good care of them that most of your recent guests have stayed in Cameron. I'd say that was a pretty good track record."

Melba's face softened again. "It's good to see you young people getting married. I've enjoyed every one of the weddings we've had lately in Cameron."

She watched them carefully. "You two take good care of each other, and of young Rafael." She smiled once more. "But I don't think anyone has to tell you that. You were made for each other."

Silence hung between them, heavy and uncomfortable, as Melba turned and walked away. Finally Janie spoke, trying to lighten the mood. "I guess that's one positive vote for the social worker."

Ben took her upper arms in his hands and turned her to face him. "This is hard for you, Janie. I'm sorry."

She wanted to snap back at him, give him a sharp answer that would vent her frustration. But she saw the lines on his face, the strain in his eyes, and she sighed. "It's not easy for you, either. We'll get through the day."

"It's not today I'm worried about," he muttered.

A flash of heat seared her as she thought about the coming night, and all the nights to follow. She hadn't wanted to move into Ben's house. Even though she'd only been inside one time, memories of that one night still consumed her.

Ben had found her sitting on a bench in the park late at night. It had been one of the nights when the loneliness, the hopelessness of her situation had overwhelmed her. And when Ben sat down beside her, she had seen the pain in his eyes.

It had been a night of mutual comfort. She'd told herself so countless times in the past few months. But her heart knew they had shared more than comfort. Ben had touched a place in her heart that she'd thought was forever hidden, and she'd never been the same.

But she couldn't risk thinking anymore about that night, so she chose to deliberately misunderstand him. "Everyone in town is sure that our marriage is real," she finally said, managing to keep the wobble out of her voice. "We'll do just fine with the social worker."

Ben slanted a glance at her, and the fire in his eyes told her he hadn't been thinking about the social worker, either. Then she watched as he banked the fires, and slowly nodded. "Thanks to you, Janie. If the judge approves our adoption petition, it will be thanks to you."

She shook her head. "You're the one who connected with Rafael. You're the one he trusts, the one he's bonded to. I'm just here to make things go smoothly in the legal department."

Ben watched her for a moment, then an odd little smile curled his lips. "Don't shortchange yourself, Janie. I think Rafael needs you as much as I do."

For just a moment, need filled his eyes and hope leaped to life in her chest. For just that moment, she allowed herself to think that he needed her in a far different way than as a temporary wife. Then the moment of vulnerability was gone, his need hidden carefully away. Once again his face was aloof and closed.

"We need to talk to people, eat some food, play the happy couple," he said after a moment. His voice was gruff.

"I don't think I could swallow a thing." Just the thought of eating made a large, greasy ball of anxiety swell in her stomach.

Surprisingly, he grinned at her. "No one will mind that. They'll put it down to wedding day nerves."

"They'd be right," she muttered. It was far more than nerves, she thought grimly. She'd never thought of herself as an actress. But she had to put on the performance of her life today, then follow it up with a similar act every day from now on. As far as the world was concerned, she and Ben were deliriously in love and committed to each other and Rafael.

"Where is Rafael?" she asked, realizing she hadn't seen him for a while.

Ben's face relaxed in another grin. "He's raiding the wedding cake with Cassie Farrell. The last time I checked on him, Cassie was telling him all about barrel racing. I expect the next thing he's going to want is a horse and barrel racing lessons."

Janie looked around the restaurant until she spotted Rafael and the dark-haired Cassie sitting at a table, their legs swinging back and forth as they ate cake and talked. Rafael stared at Cassie, his face rapt with attention. Janie's heart contracted in her chest as she watched the two children.

"I'm so glad he's spending more time with other children."

"The kids have been good for him." Ben's voice roughened, as if he was trying to hide his emotion. "Tom Jessup has had him out to his ranch a few times to play with Stevie, and there are a few kids in the neighborhood who've been coming around the house. It finally looks like he's opening up."

"Thanks to you," Janie murmured. She watched Rafael as she spoke, knowing that the fact he could relax with Cassie was due to Ben's loving care of him.

"I'm not doing anything special," Ben protested.

"Yes, you are." She finally looked over at Ben. "Whether you want to admit it or not, you're making a huge difference in his life. You're giving him stability, and a sense of belonging. You represent safety to Rafael. I'd say those were things that have been missing from his life for far too long."

"That's not so hard." His voice was gruff. "It's easy to feel safe and stable in Cameron."

"You're also giving him love. That's not quite as uncomplicated."

Ben's face hardened. "I'm taking care of him, Janie. I want to give him a home. That's all it is."

Janie looked over at him, studied his eyes and the pain that simmered deep inside him. The middle of their wedding reception wasn't the time for a debate about the meaning of love. "We'll see," she said.

"Let's go check on him." Ben's voice was abrupt. "He's always a little nervous in a crowd if he doesn't know where I am."

Janie had to clamp her lips together. If Ben's concern for the child's state of mind wasn't love, she didn't know the meaning of the word. But if Ben chose to deny that he loved Rafael, it wasn't her place to challenge him on it.

After all, he doesn't love you, either.

The pain stabbed at her again, sharp and fierce. As she followed Ben over to the table, she told herself to get used to it. If she expected to be successful at this sham of a marriage, she was going to have to accept the fact that theirs was a marriage of convenience. Love had nothing to do with it.

Rafael looked up when they approached the table, and the quick light in his eyes told Janie how he felt about Ben. Then he turned to her and gave her a shy smile, and her heart turned over in her chest.

"Hey, buddy." Ben reached out and ruffled Rafael's hair. The gesture was automatic, the kind of touching that all parents indulged in. Janie wondered if Ben even realized how much he cared about this child. "Don't you think the rest of us would like some of that cake?"

Ben pretended to scowl and Rafael giggled, much to Janie's surprise and delight. She hadn't seen the playful side of either the man or the child.

"We left half for the rest of you." Cassie piped up, grinning at them, and Rafael's eyes sparkled.

"Yes, we only ate half," Rafael echoed.

Ben turned to her, feigning a stern look. "What do you think about this, Janie?"

She tried to look thoughtful. "I don't know. It looks to me like they could each use another piece of cake. I don't think they've had enough."

Both children giggled again, and Ben threw her a grateful look, laughter stirring in the back of his eyes. "Am I going to be outnumbered here?"

"Right now it looks like it's three to one." Janie kept her face bland as she watched Rafael. His eyes darted from one of them to the other. His shocked delight at being the center of attention made her heart ache.

Ben heaved a huge sigh. "It's a sad thing when a man is outnumbered. Go ahead and get more cake. But I don't want to hear about any stomachaches tonight."

Both children scrambled away from the table, laughing, and Ben turned to look at her. "Thank you," he said quietly.

"For what? For teasing a couple of children?" she said, her voice light.

"No, for making Rafael feel like a part of a family."

"That's what he is, Ben. The day you took him into your home, he became your family. All I'm doing is helping to make it a legal bond as well as an emotional one."

"Not everyone would know how to handle him."

"I'm no expert. I've never lived with an eight-year-old boy. But my nephew is a little older than Ben." Her heart quivered once with remembered pain, then she firmly put it out of her mind. Her family was safe and happy somewhere. She had to believe that. "I know how to push their buttons."

"How am I ever going to make it up to you?" Ben asked.

"There is no need to make it up to me," she said, her voice sharp. "I'm already crazy about Rafael. He deserves all the happiness he can get out of life. And it doesn't take a rocket scientist to see that he's happy with you. If I didn't think the two of you belonged together, I wouldn't have agreed to this...this sham. So don't talk about making it up to me."

Ben stood watching her, a strange light in his eyes. "Every day I learn more about you, Janie. I'm not sure if that's a good thing, or not."

"You'd better learn enough about me so we can fool the social worker and the judge." Her voice was sharper than she intended, to mask the pain that washed over her. "This isn't about you and me, it's about Rafael."

His eyes cooled and hardened. "You're right. And thank you for the reminder. You won't have to remind me again."

Chapter 5

Several hours later, Janie took a deep breath and watched the last person leave the restaurant. She wanted to lock the door behind him and hide away from the world, but that was impossible. The person she most wanted to hide from was standing next to her.

After this stress-filled day, she desperately wished she could let the mask slip, to stop pretending, but she couldn't do that. She was committed to this sham of a marriage, and she would do her best to keep up the facade. Because there was someone who mattered more than her comfort, someone who was more important than her pride.

He stood next to Ben, watching her with uncertain eyes.

"What's wrong?" she asked, her voice sharpening as her gaze whipped back to the child. "Are you all right, Rafael?"

Ben cleared his throat again. "He's fine. There's just something that I haven't told you."

"What's that?"

"Shea is going to have Rafael stay out at the ranch for the night. She said that we...ah...needed to have privacy on our wedding night."

"And you agreed?" Janie fought to keep the rising panic from filling her voice. She didn't want to alarm Rafael.

"What was I supposed to say, Janie?" he demanded. "That we weren't interested in having a wedding night?"

Janie struggled to control her reaction. She was too aware of Rafael watching. "You could have said I wanted time with Rafael, to get to know him." She was cornered, and she knew it. Sighing, she said, "Are you sure you want to go to Shea's, Rafael?"

He nodded eagerly. "I like the ranch," he said. "I like to play with Buster."

Janie touched the boy's head. There was no way she could compete with Shea's dog. "Okay. Why don't we get your bag packed?"

The three of them left the restaurant, and Janie locked the door carefully behind her. But instead of walking to her own house, as she usually did, they climbed into Ben's vehicle and headed the few blocks in the other direction to Ben's tiny home.

Rafael was out of the car and running to the house almost before the car had stopped. She tried to climb out after him, but Ben put his hand on her arm. When she froze, he pulled it away, but it was too late. Her nerves tingled, and her heart was racing. She slowly turned to face him.

"I'm sorry, Janie," he said quietly, when she finally turned to face him. "There was nothing I could say to Shea to head her off. You know how she is when she gets an idea. And if we were truly married, we'd want privacy for our wedding night." He nodded at the house, where Rafael was heading back out the door, a backpack in his hand.

"You can see that Rafael is excited about going to Shea's." He compressed his lips as the boy approached the truck. "We'll talk about this later."

As Rafael got into the truck, Ben said, "You have everything you need, buddy?"

Rafael nodded vigorously. "I have clean clothes and underwear, and my hairbrush. And my deedee."

Before Janie could ask what a deedee was, Ben turned and gave Rafael a stern look. "How about your toothbrush?"

The boy gave him a mulish look in return. "I forgot it."

For a moment Ben watched the child, then he grinned at him. "That's okay. I'm sure Shea has one you can use."

Janie almost chuckled at the chagrined look on Rafael's face. Some things never changed, and apparently getting kids to brush their teeth was one of them. But her smile faded as they drove down the two-lane highway toward the Red Rock Ranch. Soon Rafael would be with Shea and Jesse, and she and Ben would be alone.

On their wedding night.

The thought stirred images she didn't dare allow to linger. Turning away from Ben, she stared out the window at the gathering dusk and tried to force herself to think about something else.

"Hey, Rafael," she said, turning around to face the child, "what's your deedee?"

He watched her for a moment, as if trying to decide if she could be trusted, then he reached into his backpack and pulled out a small square of multicolored cloth. She saw his fingers stroke it once, then he slipped it back into the pack.

She opened her mouth to ask him where he'd gotten it, but Ben touched her hand once, then immediately withdrew his fingers. When she glanced over at him, he gave a quick, silent shake of his head.

"It's beautiful," she said, instead of the question she'd bitten back. "I can see why it's special to you."

He nodded once, then shifted his hands on his pack. Almost, she thought, as if protecting the scrap of material. Her heart ached for him and all he had suffered.

"Here we are," Ben said as he slowed the truck. He turned into a curving driveway and headed around a cliff that blocked the view of the rest of the ranch. Once past the cliff, the beauty of the Red Rock Ranch unfolded in front of her, under the rising moon.

The green pastures stood in front of them, almost black in the moonlight. Cattle were mere shadows, darker blurs on the velvet of the grass. Only the buildings were full of light. The house stood as a welcoming beacon in the rapidly darkening Utah dusk.

He glanced into the back seat of the truck. "We'll come get you in the morning, okay, buddy?"

"Can I stay until the afternoon?"

Janie smiled in the darkness. The wheedling tone of Rafael's voice was one of the sweetest sounds she'd ever heard. Only a child who was completely confident of his relationship with the adult in his life would whine that way.

Ben pretended to consider. "I'll have to talk to Shea. They may have things planned for tomorrow."

"Shea says I'm never a bother," Rafael replied. "She says I can help out here on the ranch any time I want."

"I'll talk to her."

But before they could get out of the car, Shea burst out of the house. Janie didn't think she'd ever seen Shea moving at less than warp speed.

"Hey," she called. "Is that the guy who's going to help me with all those cattle tomorrow?"

Janie could feel Rafael beaming from the back seat. "Ben doesn't think I help," he said, and she smiled again to hear the scorn in his voice. "Tell him I'm a big help, Shea."

"The biggest." Shea's face was solemn as she leaned through Janie's open window. "I've got all kinds of work planned for tomorrow. How about letting him stay two nights?"

Panic rose up inside of Janie. That would mean two nights and a whole day alone with Ben. And she wouldn't even have the excuse of the restaurant to get away from him. Heaven on Seventh was closed on Sunday.

"I don't know, Shea. Maybe we should come for him tomorrow afternoon." She heard the strain in Ben's voice. Apparently he felt the same way about being alone with her. She should be glad, she told herself fiercely. But a small corner of her heart folded in on itself, trying to protect her from the pain.

"Why don't you give me a call?" Shea said easily. Then she grinned at them, a wicked look in her eyes. "And if I don't hear from you, I'll assume you found other things to think about."

The only things they would be thinking about, Janie told herself, were ways to avoid each other in that tiny house of his. And ways to avoid the memories that lingered there.

Then Shea stepped away from the truck, and Rafael bounded out of the back seat. Ben slid out of his seat and went over to stand in front of the boy, and Janie slipped out of the truck to stand nearby.

Ben squatted down in the red dust and put his hands on Rafael's shoulders. "You have a good time, you hear?" he said, and his voice was gruff. "And you mind Shea and Jesse."

Rafael nodded hard. "I will, Ben."

Almost as if he couldn't stop himself, Ben's arms

snaked around the boy in a quick, hard hug. "I'll miss you," he said, then he set Rafael away from him and stood up. "We'll see you tomorrow."

Rafael nodded and hugged his pack to his chest more closely. When he gave her a quick glance, Janie stepped forward. "I'll miss you, too," she said in a low voice. But she didn't touch him again. She remembered the way he'd tensed the last time she'd touched him.

"Is he going to be scared?" she asked Ben when they were in his truck and out of sight of the house.

"I don't think so." He glanced over at her, and she saw understanding in his eyes. "I think most eight-year-old kids have a hard time with their first few sleepovers. And Rafael is not a typical eight-year-old. He'll be fine. And if he's not, Shea will give me a call."

They drove through the darkness, the silence humming in the truck between them. Janie didn't want to think about the fact that they were alone, and married. She didn't want to think about the long night facing them. So she searched for a safe topic of conversation.

"What's that piece of cloth he has that you called his deedee?"

Ben's face tensed. Apparently this wasn't a safe topic of conversation after all. "When he arrived in this country from San Rafael, he had only a few things in his pack. The other children brought food or clothes, but all he had was a tattered lace shawl, a silver comb, a chipped white mug and that scrap of cloth. I've asked him if he wanted to tell me about them, but so far he hasn't. He keeps the other things underneath his bed, but he takes that piece of cloth everywhere. And he sleeps with it every night."

"Deedee doesn't sound like any Spanish word I've ever heard," she said, trying to keep her voice light.

Ben's hands tightened on the steering wheel, and his face looked as if it could have been carved from the rock that surrounded them. He didn't say anything for so long that Janie was certain he wasn't going to answer. Finally he spoke, and the words sounded like they had been torn from his throat.

"It's not. He got that word from me."

"Is that what you called your comfort blanket as a child?"

"No." His hands curled so tightly around the steering wheel that his knuckles whitened. "It's what another child I knew called it."

"You seem to have figured out the right way to handle it." She wanted desperately to ask him about that other child, but her heart told her she didn't have the right. And Ben certainly had no obligation to share any part of himself with her. Wasn't that the bargain they'd made?

Ignoring the pain in her chest, the emptiness that wanted to swallow her, she said, "Rafael seems to be adjusting pretty well."

Ben didn't answer right away, but she saw his hands loosen their grip on the steering wheel. Finally he said, "Yeah, I think he is. He won't talk about his life in San Rafael at all, or any of the things he brought with him. But he's smiling more, and he lets me hug him now. He didn't want to be touched when he first came to live with me."

Rafael was a safe topic, she thought. They could talk about Rafael all night and never have to touch on the subject they both clearly wanted to avoid—their so-called marriage. So she asked Ben another question about Rafael, and Ben relaxed even more as he answered it. By the time he turned into the driveway of his home, she had almost forgotten the tension that hummed beneath the surface.

Almost, but not quite. Because as soon as she faced that house, all the strain came roaring back.

Ben's voice trailed away as they sat in the darkness and

looked at the small, one-story house. There was too much history here, she thought in a panic. Too many memories. They should have chosen to live at her house.

But they couldn't do that. They had Rafael to consider, and he needed the stability and sameness of Ben's house.

So she sat and stared at the house, willing herself to walk inside. She'd been inside several times in the last few days, to move her clothes and belongings in, but she hadn't been alone with Ben at the time. Rafael had been there, and usually at least one of the other deputies who'd been helping her move. This would be the first time she and Ben were alone, truly alone, since she'd agreed to marry him.

Ben finally said, "We'd better go inside." She heard the strain in his voice and wondered if it was because of the looming night alone.

"You're right." Her lips felt stiff, and she had to struggle to get the words past them. "If I know Cameron, everyone on your block has been waiting and watching for the newlyweds to get home."

He turned to her, and even in the darkness, she saw his eyes glittering. "Then we'd better make their wait worthwhile, don't you think?"

He moved closer, and all the air whooshed out of her lungs. "I think..."

"That's a bad habit of yours, Janie. You think too much." His mouth lowered. "Sometimes you just have to *do*."

His kiss wasn't tentative or tender. He crushed his mouth to hers, devouring her, demanding a response. And in spite of her vows to herself, in spite of all her lectures these past few days, she couldn't stop herself from responding. She couldn't bite back the moan of pleasure, the burn of desire that scorched her with its heat. She couldn't stop her hands from clutching at his shirt, holding on like he was the only constant in a spinning, out of control world.

She felt the shudder that rippled through him, felt the thudding of his heart next to hers. And she felt him struggle for control, fight to pull himself back from the edge of passion. Suddenly all the promises she'd been making to herself didn't matter. She forgot the countless times she'd told herself that she and Ben could live together as emotionless, passionless strangers.

All she knew was the rightness of Ben, of touching him and caressing him. All she heard was the small voice inside her head that told her to grab on to him and hold on for all she was worth. All she wanted to do was keep on kissing him, forever.

When Ben smoothed his hand over her cheek and down her throat, she felt him trembling. And when he eased away from her, his regret lingered in the air between them, heavy and dark.

"What's wrong?" she managed to say.

"I'm sorry, Janie. That wasn't any part of the bargain we made." He moved away from her and leaned back in his seat, careful not to look at her. "I had to kiss you in church, but you're supposed to be calling all the shots in this marriage. I promise you I won't touch you again."

That would be the smart thing to do, Janie knew. But she said in a small voice, "It's not as if I was objecting."

"You should have been." He still refused to look over at her. "I don't have anything to give you, Janie. I thought I made that clear. This marriage is supposed to be for Rafael's sake, nothing more. It's not supposed to be about kissing you in a car, in full view of my neighborhood, for God's sake."

"Then think of it as part of the show." She hoped the trembling she felt inside didn't leak into her voice. "If the neighbors were watching, they saw what they expected to see. So be glad about that.''

''I don't want to take advantage of you.'' His words were a murmur of velvet in the darkness of the car, and because his voice made her shiver, she allowed his words to prick her temper.

''I'm not a child, Ben,'' she said, and her tone was sharper than she'd intended. ''I'm an adult, just like you. No one takes advantage of me without my full cooperation. If I hadn't wanted you to kiss me, I would have said so.''

''Fine. We'll think of it as part of the act. But I hope someone in the neighborhood was keeping track.''

''Don't worry,'' she said dryly, her temper vanishing. ''I'm sure any number of people will be able to testify that we couldn't keep our hands off each other, and we weren't even in the house yet.''

''Let's go.'' Ben's voice was abrupt as he climbed out of the truck and slammed the door. ''I'm not giving any more free shows.''

She wanted desperately to ask if he was tempted to do so, but she didn't want to hear the answer. They had made a bargain, after all, and it would be better for both of them if they stuck to it. When Ben kissed her, she might forget all the reasons she couldn't get involved with him, but that didn't mean that those reasons ceased to exist. Here, on the dark and quiet street, she remembered every one of them.

As Ben opened the door of the truck and waited for her to get out, she couldn't stop herself from looking into the dark shadows surrounding Ben's house and the houses close to it. When Ben laid a hand on her arm, she jumped.

''It's all right, Janie. There's no one here but the two of us.''

''How can you be sure?'' she asked. ''I can't take that

chance. Especially now. I have to think about you and Rafael.''

"Think of it this way. Now, if someone wants to get to you, he'll have to go through me. And I don't bend very easily.''

No, Ben Jackson didn't bend. She knew that for a fact. She just hoped that he didn't end up breaking before this charade of a marriage was over. "Let's go into the house.''

He nodded, but she saw a muscle working in his jaw. "I'll get the stuff in the car later.''

When they approached the front door, he took out his keys and unlocked the dead bolt, then turned on the lights. Ben stood back, but Janie hesitated. They had stood in front of the minister and said their vows, but the marriage hadn't seemed real somehow until this moment. Stepping into Ben's home tonight would seal the bargain in a way that was far too intimate. And once they were inside that door, there were far too many memories waiting to ambush her.

"Thanks for reminding me," Ben murmured, and his voice was too close. "If you hadn't hesitated, I would have forgotten the ritual. And we don't want to disappoint our audience.''

"You would have forgotten what?'' she said, turning to face him. She found he was standing right next to her, his face grim.

"This.'' He swept her up into his arms and carried her across the threshold into his house. Kicking the door shut, he stood her back on her feet, then quickly moved away from her.

"We wouldn't want to forget any of the romantic non-sense people expect from newlyweds,'' he said, walking into the kitchen to turn on the lights there. Then he headed down the short hallway that led to the bedrooms.

"It's not nonsense,'' she murmured to herself. She tried

to keep the hurt from welling up inside her. What woman didn't dream of her wedding day, of having her husband carry her across the threshold of their home? She had put such dreams out of her mind three years ago, she reminded herself. It was moments like this, though, that made the pain of all her losses stir again.

Ben emerged from the hallway, and she saw that all the lights in the house had been turned on. "I figured you'd be more comfortable if the house wasn't dark," he said.

"Thank you. That was thoughtful of you."

He paced the living room, but didn't sit down. Tension seemed to vibrate off him in tangible waves. Her heart tripped in her chest and speeded up. They were alone, and the endless night stretched ahead of them.

But she would be darned if she would let him see how nervous that made her. She was too vulnerable to Ben as it was. So she tilted her chin into the air and sat down in a chair.

"Stop pacing, Ben. We're both adults." She leaned back against the seat and forced her face into a cool, detached expression. "There's no reason we can't manage an evening spent together. There's plenty to talk about."

He stopped walking, but he didn't sit down. He swiveled to face her. "And what topics of conversation have you picked out for us, Mrs. Jackson?" There was a flash of pain in his eyes as he spoke. "Would you like to talk about which drawers you're going to have in the dresser? Or how about how I can make room in my closet for your clothes?" He paused, and she saw something flare in his eyes, heat and a need that she was sure she imagined. "Or maybe you'd like to talk about the sleeping arrangements."

She swallowed once and looked away from him. For just a moment, she wished that theirs was a real marriage. She wished she had the right to wrap her arms around him, to take away the pain she saw in his eyes. And respond to the passion that was hidden below it. But she didn't. So she swallowed again and said, "I thought maybe we could talk about Rafael."

He nodded curtly. "Yeah, we need to talk about Rafael. There's a lot I have to tell you about him. But not tonight.

"Tonight I think we need to talk about ancient history." He paused, and this time there was no mistaking the desire that heated his face. "We need to talk about what happened five months ago."

Chapter 6

Ben stopped, appalled at himself. That night was the last thing he intended to bring up to Janie. It was the last thing he wanted to think about. The events of that night still haunted him, but Janie couldn't ever find that out.

He didn't have a clue to how Janie felt about that night. Even now, when he looked over at her, she lifted her chin defiantly and pushed a few tendrils of her wavy red hair off her face. Her eyes didn't tell him anything.

Another wave of admiration swept over him for this woman he'd married. Janie had a backbone of steel. The events in her life that had led her to Cameron could have destroyed another person. But they only seemed to have made her stronger. And now, when he brought up a subject that was bound to be embarrassing, if not downright upsetting, she merely lifted her chin and watched him with that cool blue gaze of hers.

"What is it that we need to talk about? I thought we'd said everything that needed saying that morning."

Her words were as cool as her gaze, but he heard the slight tremble in her voice. For a moment, wild hope rose up in him, a hope he'd always refused to acknowledge. Maybe she hadn't been as unaffected by that night as she'd wanted him to believe. Maybe it had meant more to her than comfort and an exchange of pleasure.

And maybe he was a complete fool, Ben told himself harshly. It didn't matter what she'd felt. It couldn't matter. Because he couldn't let it matter to him.

"I thought we should clear the air," he said, shifting on the suddenly lumpy chair and wishing he'd kept his damn mouth shut.

"There's nothing in the air to clear. I was lonely that night. It had been two years, and I thought nothing was ever going to change. I was feeling sorry for myself. I shouldn't have been crying on that park bench, but I was. When you found me, I needed someone to hold me and comfort me. The comfort went too far, but I don't regret it." Her gaze shifted, and now she didn't quite meet his eyes. "I'm sorry if you do."

"I don't regret that night," he said, too quickly. God, if she only knew how he'd dreamed of that night. How he'd wished passionately, in a hidden corner of his soul, that it would happen again. "But I don't want you worrying that it'll happen again."

Her gaze snapped back to his. "I have no illusions, Ben. This wasn't a happily-ever-after kind of day. We have a marriage of convenience, not passion. But I'm committed to making it work. I'm committed to making sure that Rafael stays with you. And I'll do anything I have to do to make that happen. Including pretending to the world that we're madly in love."

For just a moment, he allowed himself the fantasy that she wouldn't have to pretend. For just a moment, he allowed himself to forget the past, forget all the vows he had made to himself. For just a moment, he actually allowed himself to hope that eventually, he and Janie would be a normal couple, with a normal marriage. Something he once believed he'd had.

That would never happen. The voice inside of him spoke harshly, castigating him for the fool that he was.

And he had to make sure that Janie felt the same way. "So that night is forgotten?"

"Completely," she said, her voice firm.

"And it's not going to be a problem for you?"

"No. How about you?"

"It won't be a problem for me," he answered, and his voice was grimmer than he'd intended. He wouldn't allow it to be a problem.

"I'm glad we got that out of the way," she said, but for a moment, he saw a trace of sadness in her eyes, a sadness that seemed to come from deep inside her. Then her eyes became aloof once again. "Why don't you tell me more about Rafael? I know school starts in a few days. I know you've been juggling your work schedule so you could spend as much time with him as possible. What are we going to do once he's in school most of the day?"

Ben wasn't sure if he was relieved or disappointed that the conversation had taken such an impersonal direction. Then he sighed. He'd better be damned glad it was impersonal. He was feeling too edgy, too restless tonight. He didn't want to do something dangerous, something that he and Janie would both regret. So he dragged his thoughts back to Rafael.

"I'm going to start working days again. That way I'll be here soon after he gets home from school. I've already talked to Laura Weston. I'll take him over to her house in the morning. Laura can take him to school with her children, Jenny and Todd. Then Rafael can go to Laura's after school until I get home."

"I can go to the restaurant a little later every day," Janie said slowly. "I've been thinking about hiring another cook, anyway. That way I could be here to see him off to school in the morning. So he'd only be with Laura for a little while after school every day."

"You don't have to do that, Janie," he said, moved by her offer. "That wasn't part of the deal."

"I guess I'm going to be breaking the deal, then." Her voice became cool again. "Don't worry, Ben. I'm not doing it for you. I'm doing it for Rafael. And think of how good it will look to the social worker who's going to be making the recommendations to the judge."

"You make it sound so cold-blooded," he muttered.

"Isn't that what it's supposed to be?" she demanded. "I thought those were the rules."

"I don't know what the rules are," he said, jumping up and pacing around the room. "All I could think about was keeping Rafael. Saving him. And marrying you was the only way I knew of to do that."

"I know." Her voice softened and she sighed. "I'm sorry, Ben. I shouldn't have snapped at you like that. I know that everything you've done has been for Rafael. I wouldn't have agreed to this marriage if I hadn't seen how much you cared about him. But you're going to have to let me do some things for him, too. Otherwise he'll figure out that there's something wrong." She tilted her head and watched him carefully. "Are you trying to protect him from me?"

"I guess I am," he answered slowly. "He's lost too much already in his eight years. I don't want him to get attached to you, then have you leave."

"You should have thought about that before you cornered me into marrying you." Her voice could have been tart, but instead it was weary. "I won't abandon him, Ben. If we go our separate ways after you get custody of him,

I'll still be a part of his life. Lots of parents get divorced, but that doesn't mean they forget about their children. I won't forget about Rafael.''

''I wasn't asking you for a lifetime commitment to him.''

''You may not have been asking for it, but that's what I hope to give him. Did you really think I could just turn my back on him and forget about him once my 'job' was finished?'' She glared at him, her eyes sparking.

Ben ran his fingers through his hair and sighed. Everything had become far more complicated than he'd planned. ''I hadn't thought that far ahead,'' he admitted. ''I couldn't see any farther than the custody hearing.''

''I know.'' She rose from her chair and stood next to him. Her hand hovered above his arm for a moment, almost as if she couldn't bring herself to touch him, then she brushed his tensed muscles with her fingertips. His muscles quivered at her touch, and she quickly pulled her hand away.

''If I hadn't seen your single-minded devotion to Rafael, I wouldn't have agreed to this marriage. But I had no doubts that he would be better off with you than with anyone else.'' She smiled, and he was struck again at the sweetness in her. ''How many times do we actually get a chance to do something that will make a real difference in a child's life? We'll get through this, Ben. We'll get permanent custody of Rafael, and we'll adopt him. And we'll deal with whatever comes along afterward.''

''I wish I had known you years ago, Janie. Before you had to run away, and before I...'' The words came out of nowhere, startling him. But he realized it was true.

''Before you what, Ben?''

''Before I became cynical and hard.'' He turned away from her, because he wanted to tell her all of it. He wanted to tell her the truth, the reason why he was alone and would always be alone. And he was appalled by the need to bare his soul to her.

"What happened to make you cynical and hard, Ben?" she asked quietly.

"Life happened." His voice was brusque. "We'd better get to bed. It's been a long day."

"And we don't want to let the neighbors see the lights on for too long in this house," she said, too lightly.

"No, we don't." He swallowed once and turned to face her again. "We need to talk about the sleeping arrangements, Janie."

"All right. Where am I going to sleep?" There was no lightness in her voice now.

"This is a two-bedroom house," he said grimly. "Rafael has one bedroom, and I have the other. And don't forget the social worker. She'll ask Rafael where we sleep. She'll make it sound like a game, and Rafael will tell her every detail about our lives."

"That's despicable!" Janie's face was pale, but her eyes flashed.

"That's her job. She's only thinking of Rafael. She wants to make sure that he's in the best possible home."

"Then all she has to do is watch you with him. And watch him when he's with you. That will tell her everything she needs to know."

Her eyes were blue fires, and Ben felt his heart weakening. Janie was so fierce in his defense. He wanted to wrap his arms around her and thank her, but he knew better. Touching her was off limits. Touching Janie tonight would be the biggest mistake he could possibly make.

He shoved his hands deep into his pockets, because his heart didn't want to listen to his head. "What we want doesn't matter, Janie." He hoped his heart was listening. "We have to think about how everyone else is going to see our marriage. And that means sleeping in the same room. In the same bed.''

Her face was even more pale and her eyes enormous. "How can we do that, Ben?" she whispered. "I can't sleep in that bed with you. I'll do nothing but remember..."

She clamped her mouth shut, but it was too late. His heart leaped. That night *had* been important to her. It had been about more than pleasure and comfort, more than mere sex. But he caught himself before he could go to her. "It's a big bed, Janie," he said, his voice even. "I promise I won't touch you. We can manage to share it."

"Do you really believe that?" Her voice was a low, agonized murmur.

"I have to believe that. Because that's the way it has to be. You can't sleep on the couch. And you can't sleep in Rafael's room. That leaves my room, and my bed."

"I can sleep in Rafael's bed tonight," she said, and there was desperation in her voice.

Ben shook his head. "Then what happens tomorrow night? Do you think we'll both be able to act perfectly normal with that hanging over our heads? Don't you think there'd be some tension in the air before we crawl into bed together? And don't think that Rafael won't notice the tension. He's a smart kid, and I have a feeling he needed his wits to survive in San Rafael. He'll figure out that something is wrong."

"And you think that sleeping together tonight is going to make it easier to sleep together tomorrow night?" she demanded.

"It'll get easier every night," he said. He hoped that was true. Because if it wasn't, his life would be hell in the next weeks and months. He wasn't sure how he was going to make it through the nights with Janie sleeping in his bed.

Janie chewed on her lip, her body quivering with tension. Finally she looked up at him. "There must be some other way." Her voice echoed with desperation and her eyes looked hunted.

"No. I'm sorry, Janie, but there's no way around this. We have to share a room, and a bed. Because if we don't, our marriage will be exposed for the sham that it is."

"I could sleep on the floor."

"There's no reason for you to do that." His voice softened. "I promised I wouldn't touch you, and I won't."

"I'm not worried about you breaking your promises," she said, slashing her hand through the air as if dismissing that concern.

"Then what are you worried about?"

She glared at him. "Do I have to spell it out for you, Ben? We're two healthy, normal people, and we shared that bed once before. What do you think is going to happen if we sleep together every night?"

The devil inside him, the one that he fought constantly, was beginning to enjoy her distress. "I can control myself, Janie. Are you telling me that you can't?"

Sparks flew from her eyes. "We're going to find out very soon. Because if I manage not to kill you right now, it will be a miracle of self-control."

Incredibly, Ben found himself smiling. "Whatever else our marriage is going to be, it won't be dull." Ignoring what his reason told him, feeling only his need to hold her, he moved closer and pulled her into his arms. He held her close in spite of the way her body stiffened. "I'm sorry I teased you, but we both need to lighten up. Yeah, it's going to be tough. It's not going to be easy to sleep in the same bed with you every night. We're going to know things about each other, intimate things that we'd rather not share with a virtual stranger. But Rafael is worth it. And if you can do it, so can I."

She didn't relax in his arms, but she stopped trying to push away from him. "I know." He felt her sigh ripple out of her body. "I know that it's not any easier for you than it is for me. But I wasn't expecting this. I thought we'd be able to keep some distance from each other, keep things impersonal and businesslike."

"I'll try, Janie. But the world isn't going to buy a businesslike marriage."

"The people in Cameron will see what they expect to see," she answered, but she didn't move away from him.

"Maybe, but the social worker is going to be a much harder sell than Cameron. And she's the one who counts." He allowed his hand to drift down her back, telling himself that he was merely comforting her. But the wave of need that flooded over him had very little to do with comfort. He told himself to move away from her, to stop touching her, but he couldn't do it.

She sighed again, and when her body trembled against his, desire stabbed into him with the force of a lightning bolt. His hand hesitated on her back, aching to drift lower and shape her hips, but he moved higher instead. She wanted comfort from him, and nothing more.

"I know you're right, Ben." She looked up at him, and he saw weariness in her eyes. He wondered if that weariness was why she'd let her guard down. "But it's going to be hard for me. I've kept to myself for so long, been careful for so long, that it would be tough to open up even if we had a real marriage."

"No one expects you to change overnight. The social worker will understand that there are a lot of adjustments in a marriage." He continued to stroke her back, his hands slow and careful. He felt every bump in her spine, every ridge of tense muscle. And he ached to burrow beneath her clothes, to massage away the tension, to touch her skin. Every part of him remembered how she felt.

"I guess we'll just have to do a good job of convincing her that anything odd she notices is one of those adjustments." She sighed again and burrowed closer. He wondered if she realized what she was doing.

"You can do it, Janie. I think you could do anything you set your mind to doing."

"I'm not sure I can do this." Her voice was muffled against his chest. "But I'll try."

"Then let's go to bed." He forced himself to step back and let her go. His body ached with the loss, and he turned away so she wouldn't see how she'd affected him. "You go ahead. I'll turn off the lights and lock up."

"Is there a, ah…" She licked her lips once, and his body tightened. The memory of her taste exploded in his mouth. "What side of the bed should I take?"

"It doesn't matter." His voice was guttural and harsh, his desire barely under control. "Wherever you're comfortable."

She looked as if she wanted to say something, then she merely nodded once and turned away. She practically ran into the bathroom.

The door clicked shut, and he waited to hear her lock it. When she didn't, he smiled to himself without humor. Janie was entirely too trusting. If she had known what he was thinking, she would have locked the door and pulled something in front of it.

The sound of running water tormented him. Was she getting undressed? Would she take a shower? He pictured her standing in the shower, water running off her body, and images were so vivid that he thought he could reach out and touch her. Cursing himself, calling himself every kind of fool, he turned abruptly and hurried away from the small bathroom.

He tried to erase the images from his mind as he concentrated on locking the doors and windows. He had to focus on his job, and right now, his job was keeping Janie safe.

If you wanted to keep her safe, you shouldn't be in the same house with her. The voice inside his head was grim. His agreement with Janie, his promise not to touch her, was in danger of falling apart. He wanted her with a desire so fierce, so intense, that it threatened to consume him. He couldn't bear to think about the coming night, when he would be forced to lie next to her, surrounded by her scent, listening to her breathe, and not touch her.

So he would concentrate on something else, he told himself, and he blocked off the sounds coming from the bathroom. He would concentrate on keeping Janie safe from the dangers that she feared from outside this house. He moved deliberately through the small house, checking every window lock, then testing the new dead bolts on the doors.

It was the least he could do. He didn't think Janie had anything to worry about, but he intended to respect her feelings about her safety. And he knew she would worry if the house wasn't locked up tight.

As he moved through the house, one part of his mind couldn't stop listening to Janie. He knew the instant the water stopped running, the instant the bathroom door opened. By the time he'd finished checking and double-checking the windows and doors, Janie was in the bedroom with the door half-closed, and his heart was pounding. Knowing she was there, knowing that she was in his bed, made his blood surge in his veins. He wanted nothing more than to go to her, to slide into bed beside her and have the right to reach for her.

But he didn't have that right. Not tonight or any night in the future. So he pushed the images out of his mind and tried to think about Rafael, or his job or anything that would take his mind off Janie.

Nothing worked. By the time he walked into the bedroom, he could think of nothing but Janie. Her scent swirled around him, filling the room with her essence. And he could focus on nothing but her slight form, curled into a ball on the edge of the bed.

She'd turned on the lamp on his side of the bed and the pool of golden light spilled across his sheets, burnishing her red hair to gold. He could tell she was pretending to be asleep. As he watched her tense body lying on the bed, a spear of tenderness moved through him. It pushed the need into the background and allowed him to regain a small part of his control.

He eased into bed and turned off the light. For a long time he lay perfectly still, his muscles tense, barely breathing. Janie didn't move, either. But he could feel her tension throbbing in the air, feel her uneasiness as though it was a living thing coiled between them.

"Janie?" His voice was a disembodied whisper in the dark room, barely audible.

She was silent for so long that he was afraid she wouldn't answer, afraid that she would stubbornly maintain the illusion of sleep. But finally she said, "What?"

"I'm not going to jump your bones, you know." No matter how much he wanted to do just that.

"I know that."

"Then why are you lying there as stiff as a board, almost falling off the edge of the bed?"

"I am not!"

"You are, Janie." Hearing the indignation in her voice, he smiled to himself in the darkness and felt a little of the tension draining away. "I can hear your fingernails digging in from here, trying to hold on."

She rolled over onto her side, and in the darkness he saw the glitter of her eyes. "Don't flatter yourself, Ben.

You sound as if I can't resist you. I can resist you just fine."

"Great. Then you don't have anything to worry about. Relax and go to sleep. I'll see you in the morning."

He heard her breath huff out in an angry whoosh. "I was asleep until you woke me up."

"Sorry." He grinned into the darkness, glad that the heavy tension had lifted. "I'll keep my mouth shut."

"You do that."

She rolled over again, but this time she wasn't on the edge of the bed and in danger of falling out. Her back was turned to him again, but he hoped that she would concentrate on being angry with him and not about how close he was. Because if she fell asleep, he might have a chance at getting some sleep himself. As long as Janie was awake, he would be awake beside her, damning himself for wanting her.

He was awake when she fell asleep some minutes later, and he was awake when she rolled over and bumped into him. He tensed, waiting for her to recoil, but she didn't back away. Instead, she murmured in her sleep and snuggled closer.

A better man would move away from her, would give her the room he knew she wanted. A better man wouldn't take advantage of a sleeping woman.

He'd never claimed to be even a good man, let alone a better one. So he turned into her embrace, allowed her to curl her hand into his chest. And when one of her legs slipped between his, he clenched his teeth, but he didn't ease away from her.

As they lay close together on the bed, her hair tickled his nose and her scent seemed to surround him. Her skin was warm and supple through the cotton gown she wore, and another spasm of need ripped through him. But beneath the desire, beneath the physical yearning for her, was an underlying tenderness.

No one could ever doubt Janie's strength. But he wondered how many people ever saw her vulnerability? How many people had she shared her fears with? Damn few, he'd bet.

His hand tightened on her and he pulled her closer. He'd keep her safe, he vowed, if he had to die trying. As long as Janie was in Cameron, nothing would hurt her. And if all they ever had together was this furtive tenderness in the middle of the night, so be it. It might be wrong to hold her like this, but it wasn't the first time he'd done something wrong.

If this was all he ever had of Janie, he'd hold on for all he was worth.

Chapter 7

Janie stirred and drifted awake, opening her eyes to see sunlight pouring in through the window curtain. She frowned at the sight, confused. Her bedroom windows weren't this bright. She kept them shuttered, so sunlight couldn't possibly get into the room.

As she glanced around, she realized this wasn't her bedroom, and then she remembered. This was Ben's bedroom. She and Ben had gotten married yesterday.

And Ben was lying next to her, his legs intimately tangled with hers, one hand curled around her chest, his fingers dangerously close to the curve of her breast.

Before she could think, before she could move away, heat and need roared through her, igniting a desire that stunned her. She had told herself last night that she wasn't interested in Ben. She'd convinced herself that getting involved with him right now would be foolish and dangerous, and she'd had enough danger in her life to last forever. She didn't need any more of that.

But apparently her body hadn't bought all those careful arguments, because she and Ben were entwined together like lovers.

From the sound of his steady, slow breathing, Ben was still asleep. Maybe if she could ease away from him and get out of the bed before he woke up, he would never know what had happened. A wave of heat flooded her face as she tried to move carefully away from him. After all she'd said to him yesterday about getting involved, about sleeping in the same bed, she'd ended up crawling all over him during the night.

He had every right to laugh at her the next time she said they could live together and behave like responsible adults.

She tried to slide away from him again, and Ben's eyes flew open. For a moment, as he focused on her, he looked as confused as she'd felt earlier. Then his eyes darkened and his gaze took on an intensity that she told herself she couldn't respond to. "Good morning, Janie."

"Good morning." She tried desperately to sound dignified and nonchalant at the same time. "It looks as though we both move around in our sleep."

Ben glanced down their bodies, his gaze lingering on their tangled legs. "I guess we do."

Slowly he pulled his legs away from hers. Before he rolled over, she felt the heavy weight of his arousal against her thigh. Then he turned and sat up on the edge of the bed, his back to her.

"I'm sorry, Janie. I didn't mean for that to happen."

"No apology is necessary. You can't help what you do in your sleep." She hated the prim sound of her voice, but told herself it was better than the alternative. Ben would be horrified if he knew how much their casual contact had aroused her. Sleeping this close together wasn't part of the deal.

"Right," he muttered. He sat on the bed for a moment

longer, almost as if he wanted to turn around and say something to her. Then he stood up and grabbed for a robe. "I'll leave and let you get out of bed."

Before she could stop him, he hurried from the room and closed the door behind him. Almost, she thought to herself, as if he was running away.

That was for the best, she told herself firmly as she slid out of bed and searched for a pair of shorts. Their movements during the night had been unconscious and unknowing. They had moved around and ended up next to each other. It was as simple as that. There was no reason to make it any more complicated.

A small voice inside her mocked her words. Nothing was going to be simple when it came to her and Ben. And the desire she'd felt this morning, waking up next to him, just added another level to the complicated feelings she already had for him.

She dressed slowly, trying to give both of them a chance to recover their equilibrium. When she finally emerged from the bedroom, the smell of coffee and bacon filled the air.

"What are you doing?" she asked as she walked into the kitchen. Ben stood at the stove, turning bacon and cooking pancakes.

"I figured you could use a morning off from cooking. You can eat someone else's cooking for a change." He handed her a cup of coffee and she stared down at it.

"How did you know how I liked my coffee?" She took a sip, and it was perfect.

He shrugged, but didn't turn around to face her. "I noticed how you fixed it at the restaurant."

"That's very observant of you."

"That's my job, Janie." Finally he turned around. "I'm supposed to notice things, and now it's just a habit. I pay attention to everything."

"And you noticed my coffee in case you had me in the lockup one day and needed to know how to fix it for me?" she asked lightly, moved more than she should have been that he'd noticed.

One side of his mouth quirked up in a grin. "You've got it. I have a catalog of everyone in Cameron's taste in coffee."

The atmosphere lightened, and she looked around the kitchen. "What can I do to help?"

"You can sit yourself down in a chair and watch me. Since Heaven on Seventh is closed today, you're not doing any cooking."

"Are you trying to butter me up?" She would keep the conversation light, or die trying.

They managed to keep up the lighthearted banter during breakfast and the cleanup that followed. But when they had finished, she saw uneasiness flicker in Ben's eyes. She understood, because she felt it, too. What did they do now? How would they spend their time today without Rafael there to act as a buffer between them, to be the focus of their attention?

Ben leaned against the kitchen counter, watching her. She stared out the window, trying to avoid his gaze. Finally he said, "What next? We have a whole day to fill."

She forced herself to look at him. "I don't know. Do you have any suggestions?"

He shrugged and pushed himself away from the counter. "Why don't we move the rest of your things into the house, then we can go out and get Rafael when we're finished."

"He's going to be disappointed to leave Shea and Jesse." She spoke without thinking.

Ben's gaze bored into her. "Do you want to leave him there for another night?"

"No!" Horrified at the thought of spending another

night alone with Ben, she shook her head vigorously. "Of course not. He just looked so happy to be playing with that dog."

"We'll get him a dog, then. He's never asked for one before."

She shook her head and managed to grin at him. "First a child, then a wife, and now a dog. It sounds like you've become completely domesticated."

But instead of the answering grin she expected, Ben's face closed and his expression became impossible to read. "Don't let outward appearances fool you, Janie. I'm the last person in the world who should be trusted with a wife and a child. I'm not even sure I should have a dog."

Horrified, she stared at him. "What do you mean by that?" she finally said.

He turned away and began folding the towel he'd used to dry the dishes. "I didn't mean anything. Forget it, Janie."

"How can I forget something like that?" she asked quietly. "You're doing a wonderful job with Rafael."

"I only meant that I wasn't cut out to be married, or have children. That's all." His back was stiff with tension, and he didn't turn around.

"How can you say that? You're exactly what Rafael needs. It's obvious that he's flourishing."

"Drop it, Janie. It's not something I want to discuss."

"I'm your wife, Ben. I told you my secrets. Don't you think I should know yours?" She held her breath, waiting for his answer.

Slowly he turned around. "Are you really my wife, Janie? In every sense of the word?" His eyes blazed with a sexual heat that scorched her.

But she refused to back down. "In the eyes of the world I am. And isn't that what counts? What am I supposed to say to the judge when he asks me a question I can't answer? 'I don't know those things about my husband, Your Honor. He didn't trust me enough to tell me.'"

"Don't push it, Janie. Don't push me." At that moment, Ben was hiding nothing. His eyes glittered with anger, and a need so all-consuming that she began to shake. She had never seen such naked desire in a man's eyes before. She felt herself swaying toward him, unable to look away. An answering desire stirred inside her, made of memories and longings that had been suppressed for too long. She wasn't sure if she could turn away now.

But it appeared Ben could. He reached for her, then drew abruptly back. "Don't, Janie. This won't solve anything."

"Are you sure?" She didn't recognize the low, throaty voice as her own.

"Damn sure." He shoved his hands into his pockets and damped the fire in his eyes. "Let's get over to your house and move the rest of your stuff." But he couldn't quite hide the regret, and Janie tucked that into her heart. It would have to do for now.

"Let me get my key, then."

They worked together into the afternoon, moving the last of her belongings into Ben's house. Finally they loaded Mimi into her carrier and Janie took one last look around the house that had been her prison.

"Are you going to miss having your own place?" Ben asked as she pulled the door shut behind them.

"Not at all." She was very certain of that. "This was never a home for me. It was only a place to live. And to hide."

"What are you going to do with it?"

"I haven't decided. I suppose I should sell it."

"That would probably be best," he agreed.

But a part of her didn't want to part with the house. Eventually, her marriage to Ben would be over. Sooner or later, she would need another place to live. Maybe if she kept this house, she would at least have someplace familiar to go and lick her wounds.

Because there were going to be wounds. She had been a fool to think she could marry Ben, then walk away months later without any regrets. She already had a boat-load of them. And once she got to know Rafael better, there would be many more.

She refused to think about that now. "Maybe I'll rent it out, instead."

Ben shot her a look that was both vulnerable and defiant. "So you always have an insurance policy?"

"Yes. Don't you think I need one? You set the limits on our so-called marriage yourself."

"Keep the house, Janie." His voice was rough. "Make sure you have someplace to run when everything falls apart. Because it's going to."

"You've already made that very clear," she said in a low voice. "Don't worry, Ben. We may have to share a house, and a bed, and our lives, but I don't intend to make any demands of you."

"That's not what I meant."

She heard the frustration in his voice, but she refused to let him off the hook. "Then what did you mean?" She hoped her face was as cool as her voice.

"You can make any demands on me that you want. I owe you, and you know it. I only meant that a divorce is inevitable. It would be nice if you had someplace familiar to go when this is all over."

"You have no idea what I need, or what I want. So don't try to tell me what to do."

"Fine. Forget I said anything. Let's get this stuff over to the house, then go get Rafael." He pushed the last arm-load of her belongings into the truck, then lifted the cat carrier into the back seat. "I miss the kid," he said gruffly.

"And I'm sure he misses you," Janie said, her anger dissipating. They had to deal with a difficult situation, but they were doing it for all the right reasons. The trick was to focus on Rafael rather than her and Ben. "I'm anxious to begin to get to know him."

A week later, she felt like she hadn't even scratched the surface with Rafael. He was always polite to her, always obedient, but she didn't have any idea what was going on behind his eyes. And he didn't want Janie to touch him.

"That's how he was with me at first," Ben told her that night, after Rafael was asleep. "He doesn't trust easily. But he's warming up to you."

"I hope so. The hearing is less than three weeks away."

"Give him more time. He's had a lot to deal with—a new family and school starting—but that cat of yours is helping."

But Janie glanced toward Rafael's bedroom, where she knew Mimi lay curled into a ball on the boy's bed. The cat now followed Rafael around the house, but this was the first night she'd slept at the end of his bed. "I'm a little surprised," she admitted. "I didn't think Mimi would be so good with children. But she's really attached herself to Rafael."

"I should have gotten him a pet a long time ago."

"Don't beat yourself up," she said, hearing the censure in his voice. "You had enough to cope with when he came to live with you."

Before Ben could answer, she heard Rafael moving around in his room. Then he came flying out the door. "Janie," he cried, and his face was white with fear. "There's something wrong with Mimi."

Janie ran into Rafael's room. She felt Ben right behind her. Rafael hovered over the cat, and Janie sank down on to her knees beside him. "What's going on, Rafael?"

"Watch her. See?" The boy's voice rose with fear. "See what she's doing? Why is her body twisting like that?"

Without thinking, Janie wrapped her arm around Rafael's shoulders. The boy flinched once, then he leaned into her. "Is Mimi going to die?" he asked, tears in his voice.

Janie reached over and kissed him, then hugged him closer. "No, she's not going to die. She's fine, Rafael."

"Then what's wrong with her?"

"She's having a dream," she said gently. "That's why her body is moving like that." Keeping her arm around the boy, she drew him closer to the bed. "See how her legs are twitching?" She touched one of Mimi's white paws. "She's dreaming that she's chasing a big bear out of our backyard."

"Is she dreaming that she's saving me?" Rafael demanded. There were no tears in his voice now, only excitement.

"I'll bet she is. See, she's moving faster now. That bear is heading out of Cameron, and Mimi is hot on his trail. She's going to make sure that bear never comes back."

"Mimi could save me, couldn't she, Janie?" He didn't seem to realize that he was still standing in the circle of her arm.

"I'll bet she could. But you know what? She'll never have to save you, because that's what Ben and I are here for. If there's ever any saving to be done, we'll be there."

Rafael seemed to think about that for a moment, then he turned to her, his face earnest. "Mimi could be in charge when you're not home. Mimi can save me when I'm staying with Mrs. Weston. She has Jenny and Todd to worry about, too. She might not be able to save me."

"I think Mrs. Weston could save you just fine. But why

don't we make Mimi her assistant? Do you think she would like that?"

Rafael nodded eagerly. "I'll tell her tomorrow."

"I think Mimi will be proud to be your assistant saver," she said gravely. She glanced over at the bed, where the cat lay quietly once more. "I guess the bear is gone. Mimi's dream is over. She's sleeping, and you should be, too."

"All right, Janie."

He slid into bed, and Janie hesitated for only a fraction of a second before she bent over him and brushed the hair out of his eyes, then dropped a kiss on his forehead. "Good night, Rafael."

His mouth curved up in a sweet smile. "Good night, Janie."

He didn't seem to mind her kiss at all, and Janie felt a lump growing in her throat. "Sleep tight," she whispered.

Ben stood in the doorway watching, and in the darkness she couldn't read the expression on his face. He stepped aside when she walked out of the room, then followed her to the living room.

"Don't you want to reassure him?" she asked quietly when they were out of Rafael's hearing range.

He shook his head. "I don't have to. He looked perfectly happy when you left him."

"He still might feel better if you said something to him." She chewed on her lip. "Maybe talking about Mimi saving him from a bear wasn't such a good idea. I'm afraid I just gave him more to worry about."

Ben's face softened, and he reached for her hand. "I think it was a brilliant idea. There are too many ghosts in Rafael's past, ghosts that hold too much power over him. Bears are real, but he knows there are no bears around here so it's a safe fear. God knows I'm no psychologist, but maybe this will help him get over whatever happened in San Rafael. Maybe if he thinks Mimi can save him from bears, he'll think she can save him from whatever happened in that hellhole in South America.''

"I hope you're right." She sighed. "The words just came out of my mouth before I could think. I'm afraid I don't know a lot about being a parent.''

"You're doing fine, Janie." His hand tightened on hers. "He let you touch him tonight, didn't he?''

"He was scared." But she hoped it was a beginning. "We'll see how he is tomorrow.''

She glanced at her watch and rolled her shoulders. "I'm going to bed. It's been a long day.''

Ben nodded. "I think I'll watch the news." He gave her a humorless smile. "I need to see what's going on in the world that could affect Cameron.''

"Great." Janie strained to smile back at him. "I'll see you in the morning.''

Since that first night together, they had taken pains to go to bed at different times. And they would both pretend to be asleep when the other finally came to bed. Tonight Janie prayed she would be able to fall asleep quickly, prayed she wouldn't still be awake when Ben slipped into bed beside her. The past week had been one night after another of torment. Neither she nor Ben would admit they had trouble sleeping. Neither of them would acknowledge the need that kept them awake and restless for most of the night. They were both so tense, both so desperate to stay on their own side of the bed, that they lay stiff and uncomfortable for hours before finally drifting off to sleep before dawn.

When Janie slid between the covers, she tried to shut everything out of her mind. She was determined to ignore the scent of Ben that clung to his pillow, disregard the way the bed seemed empty without Ben beside her. She needed to think about the restaurant, and what needed to be ordered.

But her mind stubbornly refused to cooperate. Instead of thinking about silverware and china, ketchup and salt, she thought about Ben, watching her and Rafael from the doorway. Tenderness had filled his face, a tenderness she found profoundly moving. Ben and Rafael would save each other, and she was determined to give them the chance. The past week hadn't been easy, but she knew she had made the right decision. Ben and Rafael belonged together, and she was fiercely glad to help them. She might be part of their family only temporarily, but she would do everything in her power to make sure they stayed together.

Even sleep in the same bed as Ben.

She rolled over, restless again, and found herself inhaling the scent from his pillow. Cursing herself and her stupid yearning for a man she couldn't have, she rolled over and forced herself to lie perfectly still. Maybe if she didn't move, didn't open her eyes, she would be asleep before Ben joined her.

But she was still wide awake almost an hour later when Ben walked quietly into the room. He was almost completely silent as he climbed into bed, clearly hoping she was asleep, too. He lay tense and stiff on the other side of the bed, but Janie was far too aware of his presence. She squeezed her eyelids tightly shut as tears trickled down her cheeks. Another night of hell loomed ahead of them.

The next evening, Janie slid a turkey dinner underneath the warming lights on the counter and turned to reach for the next order. The spinner was empty, and she looked over at her new cook, Jim West. "Did you take the rest of the orders?"

He didn't look up from the stove. "Isn't it about time for your family to get here? Go out and eat dinner with them." He glanced up at her. "A newlywed should spend time with her husband."

Janie tilted her chin. "Since when have you become an expert on my family?" she demanded.

"Since I've seen how hard you work in this place," he shot back. "An hour off isn't going to hurt anyone."

Janie's mouth quivered as she tried to hold in the smile. "It's customary in most businesses for the boss to give the orders, you know."

Jim grinned over at her, his smile deepening the creases that lined his cheeks. "Guess you forgot to tell me that part when you hired me."

She glanced over the counter and saw that Ben and Rafael were already seated at their usual table. Her heart fluttered in her chest at the sight of them sitting close together, their dark heads bent over a menu.

Reaching behind her, she untied her apron. She ached to join them, to share the small talk of the day and Rafael's adventures in school. "Thanks, Jim. I'm going to take you up on your offer."

"'Bout time," he said, but he grinned at her. "Everything's under control back here."

Ben looked up when she slipped into the booth next to Rafael. For a moment, his eyes brightened, then he carefully hid his reaction. "You're able to join us tonight?" he asked.

"Jim threw me out of the kitchen," she said, determined to keep things light. "So I thought I'd be a customer for a while."

"Janie," Rafael said, bouncing on his seat. "Do you know what happened in school today?"

"What happened?" She leaned back in the booth, enjoying the boy's animation. His dark eyes glowed, hiding the shadows that always lurked in them.

"Ms. Carmichael played her guitar for us. And she let me hold it while she was getting ready!"

"That's very exciting." Janie flicked his hair out of his eyes, rejoicing when he didn't even seem to notice.

"And that's not all. When she was finished, she let me touch one of the strings. It made a beautiful noise," he said, awe in his voice.

"That was very nice of Ms. Carmichael. Did you thank her?" Janie asked automatically. At least some parts of parenting seemed to be automatic, she thought wryly.

Rafael nodded vigorously. "I thanked her. She said she would show me some more next time we played the guitar."

"You're very lucky to have Ms. Carmichael for your teacher."

"Cameron is lucky to have Keara," Ben added. "She's a great addition to the school."

Janie felt a hot flash of jealousy that shocked her. She had no reason to be jealous of the music teacher. She had no reason to be jealous of anyone, she told herself. Where there was no real relationship, there could be no jealousy.

"I don't see her around town much," she forced herself to say.

"Keara keeps to herself." Ben looked down at the menu, and Janie saw that the conversation about the music teacher was over. "What's the special today?"

When a smiling Mandy took their dinner order, Janie leaned back in the booth and tried to relax. Rafael was telling them about his adventures with Stevie Jessup on the playground, and she wanted to pretend that theirs was a normal family, merely enjoying dinner together.

But nothing about their marriage was normal, including the constant tension that simmered between her and Ben. Even sitting across the booth from him in a busy restaurant, she was far too aware of him. If she took a deep breath, his scent would surround her. If she moved her legs, she would brush against him.

Instead of thinking about Ben, she tried to focus on Rafael. Every day this week, when he and Ben had come to the restaurant for dinner, he had been full of stories about school. She was delighted with the wonder in his voice as he talked about his teacher or the children. And she treasured the love on Ben's face as he watched the boy talking.

"Janie, come over here," Mandy called, waving frantically. She stared intently at the small television that sat next to the cash register.

Janie slid out of the booth, wondering why Mandy looked so excited. She felt Ben behind her as she hurried toward the front of the restaurant.

"What's the matter, Mandy?"

"It's Cameron," the waitress answered, her gaze transfixed on the screen. "The reporter is talking about Cameron."

Janie watched as the reporter for the national news show talked about Rafael's upcoming custody hearing. He recounted the story of Shea and Jesse Coulton and the refugee children from San Rafael they had saved. Then the camera panned down Main Street, cataloguing the stores and houses that were so familiar to her, and she felt a strange start of recognition.

The camera fixed on the reporter again, and a shock trembled through her as she realized he was standing in front of her restaurant. She gripped the counter as the scene changed to the inside of the restaurant. The camera panned the tables, full of smiling people, then focused on the baskets of flowers hanging from the walls. Janie didn't even hear what the reporter was saying.

Ben reached over and gripped her hand, and she blindly twined her fingers with him. *Cut away*, she prayed. *Let this be the end.*

But it wasn't the end. The camera had one final image. It was a lingering shot of her as she walked through the restaurant, stopping to talk with a customer and finally looking straight into the lens.

Terror and fear pressed in on her, choking her, making it impossible to breathe. Her heart stuttered, then raced with panic. She couldn't move, couldn't think. She could only stand and watch helplessly.

Her picture, and her location, had just been broadcast to the entire country.

Why now? she thought, despair stabbing into her. Now everything she'd ever wanted was within reach, and she'd have to leave it behind.

Chapter 8

Ben felt the shock tremble through Janie, then felt her brace herself, as if preparing for a blow. His fingers ached to rip the plug out of the television and hurl it through the window of the restaurant. He would give anything to obliterate the last five minutes of time, rewind the tape so that they were still sitting in the booth with Rafael, still trying to avoid looking at each other. That tension would be easier to face than this.

That would be far less painful than the stricken look on Janie's face, the panic that hummed just below the surface.

"It's all right," he said, going on instinct. "It'll be okay, Janie."

She turned to look at him, a dazed expression in her eyes. "No, Ben, it won't. Nothing is okay anymore."

"Let's go home," he murmured, wrapping his arm around her protectively. He turned to the waitress. "Mandy, tell Jim that he's in charge for the rest of the evening. We'll come back to help him lock up."

A small arm wrapped around his leg and gripped tightly. "Ben? What's wrong?"

Rafael looked up at him, his dark eyes huge and worried. Ben's first instinct was to protect the boy and tell him nothing was wrong. But Rafael had heard enough lies in his young life. So he squatted down on the floor next to the boy and said, "Janie is upset about something she saw on television. That's why we're going to leave. Mandy will wrap up your hamburger and fries and you can eat them at home. How would that be?"

"Okay, I guess." Rafael sounded doubtful as he glanced up at Janie. "Did she see that program you told me I couldn't watch, the one where there was too much killing?"

"Something like that." Ben's voice was grim. "She saw something that shouldn't have been on television, and it upset her."

Rafael nodded thoughtfully, and his grip on Ben's leg eased. "She was upset that time I watched the killing show, too. Why doesn't she tell Mandy to turn off the television?"

"She already did." There was no way he was going to alarm Rafael by telling him what was going on. It was far better for him to assume that Janie was upset by the violence in a television show. "Let's hit the trail, buddy."

"Okay." Rafael let go of Ben's leg and bounced for the door, apparently reassured. Ben grabbed the bags of food that Mandy pressed on them, then wrapped his arm around Janie's shoulders again. She turned to look at him, her eyes still stunned.

"Let's go, Janie," he said as he ushered her out of the restaurant. "We need to go home."

She stopped as soon as they were out the door, scanning the street. Her fear was a living thing that quivered between them. Before they took one step, she bent her head to search in her purse. When she raised her hand, he saw the pepper spray clenched tightly in her fist.

"There's no one here who doesn't belong in Cameron," he said softly. "Come on, let's get into the car."

"You take Rafael and go home in the car. I'll walk," she said. She didn't look at him. Her eyes were too busy watching the street.

"Do you really believe I would do that?" His voice had an edge he hadn't intended. "Do you really think I would leave you alone and frightened here on the street while I ran away?"

"You wouldn't be running away. You have to protect Rafael."

"There's nothing to protect him from, Janie." He steered her toward his truck. "Now let's go home and discuss this rationally."

She didn't speak at all on the ride home. Rafael talked about school for a while, but he must have sensed her distress, because eventually his voice trailed off and he looked at Janie with uncertainty.

After a few moments of strained silence, she turned around and gave the boy a weak smile. "Am I being a grump tonight, Rafael?"

He nodded. "But it's because you're mad about that television show, isn't it?" His voice was earnest.

Surprise flickered in her eyes, and Ben watched as she tried to pull herself together. "Yes, it was because of that television show."

"We shouldn't watch it anymore, then." Rafael seemed pleased with his logic.

"Maybe we won't," she answered quietly. After a moment, she swiveled around to face Rafael in the back seat. "What do you do when something scares you, Rafael?"

As Ben watched in the rearview mirror, the boy's eyes

became guarded. But to Ben's surprise, he answered Janie. "I close my eyes and pretend it's not there."

"What if it doesn't go away?" Janie asked.

"Then I run away. As fast as I can."

Rafael ducked his head and played with the straps on the backpack he took everywhere. Ben knew that the scrap of cloth he had labeled Rafael's deedee was inside.

"Sometimes running away is the only thing to do." Janie's voice was quiet in the car, and held more than a trace of sadness. Ben jerked his gaze over to her, but couldn't read the expression on her face.

"Running away doesn't always solve the problem," he said, too quietly for Rafael to hear.

"But sometimes you have no choice." Janie spoke equally quietly.

"What do you do when you're scared, Janie?" Rafael's small voice was unexpected.

Janie turned to face him again, and Ben could see her gathering herself, forcing herself to focus on Rafael's question. "It depends on what I'm scared of, Rafael. Sometimes I'm scared of something I read, or something I see on television. Then I just stop reading, or stop watching the television. Sometimes I'm afraid of the dark. Then I tell myself that the dark won't hurt me, and try to keep going." She paused and took a deep breath, then turned around to fully face Rafael. "Sometimes I'm scared that someone is trying to hurt me. Then I try to get away as fast as I can."

The boy was watching her carefully now. "You don't stay and try to fight the bad person?"

"Fighting isn't always the best thing to do. I might not be strong enough," Janie said carefully. "Or big enough. So the smart thing to do is run away. If I stayed and tried to fight, I might get hurt."

Rafael nodded thoughtfully, clutching the backpack to

his chest. Something expanded in Ben's heart as he watched the boy. Janie was in danger, and he knew she was terribly frightened. Yet she was sensitive enough, and caring enough, to reassure the worried boy. She had to know that Rafael wasn't asking her about her own problems. He was trying to resolve something that had happened to him before he left San Rafael.

"Here we are at home," he said, and he was afraid his voice was too hearty. "Everyone out."

Janie looked around again, scanning the bushes and shadows surrounding his house and the houses on either side of him. "It's all right, Janie," he said, touching her arm. "There isn't anyone around. There hasn't been time."

"I can't afford to assume anything," she said as she slid out of the car. She nodded at Rafael, who was bouncing his way up the front steps, their conversation apparently forgotten. "I can't think only of myself anymore."

Once they were in the house, he watched as Janie checked all the locks and made sure all the windows were bolted. Then he turned to Rafael. "What's the homework situation, buddy?"

"I have to do some math problems." Rafael sounded proud of the fact.

"Do you need help?" Ben asked.

The boy shook his head. "I can do them by myself."

"Good for you. Why don't you get started, then? You can use the kitchen table, and let me check them when you're done."

They listened for a while as they heard Rafael rustling papers in the kitchen, then the only sound was the child's pencil scratching on paper. Ben pulled Janie down next to him on the couch.

"Your picture wasn't on the screen for more than a few

seconds. And what's the chance that the murderer was watching that news program tonight?''

Her lips curled up, but her eyes didn't smile. ''It is the most widely watched newscast in the country,'' she said.

''Janie, chances are that whoever that man was, he's forgotten all about you. And it's been three years. Even if he saw you, he probably won't remember what you look like.''

She shook her head slowly. ''I can't afford to think that way, Ben. And even if I could, I don't think you're right. This man participated in a murder. And he knows there was a witness. Do you seriously think he'd put that fact out of his mind, or forget what that witness looked like?''

Ben felt a quick flush of shame. Janie was too smart, and too quick, to believe any patronizing words. And he owed it to her to be straight with her. ''All right. Maybe he hasn't forgotten, but I still think you have pretty good odds that he either wasn't watching the show, or wasn't paying close enough attention to recognize you. Everyone knows that the last few minutes of the news programs are fluff pieces. They're interesting, or cute, but usually not hard news. So chances are that even if he was watching, he turned the program off before your face came on screen.''

''Maybe so. But for your sake, and Rafael's, I have to assume otherwise.''

''What does that mean?''

Janie turned on the couch to face him. ''I can't stay with you now, Ben. I have to leave. I'll call my contact in the witness protection program in the morning and arrange to be moved.''

A sense of loss, so strong it was painful, stabbed through him. It was for Rafael's sake, he told himself. The child was becoming attached to Janie, and she was drawing him out. His own personal feelings had nothing to do with it.

"Don't do that," he said without thinking. "Don't leave."

Her eyes filled with pain before she looked away. "I don't have any choice. I can't stay here and endanger both you and Rafael."

He couldn't bear the thought of Janie leaving, of being alone and vulnerable someplace where he couldn't protect her. "You'll be safer here with me. If you leave, you have to start over somewhere else. Is that what you want? Do you want to leave Cameron, leave Heaven on Seventh?"

Her eyes glittered, but she didn't allow the tears to fall. "Of course it's not what I want. I love Cameron, and I love Heaven. And..." She swallowed once, and he didn't dare let himself think about what she might have intended to say. "I want to stay here and fight for Rafael. I want to make sure you're allowed to adopt him. But I can't take that kind of chance with either one of you."

"Nothing has changed, Janie." He heard the desperation in his voice, and he knew that too much had changed in the last couple of weeks. He'd allowed himself to begin to hope again, to begin to feel, and now he was getting what he deserved. "Even if the murderer saw you, you'll be safer with me than on your own." He took a deep breath. "Rafael and I need you."

"I know you do, Ben." Her voice was so low he had to strain to hear her. "Don't you think I know that? And I need you, too. You and Rafael." She gave him a tremulous smile. "I have a life again, and people around me. I don't want to give that up. But I couldn't live with myself if anything happened to you."

"Nothing is going to happen." He sounded more confident than he felt. Some of Janie's desperation was beginning to seep into him. "At least let's take a few days and talk about our options. That's not going to hurt anything. You won't ever be alone, and neither will Rafael. I'll make sure he's with me whenever he's not in school. Will that make you feel any better?''

"He'd be safer if I wasn't in Cameron at all." But he could hear the indecision in her voice, the reluctance to leave, and he pressed his advantage.

"Dev and all the deputies will keep a close eye out for strangers in town. I won't tell them why, just that there may be a problem. We'll keep you safe, Janie.''

Before she could answer, Rafael came into the living room, holding a piece of paper in one hand and his math book in the other. "I finished my homework, Ben." His eyes glowed with pride. "You said you wanted to check it.''

"That I do, buddy.''

Janie watched as Ben pulled Rafael down next to him and opened the book. Two dark heads bent over the paper, and she watched as Ben went over each problem with Rafael, praising him when he got a problem correct, and helping him figure out where he went wrong when there was a mistake.

How could she leave this?

How could she not?

She pushed away the part of her that yearned to accept Ben's reassurances, longed to ignore the danger. Of course she wanted to stay with them. But how could she stay, knowing that a killer could step into their lives at any moment? How could she stay, knowing that by doing so she put Rafael and Ben in horrible danger? She would never forgive herself if anything happened to either of them.

Ben eased the math book closed, and ruffled Rafael's hair. "Good job, buddy. Now go take a bath. It's almost time for bed.''

Rafael nodded, then he turned to her. "Janie, are you still scared?''

She forced herself to smile as she touched his cheek. "Not anymore. I'm safe at home now."

The boy nodded, apparently satisfied. "Okay." The fear and bewilderment she'd seen at the restaurant were gone. His eyes were clear again, and he gave her a shy smile. "You can hold my deedee if you get scared again." Then he darted into the bathroom and quietly shut the door.

Janie stared for a moment at the place where he'd disappeared, then she turned to Ben, her heart contracting in her chest. "I didn't think he ever let that scrap of material out of his reach."

"He doesn't." Ben reached over and took her hand, and she felt his warmth creep into the coldness inside her. "How can you leave him now, Janie? He trusts you. He's opening up to you. Don't abandon him."

"Don't do this to me, Ben." She could hear the anguish in her voice but she didn't care. She couldn't disguise how she felt. "You're putting me in an impossible position. Do I leave and keep him safe, but destroy his trust? Or do I stay and take the chance that he'll be well adjusted and happy when the murderer comes to kill him?"

"You're getting a little dramatic now, Janie."

"You're damned right I'm getting dramatic." She jumped off the couch and paced the room. "You're giving me a choice between two impossible things. After what Rafael just said to me, how can I possibly leave? And after what he said to me, and the trust that it shows, how can I stay, knowing that I'm risking his life?"

"Right now we have to get Rafael into bed." He stood up and looked over at the closed bathroom door. "But think of it this way, Janie. Physical injuries will heal. If, God forbid, this murderer finds him and hurts him, we can make him better. But if you leave now, will he ever trust anyone again?"

Ben disappeared into the bathroom and Janie stared at

the door for a long time, sick dread collecting in her stomach. She wanted to pick something up and hurl it at the door, but she clenched her hands into fists and turned away.

Ben was right, after all. He spoke nothing more than the truth.

She should have listened to her conscience and refused to marry Ben. She'd known it was wrong, but the part of her that had yearned for him wanted to believe that everything would be all right. And the longing for him that had lived in the most secret part of her heart had flooded over and allowed her to ignore her better judgment.

Now both Ben and Rafael would pay the price for her selfishness.

Her throat clogged with tears that swelled into a huge lump. How could she leave Rafael now, just when he was beginning to trust her? And what would happen to Ben's adoption hearing if his new wife disappeared? The judge would laugh him out of the courtroom, and Rafael would be given to someone else.

Someone who wouldn't, couldn't love him as much as Ben.

When Ben stepped out of Rafael's room, she was curled into a ball on the couch. "He wants to say good night to you," Ben said in a low voice.

Janie walked into the darkened room where Rafael snuggled in the bed, his scrap of material bundled under one arm. He smiled when he saw her.

"Good night, Janie," he said.

She bent and kissed his cheek, and he curled his empty arm around her neck. It was the first time he had voluntarily embraced her, and she hugged him back fiercely, feeling her heart move in her chest and fighting to keep the tears that swelled in her throat from overflowing. "Good night, Rafael. Sleep tight."

His arm clung to her for a moment, then he let go and turned over on his side. His eyes fluttered closed, and his breathing evened out as she watched him fall asleep.

Mimi strolled into the room and jumped onto the bed. She sniffed once at Rafael, then settled down in the crook of the boy's knees and began to purr. When the cat laid her head on her white paws and closed her eyes, Janie felt more tears prickle her throat. Even her cat had fallen for Rafael.

She stayed in the quiet room for a while, watching the gentle rise and fall of the quilt that covered him, and realized that he had stolen her heart the first time she'd seen him with Ben at the town picnic. She loved him completely. She couldn't imagine loving him more than she already did. And she would do anything, risk anything, to protect him.

Anything but leave him.

Ben was waiting for her in the living room when she finally left the bedroom. He had a pad of paper in one hand and a pen in the other. He looked up and said, "I'm making a list. Pros and cons about going and staying. We need to stop being emotional about this and try to discuss it rationally."

"We don't need a list. I can't go anywhere, Ben," she said, her voice low. "Rafael hugged me tonight. He offered me his most precious possession. How can I leave him now?"

Slowly he put the paper on the floor. "What about the risk to him if you stay?"

She sat down next to him on the couch and laid her hand on his arm. "I trust you," she said simply, and realized that she did. A huge weight slid off her shoulders. "You promised to keep him safe, and I believe you. I'm scared, but I'm not going anywhere. I won't call my witness protection contact, and I won't do anything different at the restaurant. As long as you take care of Rafael, I can take care of myself.''

He covered her hand with his own, and the roughness of his palm, the calluses on his fingers, reminded her that he was a tough man, and a strong one. He would be able to protect Rafael.

''I'm going to protect you, too, Janie. I'll keep you safe, or I'll die trying.''

''I know you will, Ben. I do trust you.''

His hand quivered over hers, then he pulled her into his arms. ''I'd give anything to make this go away, Janie. I hate seeing you suffering like this. I hate knowing that you're living in fear, and that I can't do a damn thing about it.''

Slowly her hands crept around him, holding onto his warmth and strength. When she leaned against his chest, his heart beat strongly next to hers. And she felt safe. ''But you are doing something about it. You're here with me, and I'm not alone. No matter what happens, I won't have to face it alone. You can't possibly understand how much that means to me.''

''I think I can.'' He leaned away and framed her face with his hands. ''Because I'm not alone, either. You've made such a difference with Rafael already.'' His eyes darkened. ''And with me. I didn't realize how hard it was to be a single parent until you came into our lives. Our marriage may be only for Rafael's sake, but it's important to me. And you are, too.''

As she looked at the sincerity in Ben's eyes, her heart contracted with pain. She wanted far more from him than gratitude. She wanted to be so much more than the woman he married so he could get custody of Rafael. But for now, she would settle for what he was able to give.

''You're important to me, too, Ben,'' she whispered.

He stared down at her for a moment, then his mouth

lowered to hers. His kiss was gentle at first, a mere brush of his lips across hers. It was no more than comfort, she told herself. That was all.

But she couldn't stop herself from responding to his kiss. She opened to him like a flower unfurling its petals to the sun. She stepped closer, vulnerable and trusting, and with a groan he pulled her against him.

"This isn't what I intended," he said into her mouth, his hands roaming over her back and urging her closer still.

"Me, either." She could barely form the words. Her brain had stopped working as soon as Ben's lips touched hers. She was no more than a mass of scrambling nerves and a frantically beating heart.

Her body molded itself to Ben's. The fit was perfect, as she'd known it would be. It had been perfect before, and she hadn't forgotten one detail of that night. The fire started low in her belly and raced along her nerves, until her entire body was burning. Still he kissed her, his mouth clinging to hers, tasting, testing, urging her lips apart.

She didn't resist. When she opened her mouth to him, he groaned again. He shaped her hips with his hand, urging her closer. His heat and his hardness burned into her belly, starting a throbbing demand deep inside her.

When Ben lowered her to the couch, she pulled him down on top of her. His body was heavy and hard on top of her, but she gloried in the weight. She yearned to feel his muscle and sinew pressing her down into the cushions, claiming her, branding her as his own.

Suddenly he moved lower, and his mouth pressed against her breast through the thin cotton of her blouse. She wanted his mouth on her bare skin, and the barrier only made his caress more erotic, more arousing. The heat and wetness of his tongue burned through the layers of clothing until her skin felt as if it were on fire. Her nipples puckered and ached for him.

But before she could beg him to touch her, he began to unfasten the blouse. She watched as he slowly moved down the row of buttons, his hands shaking. He paused at the last button, then pushed the material aside to reveal the lacy bra she wore beneath the blouse.

The delicate underwear was her one vanity, her one extravagance. And when Ben stared down at her, his eyes hot with need and his face taut with desire, she was fiercely triumphant. Clearly he wanted her as much as she wanted him.

"I thought I remembered how beautiful you were, but I was wrong." With one hand he reached out and traced the edge of her bra over the swell of her breast. "How could I have forgotten how lovely you are?"

She wanted to tell him that she'd waited for this moment for months, that nothing had been the same for her since that night they'd spent together, but instead of speaking, she reached up and kissed him. She didn't want to break the spell, didn't want to destroy the magic of the moment.

And he kissed her back. For a brief moment, he held nothing back. She tasted his passion, and the desire that he usually hid in the deepest part of his soul. For a moment, he let go of his rigid control, let go of the tight hold he kept on his emotions. Everything he wanted, everything he needed was in his kiss, a kiss that took her breath away and left her wanting so much more.

But his loss of control must have shaken him, because he slowly raised up and looked at her. Then he pulled the edges of her blouse together and lifted himself off the couch.

"I'm sorry, Janie," he said, and his voice was hoarse with suppressed desire. "I only wanted to comfort you. I didn't mean for that to happen."

"You must have noticed that I wasn't fighting you off," she said, and the tartness in her voice hid the pain she felt.

"You should have been. This wasn't part of our deal."

He turned around, and she sat up and began rebuttoning her blouse. "Maybe we need to change the deal."

"You don't want to do that, Janie. Believe me, you don't want to get involved with me."

"I'd say it's a little late to worry about that. We're married, Ben. That means we're involved."

He spun around to face her. "You know what I mean. We're not really involved now. We're living together, we're taking care of Rafael, but we're not married. But if we make love, if we bring sex into the equation, everything is going to change."

"And you don't want that to happen." Her words were quiet in the stillness of the house, but she could hear the despair in her voice.

"I can't allow that to happen. It wouldn't be fair to you."

"Why not, Ben?"

"You know nothing about me. You don't know who I am. And if you did know, you'd agree with me. You'd stay as far away from me as you could."

"I know more than you realize. I know what kind of a man you are. I know you'd give your life to protect Rafael, or me. What more do I need to know about you?"

He turned away again, but not before she saw the despair on his face. "I'm trying to protect you, Janie."

"Maybe I don't want to be protected from you." Standing up, she brushed off her shorts and let the anger flood her. It was better than the despair that wanted to overwhelm her. "Maybe you need to let me decide for myself what I want."

Slowly he nodded, but she saw the stubbornness deep in his eyes. "You're right, and I'm sorry. I should have been as honest with you as you were with me. But tonight's not the time for old stories." He moved closer to her and tucked her blouse into her shorts. "Those will keep. There'll be plenty of time for stories tomorrow."

Chapter 9

But they didn't get to those stories the next day, or the day after that. Ben was always busy, and Rafael was always around. Janie began to wonder if Ben was avoiding her on purpose, but she told herself that was impossible. He was always with her, at the restaurant, at the house, when she went to the store for groceries. But there were always a lot of other people around, too.

Suddenly, after avoiding people for three years, she was surrounded by people.

And deep down, maybe she was afraid of what Ben would tell her. She wasn't sure she wanted to hear his secrets. She really *didn't* know anything about him. He'd been as solitary a figure in Cameron as she had been before they got married.

It didn't matter, she told herself. She knew all she needed to know. She knew the kind of man he was. He couldn't have done anything that would change her opinion of him.

But that kernel of doubt niggled at her brain, whispering ugly suggestions. No one in Cameron knew anything about Ben, or where he'd come from. He'd just appeared in town one day over four years ago and applied for a job with the sheriff's department. No one knew anything about his past.

So she didn't press him to tell her about himself, and he didn't volunteer. They spent their evenings with Rafael, and tormented nights in the big bed together, trying not to touch each other.

A week after her picture had been broadcast on television, Janie began to relax. She still paid attention to everyone who came into the restaurant, still watched when she left at night, but there had been no sign of strangers in Cameron, no evidence that anyone was watching her.

She began to believe that Ben was right, that she had been lucky. The murderer hadn't seen her picture on television.

Then one morning, as she stood at the front window watching Rafael get on the school bus, she saw Ben's familiar white Blazer roll to a stop at the curb. The truck had barely stopped before Ben jumped out and hurried to the house. She had just gotten the door open when Ben reached the porch.

"Let's go back in the house," he said quietly, then locked the door behind him.

He stood watching her for a moment then stepped closer and took her hand. "You had a burglary at the restaurant last night," he said, his voice flat and without inflection. "Someone broke in through the back door. Jim and Phyllis found the door broken when they got there this morning. As far as anyone can tell, nothing is missing except the sixty dollars you keep in the cash register." His face hardened. "But it doesn't smell right. There were other valuable things that weren't taken, like the stereo and the computer in the office. If the burglar was someone after money, they should have taken things that would be easily sold. I think that someone took the money to make it look like a regular burglary.''

"You think it was someone looking for me." Her voice was barely above a whisper.

He nodded grimly. "Whoever broke in went through your desk, but as far as I could tell, he put everything back. And he did it carefully, like he was hoping you wouldn't notice your desk had been searched.''

"Then how do you know he searched my desk?''

"That's my job, Janie. I've been trained in tracking. I can tell when something's been disturbed. Your desk was definitely disturbed.''

She held tightly to his hand. "What do we do now?''

"I think you need to look at everything in the restaurant, see if anything is missing. You're the only one who would know for sure. Then you need to go through your desk, see if anything's missing there. I would love for you to tell me that there is a stash of cash in your office that the thief found, or that there is some expensive equipment missing.''

"But you don't think that will be the case.''

He shook his head. "I don't think so.'' He looked at her for a moment, then pulled her into his arms. "I don't want to scare you, but we have to think the worst.''

Wrapping her arms around him, thankful for the comfort of his steady heartbeat next to her ear, she said, "Should we get Rafael from school?''

She felt him shake his head. "We'll leave him there for today. I already called and talked to the principal. She'll make sure no strangers get into the building, and she'll have his teacher find some excuse to keep him in the building at recess.''

She didn't want to give up the comfort of Ben's arms, but she needed to know the truth. So she slowly pulled away. "Let's go to the restaurant, Ben. I want to look for myself. I want to make sure there was nothing there that would give away my former identity."

Some of the hardness disappeared from his eyes. "I thought that's what you would say." He touched her cheek, then let his hand drop. "Thank you for not panicking on me, Janie."

"Panic isn't going to help us." For three years she'd dreaded this day. Now that it was here, she couldn't feel anything. All she could do was focus on what had to be done. She looked around for her purse, then checked the doors again. "What about the house?"

"I called Matt Packer, one of the other deputies. He's off duty today, but he's going to come and stay in the house. He'll get overtime, and someone will be here, just in case." Ben took her hand again. "I'm probably overreacting. But I don't want to take any chances."

"I don't think you're overreacting, Ben." She gripped his hand more tightly and realized she was shaking. "I've seen what this man can do. And I'm glad you're taking me seriously."

"Of course I'm taking you seriously!" His eyes flashed, and for a moment Janie thought he was going to say something else. Then he clamped his mouth shut and glanced out the window. "Here's Matt now."

As they walked toward Ben's truck, she said, "Matt's going to be all right alone, isn't he? I'd hate to think he's putting himself in danger for me."

"This isn't just for you, Janie. This is his job, and he's good at it. He'll be fine." Ben compressed his lips again. "And whatever else he is, the guy who broke into the restaurant is smart. He's not going to do something stupid like break into a house where a cop is waiting for him."

She didn't say anything on the short drive to Heaven on Seventh, but Ben reached out and took her hand. She clung to him, afraid to voice her fears, knowing that he understood them, anyway. When they pulled up in front of the restaurant, he turned to her and said, "Do you want to go in through the back door? Everyone is going to want to talk to you. I'm afraid that your break-in is the talk of Cameron already."

She shook her head. "I'll have to face it sometime. And maybe someone heard or saw something." She swallowed hard. "I guess my days of hiding like a hermit from the world are over. Everyone's going to know all about me after this."

"Only if you want them to, Janie. I haven't told a soul, and I don't intend to tell anyone. If you give me permission, I'll tell Devlin, but no one else. I think he needs to know, but it's no one's business but yours."

"Thank you, Ben." She turned to face him, holding his hand. "I'm very glad you're here with me. If I was facing this alone…" She shuddered, thinking about how frightened she would be, and how isolated she would feel. "I don't know what I would do."

"You'd do fine. I know enough about you to realize that." He pulled her closer and wrapped his arms around her. "You're a remarkable woman, Janie Murphy. I don't think there's anything you can't cope with."

She clung to him, feeling the comfort seeping into her. "My name is Janie Jackson now," she said quietly.

She felt him tense, and for a moment he crushed her to him. Then he sat back and let her go. "I haven't forgotten that," he said quietly. "I just wasn't sure how you felt."

"I'm proud to have your name, Ben. Even if it's only temporarily."

His eyes darkened, and he opened his mouth to say something. Then he looked behind her. "People are watching us," he said, and his voice hardened. "I'm not about to give them a show. Let's go into the restaurant."

She didn't think that was what he'd intended to say, but he was right. This wasn't the place or time for confidences. So she slid out of the truck and headed for the door of the restaurant.

There were too many people in the area for her to get a good look at all of them. Men and women walked in and out of the stores and businesses, and traffic moved slowly down the street. She walked slowly, craning her neck to get a look at everything, but Ben hustled her into the building before she could satisfy herself.

"Let me look out the window for a moment," she said quietly. "What if someone was waiting for me to come to the restaurant this morning? Shouldn't I look and see if there are any strangers on the street?"

"One of the deputies is doing that." Ben nodded toward a young man who looked like he was writing a parking ticket across the street from the restaurant. "I told him to go out there and keep his eyes open. If there are any strangers, he'll see them."

"Thank you, Ben." She looked over at him, suddenly overwhelmed. "I always thought I would be facing this alone. I'm very glad you're here with me."

"So am I," he said gruffly. "I wouldn't want to think about you facing this by yourself."

"It doesn't seem so overwhelming anymore," she said as she turned away from the window. "Even such a small thing as having someone else watch for strangers in town makes a huge difference."

"I said 'For better or worse,' and I meant it." He steered her toward the back of the restaurant. "Let's get a look at your office."

"Let me see the back door first," she said, veering in that direction.

"He certainly wasn't a pro," Ben said as he watched her examine the broken door. "If he had been, a decent set of lock picks would have had that door open in about thirty seconds. Breaking the lock was a real waste of time and energy. It's also one of the reasons I don't think whoever broke in was looking for money. They'd get in and out in the minimum amount of time, and they'd have the tools to do it right.''

"You make this guy sound like a bumbling fool." She turned and faced him, leaving the evidence of her shattered secret life behind her. "He's anything but that."

"Maybe so, but he's an amateur when it comes to burglary.''

"I think all that means is he usually has someone else to do his dirty work. He certainly did at the greenhouse when his employee murdered my boss."

Ben watched Janie fingering the broken lock that was now covered with black fingerprint powder and didn't say anything. If it was her murderer who had broken into the restaurant, clearly he'd decided that this job was too important to trust to anyone else. He didn't have to tell her that. She was already frightened enough, and he suspected that she had already figured that out for herself, anyway.

Even though she'd never say so to him. Janie was a remarkably strong woman. And a remarkably brave one. Her first questions to him that morning had been about Rafael. She hadn't said a thing about herself, although she had to know that she was the killer's primary target.

"There were no fingerprints on the door," he said gently. "And there should have been lots of them. Everyone who works here goes out that door several times a day. So our burglar wiped the door clean."

"I would be surprised if he hadn't," she said, and although her voice was calm, he could hear a quiver of fear, deep in her throat. "He's not going to allow himself to be caught by something as mundane as fingerprints."

"We got a lot of prints from the office and the cash

register, and it's going to take a few days to process them. Chances are, though, that they'll all be from people who work here."

"I didn't think it was going to be easy, Ben." She swallowed once, and he followed the ripple of her throat down past her collar before he could stop himself.

Shoving his hands into his pockets to keep from reaching for her again, he turned away. "Let's go take a look at the office."

She stood in the doorway and stared at her desk for a moment, then turned to him. "If you hadn't told me, I would never have known that someone went through this room."

"You see what you expect to see. You wouldn't have remembered where you left the papers, or if the pens had been moved."

She started toward the desk, but her movements were slow and pained. His heart ached for her pain, and suddenly he couldn't endure prolonging it. He put his hand on her arm. "You don't have to do this right now if you'd rather wait."

Shaking her head, she said, "No, I want to get it over with. Besides, we need to know if he took anything. And I want to make sure there's nothing in the desk that would connect me to my past identity."

Janie sat down in her desk chair and he saw her tremble as she took a deep breath. Then she opened the first drawer in her desk.

A half hour later she turned to him and shook her head. "As far as I can tell, there's nothing missing. And I couldn't find a thing that would connect me to the woman who left Chicago three years ago."

Ben leaned forward. "Have you kept anything from your previous identity? I thought you were supposed to get rid of everything."

"You are." Janie met his gaze with defiant eyes. "But I couldn't do it. If I had destroyed everything from my past, I knew there would come a time when I would look in the mirror and wonder if it had all been a dream. I don't know if I'll ever see my family again, or my friends. So I kept some pictures and some papers. They're in a safe-deposit box in a bank, along with the information about my contact with the witness protection program. Don't worry," she said, and she must have seen the concern in his eyes, because she gave him a bleak smile. "They're not in the bank in Cameron." She hesitated, then leaned close. "They're stored eighty miles away in a bank in Panguitch. I keep the key in the house. I'll show you where it's hidden."

"You don't have to do that if it makes you uncomfortable." He was overwhelmed by her trust in him.

She shook her head. "No, I want you to know. You're my husband, and you need to know." She swallowed hard. "If anything should happen to me, I want you to be able to get in touch with my family and let them know."

"Nothing is going to happen, Janie." He bent closer, so she could see the truth in his eyes. "I won't let anything happen to you."

"You need to take care of Rafael," she said, but her voice was shaky.

"I'll take care of both of you." He leaned closer, needing to touch her, aching for contact with her. His lips brushed hers, and he felt her cling to him. He wanted, more than anything, to take her in his arms and shelter her from the ugly truth of what had happened to her today. He wanted to make her forget all about the murderer who might have found her, and the danger she was in. But he couldn't allow himself to do that. He had to focus on keeping her safe.

So he stepped away, ignoring the emptiness in his heart

and the ache in his arms. "Let's go back to the house," he said, his voice grim. "Jim can carry on here, can't he?"

"I guess he can." She looked around the office once more, then back at him. "This will be the first day that I won't be at Heaven on Seventh since I bought it." Her voice was wistful.

"Then it's about time you took a day off." He purposely made his voice brisk. "Go talk to Jim and Phyllis, then we'll go."

"All right."

She stood up and headed for the kitchen, and Ben walked out into the dining area. His boss, Devlin McAllister, stood talking with his sister Shea and her husband Jesse, who were eating breakfast. He walked over to the group.

"Good morning, Shea. Jesse." He shook hands with the former FBI agent who had married his friend's sister and relaxed enough to smile at the couple. "What are you doing here for breakfast? And does Maria know you snuck away from her breakfast?"

"We didn't have to sneak. Maria is taking a vacation. She's gone back to San Rafael to visit her family now that the civil war is over." Shea beamed up at him. "And since we're without our housekeeper for a couple of weeks, Jesse and I decided it would be safer to eat Janie's cooking than our own."

"It's good to see you." He turned to Dev. "This is supposed to be your day off. What are you doing in town?"

"Marge the dispatcher called me and told me what's going on, and I was concerned. I thought you could use another set of hands."

"Thanks, Dev. But doesn't Shea need you on the ranch?"

"She told me to get lost."

"We can survive without him today, Ben." Shea wasn't smiling now. "I want to make sure that you both take care of Janie."

"I'll take good care of her, you can be sure of that." He heard the grim determination in his voice and tried to soften it. "We'll find whoever did this."

"I know you will, Ben. But I didn't just mean finding the person who broke into her restaurant." Shea's eyes softened and she smiled at him again. "But I can see I don't have to tell you how to take care of Janie. I can see you'll do a perfect job all by yourself."

"Of course I'll take care of her. She's my wife," he said stiffly.

"You're an idiot, Ben Jackson." She gave him a warm smile as she turned to her brother. "Isn't he, Dev?"

The sheriff rolled his eyes. "Whatever you say, Shea." He pulled Ben to the side. "Let's talk about this break-in. Phyllis said nothing was taken besides the cash in the cash register. What's going on?"

"Meet us back at our house in about a half hour," Ben said. "We'll tell you about it then."

Dev's eyes sharpened, but he didn't ask any more questions. Nodding, he walked back over to Shea and Jesse and sat down. Ben turned away, uncomfortable with Shea's perception. He didn't want to think about the knowing look in her eyes, or what it meant. He didn't want to think about what Shea thought she saw when she looked at him and Janie.

Janie came out of the kitchen then, and he stood up. "Ready to go?"

She nodded. "Jim is set for the day, and Phyllis is fine up front here. I told both of them to call if there was a problem."

Ben led her out of the restaurant and over to his truck. Again, he felt her watching, felt her tense as she surveyed the street. But there was nothing to see. The street in front of the restaurant was momentarily deserted, except for the sheriff's deputy who was pretending to write parking tickets. He was far down the street now, still scanning the street, but his posture was more relaxed. Apparently he hadn't seen a thing.

No one followed them home, either. And Janie's house hadn't been disturbed. But that didn't mean a thing, he reminded himself grimly. It would be far too easy, in a small town like Cameron, for anyone to find out where Janie was living now. The people were wary of strangers asking about Rafael, but his and Janie's wedding was still big news in the town. Most of the people would be only too happy to strike up a conversation about them.

"He probably knows where I'm living by now," Janie said, her words an eerie echo of what he'd just been thinking.

"Probably," he said, after hesitating for a moment. She was probably hoping he would reassure her, but he couldn't do that. He'd vowed early on never to deceive her, and that included this situation. "It would be easy enough to find out."

"There were papers in my desk with my home address on them. I don't think there was anything there yet with your address, though."

"It doesn't matter. If he found Cameron, and your restaurant, he'll find the house."

"What do we do now, Ben? What about Rafael?"

He heard the anguish in her voice, and wished he could snap his fingers and make all three of them disappear. But he couldn't do that. So he would do the next best thing. "I have an idea. Let's wait until we get home, then I'll tell you about it." When they arrived at the house, Matt told them he hadn't seen or heard a thing. After thanking the deputy again, he sent him home, then turned to Janie.

"Dev was in the restaurant. Marge called and told him about the break-in, and he wanted to help. I think we should tell him everything. What do you think?"

She only hesitated for a moment. "Yes. At this point, I don't have much reason to hide, do I?"

"No, you don't. And the more people who know, the safer you'll be."

She swallowed and nodded, but he saw the misery in her eyes. "I suppose you're right. And, I should call my contact in the witness protection program, too."

"You should. But other than Dev, let's not bring anyone else into it yet, until we see what's going on."

"Thank you," she said, and her mouth trembled. "I know it's stupid, but I don't want anyone else to know. I don't want to know that people are looking at me and talking about me."

"Then you shouldn't have married me," he said, trying to keep a teasing note in his voice. "Everyone is wondering what you saw in a bum like me."

"They know exactly what I saw in you, Ben Jackson." She lifted her head and looked him in the eyes. "The only reason anyone would be talking about me is to envy the fact that I finally caught Cameron's most elusive bachelor."

If only her words were true. The thought stunned him and he tried to banish it, but it lingered in his mind, making him uneasy. Was Janie becoming more important to him than he could allow her to be?

It didn't matter now, he told himself. He had more important things to worry about, and so did Janie. An examination of their marriage would have to wait for this crisis to be resolved.

He wasn't sure if he was relieved or angry, and that was the most frightening thing of all.

Chapter 10

"You need more information to know what is going on, Sheriff. I need to tell you who I really am."

Ben took her hand as Devlin sat forward on the couch and narrowed his eyes. "What does that mean?" His voice was low and quiet, but Ben wasn't fooled. He'd heard Devlin use that voice before.

"It doesn't mean she's a criminal," Ben shot back at his boss.

Devlin gave him a startled glance, then leaned back in his chair. His gaze became thoughtful as it lingered on him and Janie. "I wasn't implying anything, Ben. Why don't we just let Janie tell me what she means?"

Janie took a deep breath and sat up straight. Ben tightened his hold on her hand, and she glanced over at him. He saw the trust in her eyes, and wondered why she'd given it to him. Then she nodded once and looking over at Devlin began telling him about the murder she'd witnessed.

An hour later, Janie leaned back against the cushion of

the couch and watched the sheriff try to absorb the story she'd just told him. Ben hadn't let go of her hand, and she wanted to thank him for holding on to her, for helping her get through the story one more time. But she wouldn't do that in front of the sheriff.

"I'm sorry, Janie." They were Devlin's first words, and she could see the regret in his eyes. "This must have been an awful three years for you. I wish someone could have been there to help you."

"Someone is now." The words slipped out by mistake, but she wouldn't take them back, even if she were able to. Ben's support meant more to her than she could express.

"Thank goodness for that." Devlin looked over at Ben. "What about the boy?"

"Rafael's in school," Ben answered. "But I have an idea to keep him safe."

Janie leaned forward. She had been thinking about Rafael all morning, torturing herself with images of him in danger. "That's what's most important right now. What's your idea?"

"We've never taken a honeymoon," Ben said slowly. He didn't look at her, but Janie felt red heat creeping up her cheeks. "We had Rafael starting school and your restaurant to worry about. Maybe we should go away now."

"What good would that do? If the killer is in Cameron, why wouldn't he just wait for us to come back?" she asked.

"It would give Devlin and the other deputies a chance to look around for a stranger here in town while you're out of sight."

"But what if he follows us? Then all three of us are at risk, and isolated from the people who know us."

"We wouldn't take Rafael on a honeymoon with us," Ben said quietly.

Something stirred inside Janie that wasn't fear, something she couldn't allow herself to think about. She wanted to spend time with Ben, alone and isolated. Trying to banish the wisps of desire, she said, "You would trust someone else to keep him safe?"

"This murderer isn't after Rafael. He's after you, Janie. So why would he even bother to go after Rafael if he wasn't with us? If we're lucky, he may not even know Rafael exists. I thought, if it was all right with Dev and Shea and Jesse, that Rafe could stay at the Red Rock Ranch for a few days. He'll be safe and out of the way, and we wouldn't have to worry about him."

Fear gripped her at the thought of Rafael being with someone else when he might be in danger, but she was forced to admit Ben's idea was logical. "What do you think, Sheriff?"

"I think it's a good idea," he said slowly. "Carly and I could stay out there for a few days, too, so there would be extra people around. I know Shea wouldn't mind. She's crazy about the kid."

"Then where would we go?" She turned to Ben.

He slipped an arm around her waist and hugged her reassuringly. "I thought we could go up to that cabin in the mountains on the Red Rock Ranch. It's isolated enough to be a good 'honeymoon cabin,' but close enough that we could get back to town quickly if we needed to."

"Of course," Devlin said immediately. "That's a great idea. I don't think anyone is using the cabin right now." He stood up. "Let me call Shea and ask her."

He disappeared into the kitchen, and Janie turned to face Ben. She trembled inside at the thought of being alone with Ben, isolated in the mountains, for several days. She wasn't sure if it was fear or excitement that quivered through her.

"Are you sure this is a good idea?"

Ben slowly shook his head. "I don't know if it's a good idea or a terrible one. But I can't think of anything better. I know this will protect Rafael. I think I can protect you."

"What if his social worker finds out that we've left him

with Shea and Jesse? Our hearing is coming up in a couple of weeks. Won't that be a problem?''

Ben's eyes softened. "Janie, every newly married couple is entitled to a honeymoon, even a couple who has a child. No judge in the world is going to fault us for going away together. And it's not like we'll be gone for a long time.''

"But is this going to gain us anything but a few more days before the murderer finds us?''

"I don't know. But while we're trying to figure out the next step, Rafael will be safe, and so will you. In town, you're too predictable. Everyone knows where you live, they know you'll be at the restaurant every day, and everyone knows what time you get there and what time you leave. A clever man could arrange all kinds of accidents with that information.

"If we disappear for a few days, Devlin and the other deputies might be able to flush out any strangers in Cameron. If we're gone and everyone in town knows we're on our honeymoon, people are going to notice anyone asking questions about you.''

"And if the worst happens and he finds us in the cabin, you're the one who's going to get hurt." Janie spoke softly, but Ben heard her. He tightened his hold on her.

"I'm not going to get hurt. I'll be watching for him. And if he finds us, I have a better chance of catching him if we're at the cabin. I know those mountains above the Red Rock, and we'd have the advantage. But the worst isn't going to happen.''

Before she could answer, Devlin came back into the room. "Shea thought it was a great idea. She's expecting Rafael this afternoon.''

Ben nodded once and stood up. "We'll pick him up from school and go directly there.''

Dev nodded to her, then looked at Ben. "I've got a lot to do between now and this afternoon. I'll see you at the ranch.''

He slipped out the door, and Ben locked it behind him. Then he looked down at her. "Is that all right with you, Janie?"

"Do we have any choice?" Her nightmare was happening all over again, but this time, Ben was involved. A sick feeling gathered inside her at the thought of Ben getting hurt. "Maybe we should all leave Cameron altogether for a while."

Ben took her hand, and she could read understanding in his eyes. "It'll be all right, Janie. No one is going to get hurt. Rafael will be safe, and so will you."

"It's you I'm worried about," she said, her voice barely above a whisper. "You'll be with me, so you're the one who's going to be in the line of fire."

"I can take care of myself, Janie. This is what I'm trained for." His face relaxed into a small smile. "Maybe Devlin will get a chance to see if all our fancy training was worth the money."

Fear splintered through Janie, and the too-familiar feeling of helplessness threatened to overcome her. Once again, people she cared about were in danger because of her. And once again, she was powerless to help them. She didn't even know who they were fighting.

Ben pulled her against him and murmured, "It's all right, Janie."

She burrowed into him, wanting the comfort of his presence, the reassuring strength of his body. She wanted to feel him surrounding her. Because when Ben held her, she could believe, even if only for a while, that everything would be all right.

"It's not like three years ago," he said, as if he could read her mind. "You're not alone anymore. This time, you have people who will fight for you. Whoever this man is, he's not going to get to you so easily here in Cameron. We take care of our own. And you're one of ours, Janie."

A lump swelled in her throat at his words. She wanted so desperately to believe him, to let someone else share the burden of worry and fear. But she couldn't allow Ben to give her that. "Thank you, Ben. But this isn't your fight."

"It is now. I said 'for better or worse,' and I meant it." He cupped her chin in his hand and stared down at her, and she saw the resolution in his eyes. "You're my wife. We're in this together."

Every fiber of her being wished that his words were true. But they weren't. She might be his wife in the eyes of the world, but in his heart, where it counted, she was only the woman who was helping him adopt Rafael. "What would happen to Rafael if you were hurt or killed?"

"What would I tell him if you were hurt or killed because I wasn't there for you?" he countered. "What kind of example would that be? You're not getting rid of me, no matter what you say. Now why don't you pack some things for yourself then help me pack a bag for Rafael."

She should tell him no, make him leave and take Rafael somewhere safe. But she couldn't force the words out of her mouth. She needed his faith in his town and his confidence in himself. She needed his quiet courage and his rock-steady strength. She needed *him*. So she went into their bedroom to pack a suitcase, hoping that it wouldn't be the last time they'd be in this house together.

Several hours later, Ben watched in the rearview mirror of his truck as Rafael stood on the porch of the Red Rock, next to Shea and Jesse, and waved goodbye to him and Janie. One of his hands rested on the head of Buster, and the boy had a huge grin on his face. Mimi stood inside the screen door, glaring out at the dog. "Rafael will be fine," he said to Janie, who sat too quietly in the seat next to him, twisted around so she could watch Rafael. "He's thrilled to be staying at the ranch."

"I know." She turned back to face him. "I know that Shea and Jesse will take good care of him. And with Devlin and Carly staying at the house, too, he'll be safe. But I can't help worrying."

"I'm worried, too," he admitted. He looked over at Janie and gave her a small smile. "It's part of a parent's job description. But he's going to be fine. Dev promised me that he wouldn't ever be out of someone's sight. Even in school, there'll be a deputy in the building."

"How far is the cabin?" she asked.

"I'd forgotten that you've never been there." He shifted into a lower gear as the truck started up the incline. "It's a couple of miles, but it seems longer because the road is pretty primitive. We'll be completely isolated."

"That's what I'm worried about," she muttered, and Ben felt the now-familiar tightening low in his abdomen. He was in a constant state of semiarousal whenever he was around Janie. But so far, other than their wedding night, he'd made sure they were never alone. When they were at home, Rafael was always there. And when he was at Heaven on Seventh, half of Cameron was there, too.

Now he and Janie would be completely alone, isolated in a cabin miles from the nearest people. *What are you going to do?*

He was going to pretend like nothing had changed between them. He was going to act no different than he would if they were home, and Rafael was watching their every move. He would make it through these next few days, no matter what. Even if he felt like he was going to explode.

He pointed out different parts of the Red Rock as they drove along, trying to keep the conversation light. Janie responded eagerly, as if she, too, was trying to pretend that nothing was different. Finally they pulled up in front of the tiny cabin, tucked against the shore of a small lake, and Janie's voice died away.

"It's awfully small," she finally said, a desperate tone in her voice.

"It'll be easier to keep an eye on what's happening outside," he said, and he knew his voice was too hearty. "We'll only have to take a few steps in any direction."

She glanced over at him, and he saw the awareness in her eyes, an awareness she tried to hide. She must be thinking the same thing, he thought as he looked away. It would only take a few steps in any direction to be in each other's arms, too.

"Let's get unloaded, then we'll take a look around outside the cabin." He would keep as busy as possible during the day, and hope that he'd be exhausted enough at night to fall asleep.

A minute later they stood in the kitchen of the cabin, looking around. Ben carefully plugged his cell phone into the wall and turned it on. Devlin needed to be able to reach them. When he turned back to Janie, he could feel her anxiety rising as they surveyed the cabin. There wasn't going to be anywhere to hide, he realized. There was only the tiny kitchen that opened onto a small living area, and two small bedrooms. He knew that both held a set of bunk beds and one single bed.

"Which room do you want to sleep in?" he finally said.

"Does it make a difference?" Her windblown hair curled wildly around her face, and she licked her lips as she stared at the two rooms. Ben closed his eyes as heat seared him.

"Let me take a look." He dropped his pack and escaped into the closer room. Closing his eyes, he waited for the fierce desire to ease. When he thought he could control himself, he looked carefully out of the window, judging the room's accessibility, then went and checked out the other room.

"I think this room would be better," he said as he walked back into the living room. Janie had pulled her hair away from her face, he saw with relief.

"All right." She avoided his eyes as she set her suitcase down in the room he indicated. She lingered in the room for longer than she needed to, then walked slowly into the living area again.

"I looked through the kitchen. There's enough food here to feed an army for a week," she said, trying to make her voice light.

"Dev told me there are trout in the lake. Do you fish?"

She shook her head, but her eyes lit up. "I've always wanted to learn, though."

"Great. That'll give us something to do." *And an excuse to get out of the cabin.*

"If you want to look around outside, I'll fix dinner. You must be hungry. I know I am." She was chattering, and her nervous energy seemed to fill the room. "How does spaghetti sound?"

"Sounds great." He hurried through the door, letting it bang shut behind him. He had to leave. His mind was filled with ways of using that energy of hers, and none of them was a good idea. "I'll be close by."

"I'll call when dinner's ready."

Refusing to turn around and look at Janie, Ben took a deep breath and tried to steady himself. He couldn't allow this. He couldn't let himself want Janie this way. It was too dangerous. He had to focus on their situation, not on how she tasted and felt in his arms.

And it wasn't fair to Janie. She deserved more from life than the little he could give her. She deserved to have it all—a husband who loved her, a family of her own. He couldn't give her any of those things, so he had no right to touch her.

Keeping that thought in his mind, he tried to focus on checking out the area around the cabin. He couldn't completely get Janie out of his head, but after a while he was able to concentrate on his job. Using his tracking skills, he determined that no one had been around the cabin for at least a couple of weeks.

That confirmed what Shea and Jesse had told him. Working quickly, he constructed a crude warning system that would tell him if someone tried to approach the cabin. It wasn't much, but it was better than nothing.

When he went back into the cabin, the smell of spaghetti sauce filled the air. Janie looked up from a bowl where she was mixing canned fruit for a salad. Garlic bread sat on the counter next to her. "Dinner's just about ready."

"Shall I open the wine to let it breathe?" he asked gravely.

Janie's eyes twinkled at him, and he saw her relax. "I don't know about wine, but there are a few cans of beer in the refrigerator."

Ben shook his head. "No, thanks. I don't want alcohol to dull my wits. I need to be alert."

Her face tightened and the twinkle disappeared from her eyes. "You're right. I don't know what I was thinking of."

He swept her into his arms before he could stop himself. He couldn't stand the way the light had disappeared from her eyes. "It's all right. I was the one who made the stupid joke about the wine."

"It wasn't a stupid joke." She tried to smile, and failed miserably. "You were trying to cheer me up, and it worked."

"I was trying to make you smile." When her lips turned up involuntarily, he pulled her closer. "I can't resist you when you smile."

Her eyes widened. "I didn't know you were trying to resist me."

"All the time," he muttered, unable to let her go. He knew it was wrong, knew it was stupid, but the light in Janie's eyes and the stunned delight curving her lips held him mesmerized. She couldn't possibly want him as much as he wanted her.

But apparently she did. Instead of moving away, Janie moved closer. She was so close now that every part of her body pressed against his. The softness of her breasts was crushed against the plane of his chest. Her legs trembled where they touched his. Heat and passion flashed through him, scorching him with their intensity. And Janie must have felt it, too, because he saw an answering echo in her eyes.

"We can't do this, Janie," he said, and he heard the desperation in his voice.

"Why not?" Her answer was fierce. "We're married. And there's nobody here to see us or stop us. Why would it be wrong?"

"Because it wouldn't be fair to you. Because it wasn't part of the deal. Because I can't give you what you need."

"You have no idea what I need, Ben Jackson. And you have no idea what I want."

"No, I don't, and it has to stay that way."

She leaned back slowly, looking up at his face, but she didn't move away. "You have so much to give, Ben. Why are you so afraid of giving it?"

"You know nothing about me, Janie. You wouldn't be so eager to take anything from me if you knew who I really was."

"Why don't you tell me, then? We have all kinds of time and nothing to do. I can listen for as long as you want to talk."

He wanted to tell her, he realized. He wanted her to hear the whole ugly story. He wanted her to say it didn't matter, that what happened five years ago wasn't his fault, that he didn't have anything to be guilty about.

And that frightened him. It frightened him almost as much as the desire that clutched at him whenever he was near Janie. So he let her go and took a step backward. "We don't have all kinds of time right now." He tried to make his voice light, and suspected he failed miserably. "It looks like that spaghetti is getting cold."

She watched him for a moment, and then she nodded. He realized uneasily that instead of the anger he expected, or even frustration, there was nothing but understanding and compassion in her eyes. And that was the last thing he wanted to see. "I guess you're right," she finally said.

"We have a lot to do this afternoon." She smiled, but it didn't reach her eyes. "Let's eat."

The silence was strained during dinner. Occasionally Janie would ask something about the cabin, or about the area surrounding it. He tried to lighten the atmosphere by telling her stories about the cabin. He told her how Abby and Damien Kane had stayed there while they were protecting Abby's twin nieces, and how Jesse had found Shea hiding the refugee children in the cabin. She smiled and made the right comments at the right time.

But nothing could ease the tension that lingered in the air, hovering between them like an uninvited guest that couldn't be dislodged. Every time he looked at Janie he remembered how she felt, how she looked when he held her in his arms. And every time he looked at her, he remembered her words.

She apparently wanted him as much as he wanted her. Or almost as much, anyway. She couldn't possibly want him with as much urgency, as much heat, as much need as he wanted her. It simply wasn't possible.

As soon as he'd finished his dinner, he pushed his chair away from the table. "Why don't I clean up, since you did the cooking?"

"Thank you, Ben, but don't you have things to take care of outside?" She stood and grabbed the plates as if they would shield her from the tension that simmered between them. "I'll clean up if you want to finish whatever you were doing."

He didn't need another invitation to escape from the cabin. He practically ran down to the lake, where he stood and looked out over the clear blue water and tried to put the woman in the cabin out of his thoughts.

But that was impossible. Janie was part of him now, and even when she eventually left, as he knew she would, he wouldn't be able to forget her.

He stared out at the water as he thought about the last few weeks of his life. Janie had been right. He should have asked someone else to marry him. She was far too dangerous to his peace of mind. She was temptation and seduction: she was everything he'd ever wanted. He hadn't counted on the fact that she would want him, too. Janie was making it almost impossible to do what he knew was right.

He wasn't sure how long he'd been standing there, absorbed in his thoughts, when he realized Janie was close by. He always knew when Janie was around. It was a sixth sense that had developed since the day she'd come to Cameron. It had gotten much more refined since she'd been living with him.

"I saw you standing down here," she said, her voice quiet as she stopped next to him. "Are you thinking about what we'll do if the murderer finds us here?"

Hell, no, he wanted to tell her. He was thinking about how he was going to survive the next few days. Right now, the murderer would be a welcome distraction.

"I was wondering how smart the trout are," he said, scrambling for an answer. "I'll give you a fishing lesson tomorrow, if you like."

"I'd like that." There was genuine enthusiasm in her voice, and he chanced a look over at her. "There weren't many opportunities to go fishing back in Chicago."

"With any luck, we'll have fresh fish for dinner tomorrow."

Janie stepped closer and slipped her arm through his. He tensed, but she didn't pull away. She just stood and looked out at the lake, her arm linked with his. "Under other circumstances, I think I would really enjoy this cabin."

There was a note of sadness in her voice, and he instinctively moved closer. "There's no reason we can't enjoy it now. He's not going to find us here, Janie."

She sighed, and the sadness in the sound pierced his heart. Without thinking, he put his arm around her shoulders. "I won't let anyone hurt you," he murmured.

She turned to look at him, and he saw the pain in her eyes. "I know you won't, Ben. And that's what worries me. I don't want to be responsible for you getting hurt. Or worse."

"Nothing is going to happen to me, either." He managed to dredge up a smile. "Don't you know that criminals are generally pretty stupid? I haven't met one yet I couldn't outwit."

But Janie didn't smile back. "This man isn't stupid," she said quietly. "If he was, he'd have been caught a long time ago."

"I was joking, Janie." Refusing to listen to the warnings in his head, he pulled her into his arms. "Believe me, I'm not underestimating this guy. If your murderer is the person who broke into Heaven on Seventh, he's one smart guy. I'm just trying to cheer you up."

Her softness nestled against him like she belonged there. Suddenly, all the warnings that his head was screaming were not enough. His good sense disappeared in a wave of heat. All he knew was that he was holding Janie, and she felt too good to let her go.

Before he could stop himself, he bent to kiss her. Desire flashed through him at the first taste of her lips. When she opened her mouth to him, pressing closer, he groaned and forgot every vow he'd made. His body throbbed with need and urgency, and nothing mattered anymore except the woman in his arms.

When she pulled his shirt out of his jeans and began unfastening the buttons, he drew in a sharp breath. When she touched his chest, her fingers lingering over the smooth skin of his chest, he couldn't breathe at all. And when he bent his head to trace the curve of her breast with his mouth, she moaned and quivered beneath him, and every bit of air left in his body exploded out of him.

"Please don't stop," she said, her voice husky and low.

"I can't," he said, and his words were ragged. His fingers trembled as he opened the buttons on her shirt. "God help me, Janie, but I can't stop."

"Good." Her voice was fierce with desire, and he felt her fingers fumbling with the buckle of his belt. When the last of her buttons gaped open, he pushed the shirt aside to find a lacy bra beneath. His whole body hardened painfully. "Janie," he whispered, not sure what he was asking.

"I want you, Ben," she said, her voice shaky. "I always have."

He reached out to trace the darkness of her nipple through the lace of her bra, and she drew a sharp breath and clutched at him. His own legs felt wobbly, and he knew that if they stayed here another moment, they would be making love on the rocky shore of the lake.

"You deserve better than this," he said, sweeping her up into his arms. "Let's go inside."

"As long as you don't let me go." She linked her arms round his neck and held on tightly.

Just as he opened the door, the telephone he'd left on the kitchen counter rang shrilly. He stared at it for a moment, then slowly put Janie on her feet.

Chapter 11

Frustration screamed through Janie as Ben set her on the floor. He moved away from her quickly, reaching for the phone.

"I have to answer it," he said, finally looking at her. "It's probably Devlin, and if he's calling, it's important."

She nodded, not sure she could trust her voice. Even the telephone was conspiring against her. And Ben had grabbed for the shrilling handset like it was his salvation.

"Jackson." Ben's voice was terse, and Janie watched as he listened to the voice on the other end of the phone.

His face hardened, and she instinctively moved closer to him. Something was wrong.

"Thanks, Dev," he finally said. "I'll keep my eyes open." He paused. "Yeah, I know. I'll keep in touch."

Ben laid the telephone gently on the counter, then looked up at her. "That was Devlin," he said. "Ron Perkins just called him. Do you know Ron?"

"He's Grady Farrell's ranch manager," Janie said, nodding. Everyone in Cameron eventually came into Heaven on Seventh.

"That's him." Ben's voice was grim. "Grady seems to think a lot of him. And Dev thinks he's okay."

"What did Ron want?" Premonition hummed through Janie, and it wasn't a pleasant one.

"He told Dev that someone had been asking about you at May's. He didn't think anything of it until he heard about your burglary. Then he remembered the guy."

"Did he tell the sheriff what this man looked like?" Janie asked, hope rising inside her.

Ben shook his head. "Perkins said that the guy was average looking. He said he looked like everyone else in the bar, and that's not much to go on. And Perkins said the guy wasn't asking about you directly. He would have remembered that. He was talking about Heaven and the food, and the discussion came around to the owner of the restaurant. Perkins said he never would have given it a second thought if it hadn't been for the break-in. But when he heard the news, he wondered. He thought some of the guy's questions were kind of odd. That's why he called Dev."

"So what do we do now?" Janie shivered and wrapped her arms around herself. The early autumn day was warm, but she was suddenly cold.

"I don't think we do anything." Ben paced from one window to the next, staring out at the mountains surrounding them. "But we have to assume that the murderer from Chicago has found you. It would be stupid to dismiss this conversation Perkins had with a stranger as a coincidence. But that doesn't mean he knows where we are right now. Only Shea, Jesse, Carly and Dev know that, and I trust all of them. As far as anyone else in town is concerned, we went on a honeymoon, and nobody knows where we are."

"Couldn't Ron Perkins point this man out to the sheriff?" Janie asked.

"Maybe. Perkins said he'd probably recognize him, but he hasn't seen him at May's since that evening. He did promise that he'd call Dev right away if he saw the guy again."

"Maybe we all should leave." Janie felt panic pressing in on her, and was bitterly ashamed of her weakness. But she was terribly afraid for Ben. And Rafael. "Why don't we pick Rafael up from Shea and Jesse and take off? We can go anywhere for a few days. Maybe Ron Perkins will see the guy again while we're gone, and the sheriff can arrest him."

"He hasn't done anything wrong, Janie." He reached out to touch her arm, then quickly drew his hand away. "You can't identify him as the second man at the murder because you never saw him. So Dev wouldn't have any excuse to arrest him."

"I heard him. I could identify his voice."

Ben shook his head. "Are you sure, Janie?" His voice was gentle. "It's been three years, and you had just seen your boss murdered. No one's memory would be good under those circumstances."

"There must be *something* we can do." Her voice rose in a wail of frustration.

"Dev is keeping a close eye on the restaurant. I hope that if we don't show up soon, this guy will get impatient and do something stupid, like try to break in again. Then Dev will have him." His eyes softened. "It wouldn't be smart to go back to town with this guy on the loose."

"So we just wait."

"That's all we can do."

The rest of the day was spent in edgy tension, both of them too aware of the other, both doing their best to ignore it. When Janie's frustration reached the screaming point, she hurried into the bathroom to brush her teeth and regain her composure. There had been too many emotional swings today. After she'd changed into her nightgown and walked back into the bedroom, she was surprised to see Ben sitting on the twin bed, examining a pair of binoculars. "What are you doing in here?" she blurted out.

He looked up in surprise. "I thought you understood. We're both going to sleep in this room. I don't want us to be in separate rooms if something happens." He was all business. There wasn't a trace of the desire that had filled his face earlier.

Janie swallowed hard. "I didn't realize that's what you meant."

"I can't protect you if I'm not close to you."

"I would have thought the other bedroom would be plenty close," she muttered.

"We've been sleeping in the same bed for a couple of weeks now," he answered, his words clipped. "There's no reason to get your shorts in a knot."

"Fine," she said coolly. "Just tell me where to sleep."

He jerked his head toward the bunk beds. "Use the bottom bunk. It's more protected than this twin bed."

She slipped between the sheets and closed her eyes, trying to force herself to fall asleep. But Ben seemed to fill the room. His scent surrounded her, and every noise he made was magnified about a hundred times. She even imagined she could feel his heat wrapping around her in the narrow bed.

Finally, frustrated, she turned over and faced the wall and tried to force her mind to think of other things. Suddenly the room went dark and she heard Ben settling on the bed so close to hers.

She hadn't wanted to sleep in the same bed with Ben, but now she realized she'd gotten used to it. She missed his presence next to her, missed his solid, comforting warmth. She loved waking up in the middle of the night to find that she'd cuddled against him while sleeping, and falling back to sleep without moving away.

Restless and unsatisfied, she tossed and turned for what seemed like hours. And she knew Ben wasn't asleep, either.

Finally, after she'd turned over one more time, she heard him whisper, "Janie?"

"What?" Her voice was equally hushed.

"Why can't you sleep?"

"I guess it's just all the excitement around us. All that noise and activity outside makes it tough to sleep," she said tartly.

His chuckle warmed the air around her. "You just miss sleeping with me, don't you? Come on over here."

"You're pretty cocky, aren't you?"

"I miss sleeping with you."

The laughter had disappeared from his voice. Instead, she heard a need that he rarely allowed himself to show. And she couldn't resist it.

She slid into the narrow bed alongside him, and immediately realized that it might not have been such a great idea. They could make no pretense of not touching, not in this twin bed. Their bodies were touching from chest to toe. And when he slid his arms around her and pulled her close so that her back nestled against his chest, it was obvious that he was aroused.

"Let me hold you tonight," he whispered in her ear, and his breath caressed her cheek, making her shiver.

She yearned to turn around and face him, to finish what they had started earlier that evening. But his arms held her snugly against him, and she knew that he didn't want her to turn around.

She lay as taut as a coiled spring next to him, but as their breathing steadied, she was surprised to find herself relaxing. And she realized that Ben was relaxing, too. Just before she fell asleep she sighed and moved closer to him.

When she woke in the morning, she found that she and Ben were tangled together, their legs intimately entwined. And sometime during the night she had turned to face him. Now her cheek rested against his chest, and her hand was tucked between their bodies.

For a moment she kept her eyes closed and pretended this was normal, pretended that she and Ben would wake up this way every day for the rest of their lives. But the image was too seductive, too alluring, so she reluctantly eased away from him and sat up on the edge of the bed. Ben had made his feelings about their future very clear.

"Where are you going?" His voice was slightly hoarse from sleep and thoroughly sexy.

"The sun is up. I thought we had to be up, too." She turned to face him, and found him looking at her with longing in his eyes.

She wanted to leap back into the bed with him. But before she could move, he shuttered his eyes and rolled over on his back. "You're right. There are fish waiting to be caught."

"Let's not disappoint them, then," she said lightly as she headed toward the bathroom.

By the time she was dressed, all evidence of the longing in Ben's eyes was gone. She tried to tell herself that it didn't matter. That it was there at all was a good sign. Two weeks ago, he never would have allowed her to see any weakness in him, any need for her. But they still had a long way to go.

She hummed to herself as she poured water into the coffeepot. Clearly, Ben wasn't as immune to her as he wanted her to think. Maybe they could make a real marriage together after all.

When he walked into the kitchen a few minutes later, she couldn't stop herself from staring at him. She rarely saw him without his deputy's uniform. Today he wore worn, faded jeans and a flannel shirt that was clearly an old favorite. Its soft cotton hugged his shoulders and clung to his chest. He'd rolled the sleeves up to his elbows, and muscles rippled in his forearms. She'd always thought he looked good in his uniform, but her mouth went dry as she looked at him in the worn denim and soft flannel.

"Are you ready to go fishing?" he asked.

She pulled herself together and turned away to pour a cup of coffee. "I don't do anything until I've had my morning coffee," she said firmly.

"I didn't know you were such a slave to the coffeepot." He lounged against the counter and watched her as she poured two cups.

"There's a lot you don't know about me," she said quietly.

Ben straightened and set his cup on the counter. "I know that, Janie," he said, and she heard a wisp of regret in his voice. "I guess I thought that if I didn't know you, it wouldn't be so hard to end our marriage."

"Now that we're stuck in this cabin together, you're going to learn about me whether you want to or not." She took a sip of coffee rather than meet his eyes.

"Maybe I want to know more about you now."

She jerked her head around to stare at him. "Why, Ben?"

He shrugged, deliberately casual, but he didn't look at her. "Maybe the judge at Rafael's hearing will ask us questions about each other. It just seems like good insurance."

Janie ignored the crushing disappointment and took another sip of coffee. "Ask anything you like," she said coolly. "We might as well make use of this time together."

He nodded once, then moved away to watch out the windows as he finished his coffee. Janie allowed her gaze to follow him around the room. He wasn't looking at her. He wouldn't realize that she was staring.

Ben was such a complicated man. There was so much of himself that he kept hidden. But what he'd shown her these past couple of weeks had done nothing but increase her admiration for him. He was an honorable man to the core. He would give his life to protect her, and Rafael. And he was committed to his job, and the people of Cameron. There was much to admire about Ben.

"I don't see anyone out there," he said abruptly. "Let's go fishing."

"What are we going to use for poles and bait?" she asked as he made sandwiches for lunch. There was nothing in the tiny cabin that even remotely resembled a fishing rod.

He gave her an unexpected grin. "Everything we need is in my car. I'm always prepared to go fishing."

Ben grabbed the cell phone, then Janie followed him down the steps and watched as he opened the back of his pickup truck. He pulled out two fishing rods and a large tackle box, then a backpack, before he slammed the hatch closed. "This should do it for us."

They walked to the edge of the lake, and Ben stared down into the depths for a while. Then he started walking. "I don't like this spot. Let's look for a better one."

"It looks like you do a lot of fishing," Janie said.

He looked over at her with a smile. "Whenever I can."

"I had no idea."

His smile disappeared. "I guess there's a lot you don't know about me, either."

"I want to learn, Ben," she said before she could think.

He looked over at her again, and this time there was need and desire in his eyes, along with regret. "You shouldn't want me, Janie."

"Maybe not, but I do."

"One of us needs to be smart about this marriage."

"I thought that was your job. You're the one with the mile-high fences around yourself."

"They seem to have gotten a lot lower recently," he muttered, then he walked a little faster. Almost as if he wanted to put some distance between them after his unwilling admission.

After a moment, Janie ran a few steps to catch up with him. "What are you looking for?" she asked, trying to change the subject. Clearly, their marriage was something Ben didn't want to talk about.

"I'm looking for the place where the big fish are hiding."

She glanced at him, startled, but realized that it was exactly what he was doing. Every ten or fifteen feet he stopped and stared into the blue depths of the lake. Finally he set the fishing rods and tackle box down. "This will do."

For the next several hours he patiently showed her how to tie a fly onto the end of her line, how to cast her line into the water, and what kinds of places were likely to be hiding fish. He didn't laugh when her line got caught in one of the trees behind them, or when her fly plopped into the water only inches from where they stood. And he never acted frustrated or bored or irritated with her clumsy efforts.

As the morning hours crept away, they moved slowly around the shore of the lake, trying new spots. Ben caught three fish, but threw two of them back. He kept the largest one for their dinner. She had a few bites, but didn't manage to hook anything.

It didn't matter. She loved the calmness of the lake and the silence that surrounded them, the peacefulness of the repetitive motions of casting. She loved the fact that Ben seemed truly relaxed for the first time since he'd asked her to marry him. And she was thrilled to learn a new skill, one that she'd wanted to try for a long time.

"Are you about ready for lunch?" Ben asked, laying down his fishing rod.

"I guess I am," she said, surprised. "I didn't realize I was hungry."

Ben grinned at her, his eyes unshadowed and laughing. "That's a bad sign, Janie, really bad. When you forget about everything else while you're fishing, including food, you've got it bad."

They traded banter while they ate, and Janie was amazed again at the transformation in Ben. The serious, closed-off man she'd been trying to get to know had disappeared entirely. In his place was a laughing, teasing stranger. One she wanted to know a whole lot better.

When she'd finished her sandwich and the granola bar he'd pulled out of his backpack, she leaned back against the tree and closed her eyes. "Am I mistaken, or is this heaven?"

"If it's not heaven, it's pretty darned close." He propped himself up on one elbow and turned to face her. "I didn't know you liked the outdoors so much."

"I guess it's another one of those things we need to find out about each other," she said lightly.

"How come you never learned to fish since you've been in Cameron? A lot of the people around here fish, and anyone would have been happy to teach you."

She shrugged. "I was too busy working in the restaurant. And I didn't want to make any friends. I was afraid they would be in danger if the man who was after me ever found me." She looked over at him. "Kind of like the situation we're in now."

"Poor Janie," he said softly. "How alone you must have felt."

"No more alone than you."

He shook his head. "I have a job where I'm in contact with people all day. You hide in that kitchen of yours and never come out from one week to the next."

"I come out into the restaurant all the time," she protested. "I know almost everyone in Cameron by sight."

"Then I guess you only hide in the kitchen when I'm in the restaurant."

She turned to face him. "The same way you leave the restaurant whenever you see me?"

Her question hung between them in the suddenly still air. His eyes darkened as he watched her, but she didn't look away. And neither did he.

"I couldn't stand being around you, Janie," he finally said in a low voice that resonated with desire. "I wanted you too much. And the night we spent together just made it worse. Then I knew what we were like together, but I knew I couldn't have you. It was easier to avoid you."

"Why did you think you couldn't have me?" she asked, holding her breath.

"Because you made it clear that you weren't interested. And I had nothing to offer you." His eyes flared with passion, but she could see the effort he made to control it. "I still don't."

"You're wrong, Ben." She leaned closer. "Since we've been married, I've been learning all kinds of things about you. And all of them are good." She held his gaze as she added, "You know now why I couldn't get involved with anyone, but it hasn't sent you running in the opposite direction. So what's your excuse now?"

He groaned. "Don't do this to me, Janie. I want you too

much. Do you know how much torture it's been, sleeping in the same bed with you for the past two weeks and not being able to touch you?''

"Don't you think I've felt the same way?" she asked fiercely. "I didn't make love with you five months ago on a whim. It wasn't just a night of pleasure for me, easily forgotten. There was a connection between us, Ben. I'll admit I've been fighting it, too, because I was afraid for you. I didn't want you to get close to me and then get hurt. But you're in this with me now, and if the killer is in town, he knows I'm married. So why are we still trying to pretend that this *thing* between us doesn't exist?''

"Because it shouldn't exist. You don't need a man like me in your life."

She took a deep breath, then recklessly played her hand. "You're exactly what I need in my life, Ben Jackson."

"You don't know what you're saying, Janie." The words sounded as if they'd been torn out of his throat. But instead of moving away, he reached for her and pulled her into his arms. "I don't want you to regret anything."

"I couldn't. I could never regret anything I feel about you, or anything we do together."

He groaned again. "You're making this too easy for me, Janie."

She looked up at him and brushed a lock of hair away from his forehead. "I don't think waiting for you for three years has been easy. It hasn't been for me, anyway."

Then his mouth found hers, and his kiss tasted of need and heat and desperation. He moved his hands over her as if he would die if he didn't touch her. When she pulled at his shirt, he ripped it open. And when she put her mouth against the smooth skin of his chest, she felt him shudder beneath her.

"This isn't the way it should be," he growled as he trailed kisses down her neck. "We should be somewhere comfortable and safe, where I can love you the way you deserve to be loved.''

"I'm safe with you, Ben, wherever we are. And what could be more magical than lying next to this beautiful lake, with nothing but wilderness around us? This is perfect.''

"You're perfect, Janie." He pushed her T-shirt up to her neck, then closed his eyes when he saw the delicate bra she wore. "You're going to drive me crazy if you keep wearing this fancy underwear.''

She smiled into his neck. "Why do you think I wear it? The cat sure doesn't appreciate it.''

He pulled the shirt over her head, then bent to kiss the sensitive skin below her bra. She jumped when his fingers brushed her nipple, then gasped when he took her into his mouth. "Ben," she whispered, her voice shaky.

"I want to look at you," he muttered. He snapped the bra open, then eased it away from her breasts. "You're so beautiful," he said, awe in his voice.

He bent to kiss her again, sucking gently at her nipple, and she shuddered as a hot wave of desire crashed over her. Blindly she reached for him, trying to unfasten his belt.

"Not yet," he said, gently pushing her hands away. "I've waited too long for you. If you touch me, it will be over far too quickly.''

He bent to kiss one nipple again, tracing his finger over her other breast. She moaned his name and twisted beneath him, heat building low in her abdomen.

And suddenly he couldn't wait, either. He tugged at her shorts, unbuttoning them and pulling them down her legs. His eyes darkened at the scrap of lace she wore beneath them, but then he pulled that away, too.

She lay naked beneath him, every part of her throbbing with need. He stared down at her, then said, "This is your last chance, Janie. You'd better say no now, because in a few moments I won't be able to stop.''

Chapter 12

"I don't want to say no," she said, aching for his touch. "Love me, Ben."

He groaned and gathered her against him. His kiss was deep and hard and hot, possessing and claiming her. It was the kiss of a man denied for too long, the kiss of a man who wouldn't be denied any longer.

As he kissed her, he touched her everywhere, his hands lingering and caressing. When he reached her waist, he hesitated, then slowly slid his hand between her legs.

She cried out in surprise at the shock of pleasure that possessed her. And when he touched her again, a spasm of release speared through her, leaving her limp and trembling in his arms.

"I need you, Ben. Now," she whispered.

He didn't take his eyes or his mouth off of her while he unbuttoned his jeans and slid them down his legs. His white briefs followed. The muscles in his legs rippled beneath his olive skin, and she saw that he was fully, heavily aroused. She needed to touch him, and he trembled beneath her hand. His muscles were rock-hard with tension, and he closed his eyes as she caressed him.

Suddenly he jerked away from her. "I have to get protection from my backpack."

"It's all right. It's not the right time of month."

He was reaching for the pack, but he stopped and looked at her. "What if you're wrong?"

"Then we'll have another child to raise besides Rafael."

He grabbed the pack and unzipped a front pocket. "I can't take that chance. And now isn't the time to make a decision like that, anyway."

In another moment he was back beside her. "I can't wait another moment, Janie."

She reached up and pulled him down to her. "Neither can I."

When he moved inside of her, she wrapped her legs and arms around him and closed her eyes. He moved slowly at first, whispering her name. She arched up to meet him as the tension spiraled higher and higher, then clutched him tightly as they flew over the edge together.

She floated for a long time, reveling in the weight of Ben's body on top of hers, the smell of his skin, the feel of his hair against her face, the smoothness of his skin. Finally he shifted and tried to move, and involuntarily she held on more tightly. "Don't move."

"I'm afraid I'm crushing you."

"You're not."

He rolled over so that she was lying on top of him. "The ground isn't soft enough for you," he said, his hand drifting down her back and lingering on her hip. "I don't want any stones to bruise that magnificent fanny of yours."

She snuggled closer. "Could we stay here forever?"

"Mmm, that's all right with me. It might get kind of chilly in a couple of months, though."

"You'll keep me warm," she said, shifting so that every part of her was touching him.

"You keep moving like that and you're going to be warm a lot more quickly than you think." He gripped her hips more tightly, and she could feel the unmistakable evidence of his arousal.

Desire flashed through her again, shocking her with its fierceness. And its speed. "Maybe we'd better practice, then," she said, and couldn't believe the low, throaty voice belonged to her. It belonged to a seductress, not Janie Murphy. "We want to be prepared."

"Preparation is everything," he agreed gravely. When he pulled her down to kiss her, everything else but Ben disappeared from her mind. Need swelled inside her again, and nothing existed but the man in her arms.

Ben opened his eyes to see the sun sinking below the mountains. Janie lay sprawled on top of him, her red hair in glorious disarray, her breathing slow and even.

He allowed himself to watch her sleep as he treasured the feel of her slight weight pressing down on him. They had made love all afternoon until they'd both fallen asleep, exhausted.

They needed to get back to the cabin, he told himself, but he couldn't force himself to move. Once they were back at the cabin, the world would press in on them again. Once they left this magical place, he would have to stop pretending that they had any kind of a future together.

But it couldn't be helped. Night was closing in, and the darkness on the mountain hid too many things. He wanted to be safely inside the cabin before the light disappeared completely.

He nuzzled Janie's neck, drinking in her scent, memorizing the way she tasted. She stirred and shifted so she was closer to him, and her arms tightened around him. He closed his eyes until he could control his reaction to her.

"It's time to wake up," he said, and he heard the desperation in his voice. "Come on, Janie. It's getting dark."

She opened her eyes, and her dark blue gaze was sleepy and satisfied. "I don't think I can move."

Her mouth curled into an intimate smile, and all he wanted to do was kiss her. Instead he eased her away from him. "You're going to have to move, or you're going to get mighty cold." He didn't want to mention what he feared more than the cold—the predators that might be on the loose in the mountains under cover of darkness. Both the four-legged and two-legged varieties.

She reached over and kissed him, and the fragrant cloud of her hair drifted over his face. "You promised to keep me warm," she said, and her low, husky voice reached inside of him, settling in a place he didn't know still existed.

Janie trusted him. She trusted him to keep her not only warm, but safe. For a moment his arms tightened around her, and he didn't want to move, either. Then he lifted her off of him and sat up. "I'd rather keep you warm in a bed, inside the cabin."

She grinned at him in the receding light as she reached for her blouse. "Now that you mention it, that sounds pretty good to me, too. And I'm starving."

"I've got the solution to that dilemma," he said lightly. "I'll cook the fish when we get back to the cabin."

They both dressed, then looked around to find anything they might have left behind. Ben tucked the blanket back into his pack, then closed it.

"That backpack is amazing," Janie said, equally lightly. "You must have been a Boy Scout, because you're certainly prepared for anything. What else do you have in there?"

His hands tightened around the pack, then he set it on the ground. "There's everything I might need for a couple of days in the mountains in this pack. I get called out on emergency tracking jobs occasionally, and I don't want to take the time to put everything in my backpack. So I just leave it in the back of the truck, ready to go."

She raised her eyebrows. "You have a lot of calls for condoms when you're tracking a missing person?"

He felt himself flush. "That's different," he muttered. "I put those in the pack after we got married."

Her delighted smile brought heat to other parts of his body. "I didn't know you were such a romantic, Ben."

"I just thought we needed to be prepared."

"And it's a good thing we were." Her smile faded for a moment. "But what did you mean when you said you couldn't take a chance on having another child?"

"Let's not discuss that here." He glanced at the sun, sinking quickly below the mountains now, and urged her along with a hand at the small of her back. "We can talk later."

And they would have to discuss it. He owed it to Janie to tell her the truth—the complete truth. She deserved to know why he couldn't ever give her what she so obviously needed. And wanted, if this afternoon was any indication.

His heart ached for her, ached to gather her close and never let her go. But he stepped away from her and shouldered his pack. "Let's get moving. I don't want to be out here after dark."

"Don't you have a flashlight in that pack of yours?"

"I do, and we'll use it if we have to. Right now, there's enough light to see where we're going."

They didn't speak for a while. He pushed himself to hurry, and he knew that Janie was struggling to keep up with him. He heard her panting slightly behind him, but she never complained. When he heard her stumble, he stopped and waited for her to catch up to him.

"Walk next to me," he said gruffly. "It'll be easier if we're together."

"We'll go more slowly that way," she retorted. "You don't have to baby me, Ben. I can make it on my own."

"I know you can, Janie." In spite of himself, he felt his heart softening. How could he resist this woman? She was everything he'd ever wanted. And more. But he had to resist her. It wouldn't be fair to her to lead her on, to make her believe they could have any kind of future together.

"We're almost there, aren't we?"

He could feel her peering through the gathering darkness, straining to see the cabin. "Yeah, we're getting close."

Suddenly he stopped. "Wait."

"What's wrong?" she said.

"Shhh." He held up one hand to silence her, and she stopped next to him.

It was too quiet. All day long, there had been a background chorus of noise filling the air around them. Small animals had rustled in the bushes and plants, insects had clicked and hummed, and birds had whistled and trilled. Louder animal cries had occasionally echoed from a distance.

As dusk fell, the animal sounds had lessened, then picked up again as the night-dwelling creatures had emerged. Now the air was heavy with silence.

The quiet filled his head, sending adrenaline coursing through his veins. Something was wrong. They weren't alone in the night.

"Back up. Slowly." There had been several large boulders off to the side of the lake a few yards back. That would work as cover for Janie while he checked out the cabin.

She didn't say anything as she began backing up, and Ben wanted to kiss her. *Later,* he told himself. He couldn't let himself be distracted. He had to concentrate on the possible threat that waited ahead of them.

When they reached the boulders, he drew Janie down into a crevice in the middle of the rocks, then squatted next to her. Gripping her forearms, he stared into her eyes. "I didn't see anything or hear anything," he whispered. "But it was suddenly much too quiet. I don't like it. I'm going to take a look around the cabin, make sure that everything is all right. You stay right here. No one can see you without coming right up to the rocks, and in a few minutes it will be too dark to see anything."

He slung his pack off his back and set it down next to her. "Don't come out, no matter what. *Stay put.* I don't care what you see or hear. If I don't come back in thirty minutes, call Dev on the cell phone in the pack. Tell him where you are, and he'll come get you."

She reached out and gripped his hand. "What do you mean, if you don't come back? What's out there, Ben?"

He clasped her hand and felt the connection arcing between them. He could allow himself that much, at least. "I don't know what's out there. If we're lucky, it's just a mountain lion looking for dinner. But I have to assume the worst. I have to think and act as though it's your murderer, and he's found the cabin."

"Why don't you just stay here with me? Why do you have to go and check? You said no one could see me here." Her voice sounded frantic in the gathering darkness, and he wedged himself between the rocks and pulled her close.

"I don't want anyone sneaking up on us. I'd rather know what's out there. Then we can decide what to do." He felt her heart pounding next to his chest, and he smoothed his hand over her hair. "It's probably an animal, and we'll have to sit here and wait for him to leave. Don't worry, Janie.''

"Don't worry? You're sneaking off into the night to stalk what might be a cold-blooded murderer, and you're telling me not to worry?''

Even though she was whispering, he could hear the panic rising in her voice. "This is what I do, and I'm good at my job.'' Her hair slipped through his fingers like strands of silk. "I'm very good, Janie. I can disappear into the shadows, and no one knows I'm there.'' He smiled against her hair. ''Believe me, if it is the guy who's after you, he won't have any idea that I'm close. I won't take any stupid chances. I'll come back here for you.''

She held him close, her arms trembling. "I'll be waiting for you.''

He wanted Janie always to be waiting for him. It was a dangerous, seductive thought, and one he should squash immediately. Instead, he hugged it close for a moment, indulging himself in its warmth. Then he let her go and wriggled out of the crevice between the boulders.

"Stay here, and be completely quiet. Remember, don't come out until you see either me or Devlin.''

He couldn't resist one last, fierce kiss. Her lips clung to his, and he allowed himself to drown in her sweetness for a long moment. Then he set her away from him, and moved away into the darkness without looking back.

Janie watched Ben melt into the darkness that surrounded them, disappearing before her eyes. He had been right, she told herself with shaky confidence. He was good at what he did. She couldn't hear him at all. She had no idea where he'd gone. All she could do was sit and wait for him to come back.

Or not come back.

Stop it, she told herself fiercely. Ben was coming back

soon. He'd figure out that there was nothing wrong, nothing waiting out there in the darkness for them, and they'd return to the cabin, laughing at themselves for their worry. They'd cook the fish he caught, and watch the moon rise over the lake. Then they'd go to bed and make love again.

That was what she needed to concentrate on. Their future. Raising Rafael together, and the other children she hoped they would have. The stillness Ben had felt had nothing to do with another person up here on the mountain. It was an animal, she told herself, on the prowl.

She felt the tension in the air ease, felt the night return to normal. Everything that had been waiting let out its breath, rustling the leaves of the bushes and the scrubby plants. The slight breeze caressed her cheek, as if reassuring her.

But Ben didn't return.

After what seemed like a long time she allowed herself to move, stretching her legs out in front of her and shifting on the ground to find a more comfortable position against the rock. As she listened intently, she told herself that Ben was just being cautious. He wanted to make sure that whatever had been lurking in the darkness was gone.

Suddenly a dark shape materialized in front of her, gliding silently between the rocks. She stifled a scream when she realized it was Ben.

"Are you all right?" she whispered, reaching for him.

His hand closed around hers. "I'm fine. But we can't go back to the cabin." His voice was barely more than a breath of air in the darkness.

She gripped his hand more tightly as her heart began to pound. "Why not?"

"There's a man hidden in the rocks and scrub about a hundred feet from the cabin. I watched him for a long time, and he hasn't moved. He's got a rifle aimed at the front door."

She could only stare at him as her heart shriveled with fear. "What?"

"It looks like he's found you, Janie. Now we have to catch him before he catches us."

"How could he have found us at the cabin? And so quickly?"

"When I get a chance, I'll check the car. He probably put some kind of tracking device on your car and my truck before he even broke into the restaurant. That way, if we took off, all he would have to do would be to follow the device." His voice filled with disgust. "I can't believe I didn't think to check the truck before we left."

"It's not your fault, Ben," she said, and she moved closer to him. "I wouldn't have thought of that, either."

"It's not your job to think like a criminal. But it is mine. And I should have thought of a tracking device." Even in the dim light, she could see the granitelike contours of his face. "Deep down, I guess I didn't take the threat to you as seriously as I should have."

"Don't blame yourself. I thought we were safe up here, too." She tightened her grip on his hand. "What are we going to do now?"

"We're going to make our way to somewhere we can spend the night. We have the advantage right now, because I know where he is, and he doesn't know where we are. But it would be too dangerous to try and take him down in the darkness. By daylight, we should have the advantage. He'll have been waiting for us all night, and he'll be tired. Maybe I can take him by surprise."

"You're not going after him by yourself." Janie heard the rising fear in her voice, but she didn't try to disguise it. "Promise me you'll call the sheriff for help."

He reached out and cupped her cheek in his hand. "I'm not stupid. Of course I'll call for backup. Devlin will come up with a few of the other deputies, and we'll catch this guy. But it's not going to happen tonight."

"Don't we need to stay and watch him?" she asked, reluctant to move from the relative safety of the boulders.

"I don't think so. He's focused on the cabin. He doesn't know I've seen him, and he'll be waiting for us to return. I'm sure he's been inside and knows we're staying there. So he won't go far."

"Where are we going?"

"The cliffs behind us are full of caves. We'll find one and stay there for the night. I have enough food and water for both of us, and some extra clothes and emergency blankets. We won't have all the comforts of home, but we won't starve or freeze, either."

Janie looked out into the darkness that was now complete. The moon hadn't yet risen, and she could barely see the lake, several yards away. Fear tried to suffocate her again, but she turned to Ben. "Tell me what you want me to do."

His hand tightened on hers. He leaned closer and brushed her cheek with his mouth. "You're something, Janie. Do you know that?"

"I'm just stiff from sitting here for so long," she retorted. "I need to move around."

"Let's get moving, then." He tried to make his voice light, but she heard something humming beneath his casual words. Something that felt important. But he had already turned away and was wriggling out from between the boulders.

She followed him, flexing her cramped legs and arms. When they reached the path, he motioned for her to stay down while he silently disappeared into the shadows once again.

In moments he was back, reappearing as mysteriously as he had vanished. "Let's go. I want to head away from the cabin. We'll intersect the cliffs before too long. I doubt that's what he's expecting us to do.''

He started walking, and she was surprised and uneasy to hear pebbles tumbling along the path. Ben had moved so silently earlier. It was almost as if he didn't care if he alerted the man waiting for them.

She was just about to ask Ben what was going on when he stopped abruptly and held up his hand. She halted immediately and stood behind him, trying to breathe in slowly and carefully. After what seemed like an eternity, he pulled her gently down beneath a large mesquite bush next to the path.

"Stay here," he breathed in her ear. "I'll be right back."

He vanished again, this time silently. He was back by her side minutes later.

"It's all right," he said, his words still barely more than a breath of air next to her head. "He didn't move, so he either didn't hear us, or assumed it was an animal making the noise."

"You kicked those pebbles on purpose?" She gave him a confused look.

"I had to make sure he wasn't going to try and follow if we made any sounds. He's still in the same place, so we should be all right. In a few minutes, we're going to be out of his hearing range, anyway."

"Let's go, then." Panic rose in her at the thought of the murderer calmly waiting for them, a gun in his hand. She struggled to master it, to force it back into hiding deep inside her. When Ben pulled her close and gave her a deep, hard kiss, she leaned into him gratefully.

"I won't let you get hurt, Janie."

"I know." She believed him. The murderer was smart and clever, but she and Ben would outwit him. And they were on Ben's turf. "I'm not worried about that. I just don't want you to get hurt. He's already hurt too many people I care about.''

His arms tightened around her almost painfully, then he set her aside. ''He's not going to hurt me, or anyone else. In the morning we'll catch him, and it'll be over.''

And then what? She ached to ask him, to find out what the future held for them, but knew it wasn't the time. Once they got past the murderer, they still had to get through Rafael's custody hearing. More than anything, she wanted them to be a real family. But was that what Ben wanted?

Ben moved silently on the path in front of her. She stared down, trying to see her way in the very faint light from the stars, but occasionally she would kick a pebble. The silence and her imagination made them sound like gunshots in the stillness, but Ben didn't seem to notice. He just kept moving toward the cliffs that rose darkly in front of them.

Every once in a while he would stop and set her down in a hidden niche in the rocks, or behind a tree. Then he would disappear for a while, only to return and take her hand to lead her on. She assumed he was checking to make sure no one had followed them, but she didn't ask. The less noise they made, the better.

Finally they reached the wall of cliffs that surrounded the lake. Ben hesitated, then he turned toward the lake. He must have felt her questions, though, because he stopped and pulled her close to whisper in her ear.

''There's more cover closer to the lake—more bushes and trees. And although I'm sure that's where he'll expect us to go, I'd rather take the chance and have the cover in the daylight.''

''You're in charge,'' she said, and realized that she meant every word. She trusted him completely to make the right choices for them.

He gave her an odd look and let her go. ''There isn't

much of a trail here. Do you want to wait here while I find a cave? It'll be easier for you.''

''I'd rather stay with you,'' she said immediately. ''If I'm not going to slow you down.''

''I'd rather have you with me,'' he said gruffly. ''Let's go, then.''

They moved through the maze of plants and trees, brushing close to the cliffs that towered about the lake. They made more noise now, but it couldn't be helped. There was no path along this side of the lake.

''Hold it,'' Ben said, and Janie stopped abruptly. ''This looks promising.''

He dropped his pack on the ground and pulled out a flashlight. ''I'll be right back,'' he said.

Ben scaled the cliff almost effortlessly, and her stomach dipped and swayed uneasily as she watched him. Suddenly he disappeared. After a few minutes, he reappeared and slid down to her.

''There's a cave, and I think it will do.'' He shouldered the pack again. ''It's not a hard climb. I'll stay behind you and tell you where to put your hands and feet.''

Janie nodded, swallowing hard and trying to hide her shaking hands. ''I can do this.'' She wanted to be Ben's partner, not a burden.

She hadn't mentioned her fear of heights to Ben. It hadn't been necessary up until now. She swallowed again and headed for the cliff, telling herself that all she had to do was not look down. She *could* do this.

''Put your hands here, and here.'' Ben pointed to two small crevices just over her head, and she slid her hands into them.

The rock was cold and crumbly beneath her fingers, and she felt her palms begin to sweat. Ignoring the voices in her head telling her to stop, she put her feet where Ben pointed and lifted herself into the air.

She took two more steps, then stopped and closed her eyes. The world spun dizzily around her, and greasy nausea roiled her stomach. She couldn't move another inch.

Chapter 13

"Keep going, Janie."

Ben's voice was filled with urgency, and she forced herself to open her eyes. "How much farther?"

Instead of answering, he moved closer. "What's wrong?" he said sharply.

"I should have told you before we started," she said swallowing. "I have this little problem with heights."

He went still for a moment, then touched her arm gently. "We're almost there. Do you want me to go ahead of you, or stay behind you?"

"I don't know." She heard the panic and desperation in her voice, and cursed her stupid weakness. "I thought I could do this."

"You can do this." His voice was calm and completely confident. "Move your left hand two inches higher."

She slowly let go of the rock, releasing the tight grip that cramped her fingers. The sharp edges of the cliff cut into her palm as she slid her hand higher. When she felt the next crack, she slid her fingers into it and held on tightly.

"Good. Now do the same with your right hand."

She repeated the agonizingly slow movement with her right hand, until she was securely holding the cliff again.

"Now you're going to move your feet." Ben shifted until he was slightly below her. "You won't slip, but if you do, I'll catch you. Now move your left foot higher."

As she eased her left foot out of its crevice, her stomach dipped and swooped. For a moment the world spun around her and she was certain she would fall. Then she felt Ben grasp her ankle and steer her foot to another toehold.

"Do the same with your other foot."

Once again, Ben guided her foot into another crevice, and she was a few inches higher on the cliff.

"You're doing fine, Janie."

She wasn't doing fine. She was endangering both of them, and she knew it. "How much farther?"

"Just a few more feet." He rested his hand on her leg, and she was absurdly grateful for the contact. "Look up to your left and you can see the opening."

A small black hole yawned in front of her, partially hidden by an outcropping of rocks. She forced herself to focus on the hole, rather than the ground below them. Staring at the spot, she fumbled for another fingerhold, then another. Suddenly she felt Ben's hand on her rear end, pushing her onto the ledge at the front of the cave.

In seconds Ben was beside her, folding her into his arms. "My God, Janie. Why didn't you tell me earlier?"

"It wasn't something that came up in conversation. And when you said we would find a cave, I didn't think you meant we would climb up to one."

"We're safer up here." He leaned away and looked at her face in the weak moonlight that was beginning to stream into the valley from behind the cliffs. "That was the bravest thing I've ever seen."

"That was the most stupid thing you've ever seen," she said wearily. "I froze out there on the cliff. If the man with the gun had seen us, I would have gotten both of us killed."

"But he didn't." Ben's voice was very quiet. "And you made it into the cave, in spite of your fear. You're safe now, Janie."

"Until I have to climb down again in the morning," she said, keeping her voice light and trying to smile.

"We'll figure out something in the morning. Don't worry about it now. Let's get back into the cave."

Janie looked at the inky darkness behind them, a blackness so complete that nothing could penetrate it. "You're lucky I'm not afraid of the dark."

"The cave curves around, so we can turn the flashlight on for a little while, until we get settled. You didn't see any light when I was up here earlier, did you?"

"No. Did you have your flashlight on?"

"Once I got to the back of the cave, I turned it on to make sure the cave would be all right. We won't leave it on for long, but at least there'll be some light."

Janie crawled into the darkness, following Ben. In a few moments a dim light shimmered around her. The cave was too small to stand up, but it was wide enough that they would be able to lie down.

"Home sweet home," she said as she stopped next to Ben and looked around.

"At least for tonight." He aimed the flashlight at the walls and the ceiling, then at the floor. "I was worried that there would be animals or bats in here, but it looks clean."

"Nothing is going to surprise us during the night?"

"I don't think so."

He set the flashlight down on the floor and opened his

backpack. "Here's an extra shirt for you." He tossed her a flannel shirt, and she pulled it around her shoulders gratefully. She had sweated as she struggled to climb the cliff, and now she was beginning to shiver. "I don't want to take your shirt," she said, looking over at him as she clutched the soft material close.

He gave her a quick smile. "I have another one. I always carry two of everything. People who get lost don't think to bring a jacket or a blanket with them."

He opened a small packet and unfolded a crinkly silver blanket. "You're shivering. Wrap this around yourself while I call Dev."

"This piece of plastic?" she said, taking the crinkly material.

"Believe me, it will warm you up quickly. It traps all your body heat. We'll be cozy tonight."

As he removed things from his pack, she wrapped the blanket around her. And sure enough, in just a few minutes she felt cocooned in warmth.

He moved to the cave opening, and in a moment she heard him talking in a low voice. Finally he returned.

"I told Dev what was going on, but he's going to wait until morning to come up here. All he'd be able to do tonight is to spook the guy. Your murderer will go into the mountains, and we'd have to wait for him to make the next move. Dev will be at the cabin at dawn with several deputies."

He set the phone on the floor of the cave and reached into his backpack.

"We'll have to eat our dinner cold tonight," he said, placing two packets on the ground. "I don't want to take a chance on building a fire."

"I'm not really hungry." Her stomach was still slightly queasy from the climb up the cliff.

"You need to eat." He opened a bottle of water and

poured some into the packet. "Your stomach will feel better if it has something in it. And you'll be weak in the morning if you don't eat now."

He handed her the packet and a plastic spoon, and she looked at the label. Beef Stroganoff. She took a tentative bite and discovered that it wasn't as bad as she'd expected. When she took another bite, he nodded in approval as he prepared his own meal. "Good job."

His casual words of praise made her glow inside, and she ducked her head, afraid he would see the neediness in her eyes. She didn't want him to feel that he had to encourage and compliment her every step of the way. Ben had too many other things to worry about.

They finished the unappetizing meal quickly, then Ben placed the empty packets back in his pack. After drinking some water and eating a piece of chocolate, she leaned against the wall of the cave and watched as he spread another of the emergency blankets on the ground, then turned off the flashlight.

"If we share that blanket you're using, we'll have one for the floor, too. It's more efficient for us to keep each other warm."

She was more than happy to share her heat with him, and she scooted over until they were touching. She handed him the blanket, and he wrapped it around both of them. He pulled her against him, as if to shield her from the hard wall of the cave, and she curled around him with a sigh of comfort.

Ben sat in the darkness, holding Janie, trying to deny how right it felt. Even in the dank darkness of the cave her scent filled the air, stirring memories of their lovemaking.

It would never be enough. He'd thought that if they made love, just once, it would prove to him that he'd been lingering in a fantasy, his memory playing tricks with him.

But it had been no trick of his memory. Their lovemaking that afternoon had been more intense, sweeter, and more consuming than he'd remembered. He wanted to hold tight to Janie, to love her every night for the rest of his life.

Which was why he had to tell her the truth about himself. And there was no time like the present, he told himself grimly. They were trapped in this cave for the rest of the night.

"There's something I need to tell you, Janie," he said, and he felt her tense.

"What, Ben?" She lifted her head to look at him, and he saw the trust in her eyes. And something more, something he didn't want to face. He damned well better tell her now, he told himself harshly. He had to erase that look from her eyes before it was too late. The last thing he could allow himself to do was believe that anything was possible, that they had any kind of a future together.

"I have to tell you who I really am. There are things about me that no one knows. And as my wife, you have a right to know them."

Janie shifted and moved so she could look into his face. "There's nothing you *have* to tell me. I know all I need to know about you, Ben."

"No, you don't." He knew his voice was grim, but he didn't try to soften it. "I should have told you before we got married, but I was too afraid that you would change your mind. But now that we've..." He stared into the weak light of the flashlight as memories of their lovemaking speared into him. Her taste, the way she felt, the way she'd given herself to him all rose up inside him, crying at him to hold on to Janie as hard as he could. He pushed the longing away. "I should have told you before we made love."

He turned to face her, taking her arms as if he could

hold her away from him. "I told you I'd been married before. What I didn't tell you is that I killed my wife."

He felt the shock ripple through her, saw the stunned look on her face. But she didn't move away from him. "What do you mean, you killed your wife?" she whispered.

"I didn't shoot her, or stab her or poison her. She was killed in a car accident. But it was my fault."

The stunned look faded from her eyes, replaced by a deep sympathy. "How can you blame yourself for a car accident?"

"We had a fight. She was upset. I got out of the car, and she sped off. An hour later the police were at my door, telling me there had been an accident." He took a deep, trembling breath. "She wasn't the only one in the car. The accident also killed my son."

She drew in a sharp breath. "Oh, Ben, I'm so sorry." Her hand tightened on his, and he twined his fingers with hers. "How did you manage to survive?"

"Barely." He held on to Janie as his gaze focused on the past. "His name was Robbie, and he was four years old. And if I hadn't lost my temper, he might be alive today."

"You can't do that to yourself, Ben. You don't know what might have been. You can't play God like that."

He tried to ignore her words. "I don't want absolution from you, Janie. I just want you to know everything about me."

"Why don't you tell me what happened?" she said in a low voice.

Her other hand settled on his chest, and he felt surrounded by warmth. He knew he should move away, but he couldn't force himself to do it.

He wanted to tell her, he realized. He wanted her to know the truth. All of it. So he took a deep breath.

"I grew up in Albuquerque and married Amber when we were both too young. I was twenty-one, and she was nineteen. We were in lust and thought we knew what we wanted, but of course we didn't. For a while, everything was fine. We partied a lot, had a lot of fun and didn't think too much about tomorrow. But then Amber got pregnant."

He remembered the day she had told him the news. "She was scared and upset. She didn't want kids, at least not so soon. But I was thrilled. From the moment I knew, I really wanted that baby.

"Things were never the same after that. We still went out, but I insisted that we come home early so Amber could get her sleep. And I wouldn't let her drink. I read everything I could about pregnancy, and all the books said a pregnant woman shouldn't drink." He stared into the beam of the flashlight. "Maybe that's where I went wrong. Maybe I should have let her have a couple of beers, like she wanted."

"You did the right thing," Janie said fiercely. "Alcohol can really damage a developing baby, even just a couple of beers."

He held her hand more tightly, but he didn't look at her. "After Robbie was born, Amber changed. She got restless and moody. She didn't like being tied down to a baby who depended on her. I took care of Robbie when I was home, but I had to work during the day. We got through the first year, and things seemed to get better. Then she started to nag me about money.

"With a baby in the house, money was tight. Robbie needed formula, diapers, clothes, medicine, you name it. I didn't mind, but I guess Amber resented that, too. There wasn't enough money to go out and party the way we used to do. And to be honest, I didn't want to go out. I was happy to stay at home with the baby. But Amber thought we needed more money, so I got a second job. I was a social worker, so I took a job working at a nursing home at night. The money was good, but I didn't see much of Robbie. I told myself that I was doing it for him. If his mother was happy, he would be happy."

He swallowed and stared at the wall of the cave, trying to push away the memories that flooded him. But they wouldn't go back into their hiding places.

"What happened?" Janie whispered.

"Amber started drinking. Heavily. And I didn't realize it, because I was never home. When I was home, I was either sleeping or playing with Robbie. My relationship with Amber disintegrated. And it's my fault. I let it die."

"It wasn't just your fault, Ben. It sounds like Amber made her own choices." Her voice was fierce in his defense, and he turned to look at her.

"I should have seen what was happening. I should have known about the drinking. She was taking care of my son, for God's sake. I should have paid more attention."

"How did you find out?" Janie asked softly.

"I came home early one day. I quit working at night, because I finally realized that I was running away from our problems. I needed to spend more time with Amber and Robbie. And when I got home, Amber was passed out on the couch. Robbie was watching television."

"What did you do?"

"I insisted that she get help. She wouldn't admit she had a problem, so I packed up Robbie and I left. After I'd been gone for a couple of days, she panicked and promised to do anything I wanted her to do. So I enrolled her in a program, and she stayed the whole thirty days. When she got out, she swore she would never take another drink. And she swore things would change in our marriage."

"But they didn't, did they?" Janie said quietly.

"For a while things were better. I was home in the evening, and Amber tried to make things work. But I guess she really wasn't cut out to be a mother. Taking care of a three-year-old is hard work. Eventually she started drinking again. But she was smarter about it this time. She hid the bottles and used breath mints to hide the smell.

"It took a while, but eventually I figured out what was going on. She swore she would stop, and for a while she did. But it didn't last long."

He wanted to block the rest of the story from his mind. He wasn't sure if he could bear reliving it again. Then Janie took his face between her hands. "You don't have to tell me the rest. I can see how much it hurts just to think about it."

Her words gave him a burst of strength. "I want to tell you, Janie. You need to know. One evening she picked me up from work because my car was in the shop. It had been raining, and the roads were slick. And she was driving too slowly. So I asked her if she'd been drinking again."

Once again he was back in the car, the angry words spilling out, the air filled with accusations, justification. He could smell the rain, the musty car, his baby's tears. "She denied it, but by that time I was an expert on drunkenness. I told her to pull over, to let me drive, but by that time she was so angry that she refused. She just kept going. So at the next stoplight, I got out of the car and opened the back door. I was going to take Robbie and catch a cab home. But before I could get him out of his car seat, the light turned green and she started to drive. I was thrown out of the car and she sped off. I flagged down a police car, but it was too late. She was gone.

"Two hours later the police came to the house. She'd been going too fast and skidded on a curve. The car rolled over twice and smashed into a light pole. Amber and Robbie were killed instantly."

"Oh, Ben." Janie wrapped her arms around him and

held him close. For a moment, he allowed himself to accept her comfort, allowed her sympathy to surround him. Then he freed himself and set her gently away from him.

"I shouldn't have lost my temper. I should have stayed in the car and tried to reason with Amber. If I had, they would both be alive today."

"Or you would be dead." Her words were blunt. "How can you blame yourself for what happened? Amber made the choice to drink. And she made the choice to drive while she was drunk. You're not responsible for that."

"I am responsible for making her angry enough to drive recklessly."

"Hindsight is always perfect, Ben." Her voice gentled. "It's always easy to know what you should have done. Your son's death must have nearly destroyed you. I have no idea of how awful that must have been, and I can only imagine your pain. But you can't keep punishing yourself. You did everything you could to protect him."

"If I'd done everything I could to protect him, he'd still be alive today." The grief and guilt remained lodged in his heart, a ball of ice that refused to melt. "Robbie would have been nine, a little older than Rafael."

"You couldn't save Robbie, but you're going to save Rafael. Surely that counts for something."

"He isn't saved yet."

"But he will be." Janie's voice was fierce, and she turned so that she faced him. "You're going to save Rafael, Ben. He's going to grow up in Cameron, surrounded by people who love him. Doesn't that count for something?"

He wanted to take the lifeline she offered, take the absolution and free himself of the guilt that always dragged at him. But he couldn't allow himself to do that. He couldn't allow himself to forget about Robbie, and what he had done. "Rafael isn't Robbie. Just because I'm helping him doesn't mean that I can forget about my son."

"Of course you can't forget about your son. He'll always have a place in your heart. But it should be filled with good memories, not pain. You have to stop feeling guilty about his death, and start celebrating his life. You can remember the good times you had with him, and the joy he brought to you. He wouldn't have wanted you to lock yourself away from the world because he was gone."

"I'm not locking myself away from the world. I'm a police officer. You can't get much more connected to the world than that."

The look she gave him was full of pity. "You help people every day, but you don't allow yourself to get involved with any of them. Now I understand why you're so insistent that you don't love Rafael. Do you think that if you admit that you love him, you'll somehow be loving your son less?"

"You don't understand," he muttered.

"Then explain it to me."

He sighed. "Janie, I don't do relationships. I can't. I destroyed the two most important people in my life, and it happened because I didn't understand how to reach my wife. And because I didn't understand how to handle her, my son died, too. Now do you understand why I can't take a chance like that again?"

"So you're afraid that anyone you get close to is going to start drinking, then kill themselves by driving drunk?" Her voice held only polite inquiry.

He ran his hand through his hair. "Of course not. But you deserve someone who is whole, someone who can give you everything you need. I'm not sure if I'll ever be whole again."

"You're exactly what I need, Ben. Can't you see that? And what about Rafael? If you have nothing inside you to give, why did you take him in? Why are you trying to adopt him?''

"Because he wants me," Ben muttered. "I don't know why, but it's clear that he feels safe with me. And as long as that's true, I'm going to keep him with me."

"He loves you, Ben. And you love him."

"I represent stability to Rafael. And that's good enough for me."

Janie sighed and rested her head against his chest again. And in spite of his vows, he wrapped his arms around her. "I'm just going to have to keep telling you until you believe me," Janie said. "Rafael is a smart boy. He knows a good thing when he sees it. And he loves you."

What about you, Janie? The thought came from somewhere deep inside him, and it shocked him speechless. He didn't want Janie to love him. He needed her help to adopt Rafael, and he wanted to help her get free of the threat that hovered over her. But he didn't want her to love him. And he didn't want to love her.

A part of him warned that it was already too late, but he refused to listen. "I took advantage of you," he said, deliberately shoving away any thoughts of a future together. "I should have told you about Amber and Robbie before we made love. Hell, I should have told you before we got married."

"Do you think it would have made a difference?" She sat up and looked at him again, and the expression in her eyes was so tender that he couldn't bear to look at her. "Did you think that if you told me about your wife and son, it would change how I felt about you?" Her eyes blazed fire at him. "If so, you don't know me very well, Ben Jackson."

"I know you better than you think," he murmured, and with a flash of shame he knew it was true. He'd known how she would react when he told her his story. Wasn't that why he'd told her? Hadn't some part of him, deep inside, wanted to hear her tell him that it wasn't his fault?

"Maybe you do. But you don't want to know me, do you?" she said, her voice low and tender in the semidarkness of the cave. "You don't want to need anyone, because you feel safer that way. But I'm not going anywhere, Ben. I'm going to be standing next to you and Rafael on the day of the hearing, and I'm going to be there for all the days before and after the hearing. You can't scare me off."

A huge bubble of joy swelled inside him before he could stop it. By some miracle, Janie still wanted him. And like a man dying of thirst, he would take the water she offered. It didn't matter that he knew he had no right to take it. He couldn't give her the love she needed—anything that resembled love had died inside of him a long time ago. But he hungered for her like he'd never hungered before. It would take a man far stronger than him to turn her away.

She pulled him close in a fierce embrace, and he closed his eyes and held on tightly. She fit against him perfectly, matched him perfectly. And he wanted her more now than he had that afternoon.

"I should turn out the flashlight," he said, trying to move away from Janie.

"No!" Her voice was fierce. "I want to see you when we make love. I want you to see me, and know I'm here with you."

Desire and heat shot through him, making him ache with need. "Believe me, Janie, I'll know you're here."

"If you can't see me, you can pretend it doesn't matter. I want you to know that it matters," she answered him. She let him go and sat up, the silver blanket slipping from her shoulders. Her gaze never wavered from his face as she began to unbutton the flannel shirt she wore.

When the shirt fell to the floor of the cave, she pulled her T-shirt over her head and tossed that aside. But when her fingers fumbled with the clasp of her bra, he reached out and pushed her hands away.

"Let me," he said. Her skin was soft and warm, and the scent of her filled the air around him. When her breasts spilled into his hands, he closed his eyes as desire ripped through him.

He wanted to plunge into her, to claim her and brand her as his. He wanted his mark on her, so that any other man who looked at her would know she belonged to him.

He waited until he was sure he could control himself, then he bent his head to taste her. When he took one nipple into his mouth, she shuddered and gasped as she clutched his arms.

He lowered her to the floor without taking his mouth off her. She writhed beneath him, wrapping her legs around his and arching up to meet him. When he felt himself begin to shake, he eased away from her.

"You deserve more than the cold floor of a cave," he said, watching her in the dim light that etched shadows on the walls.

Her eyes were heavy-lidded, but she managed to open them. Her smile was sultry and full of promises. "We can make love anytime in a bed. But you're not going to get me up into this cave again. So if you have fantasies about making love in a cave, it's now or never, Ben."

Chapter 14

Janie opened her eyes to find a dim light suffusing the cave. She was lying on Ben's chest, her head pillowed on his shoulder. They had made love until they were both too exhausted to move, then fallen asleep tangled together. Ben must have shifted her on top of him while they slept.

She closed her eyes again, inhaling the subtle smell of his soap and the musky scent of their lovemaking. They would have to face reality soon, but right now she wanted nothing more than to stay here with Ben, enjoying the closeness and the intimacy. She wanted nothing to mar the memories of last night. She knew that as soon as Ben woke up, they would leave the cave and begin another cat and mouse game through the mountains.

"Good morning." Ben's voice rasped in her ear, and she turned her head so she could kiss his neck.

"Good morning to you."

He eased her away from him, then sat up and reached for his shirt. "We need to get moving, Janie."

For a moment she was disappointed. She wanted to grab back the intimacy, the closeness, the sense of timelessness they'd had the night before. But she knew that Ben was focused on her safety, and that meant leaving the cave. So she nodded. "I know."

He studied her for a moment, then suddenly pulled her close for a long, deep kiss. "Hold that thought until we're safe again," he said, brushing the hair away from her face.

She nodded again, a lump growing in her throat. "I will." He wouldn't say anything more, but he didn't need to. She had seen the look in his eyes, felt the tenderness in his kiss.

Trying to hide her reaction to his kiss, she looked around the cave for her clothes, then fumbled to pull them on in the small space. "Funny," she said, trying to make her voice cheerful. "This cave seemed a lot bigger last night."

"A lot of things were different last night." Ben pulled the phone out of his pack. "I'm going to take a look around. If I don't see anyone, I'll call Devlin and find out what's going on at the cabin."

Janie threw her clothes on as she listened to Ben. There was complete silence from around the corner, and when she had finished dressing she crawled around to look at him. He was lying perfectly still on the floor of the cave, surveying the area below them.

Janie eased her way back into the small room that had sheltered them and leaned against the wall, waiting. She felt more alive than she ever had, and more aware of her body. Her muscles tingled and there was a pleasant soreness between her legs. She grinned to herself. She was going to have to stay in better shape.

After what seemed like a very long time, she heard Ben's voice, talking to Devlin. She couldn't make out the words, but she knew that he and Dev would know what to do.

"Ready to go?" Ben slid next to her and dropped a quick kiss on her mouth.

"What did the sheriff say?"

"The guy isn't at the cabin. Dev and the deputies are going to start circling the lake. He wanted us to stay here, but I told him we were going to move. If your murderer finds us in the cave, we won't have a chance. I'd rather be in the open. The odds are more in our favor that way."

"We still have to get down from the cave without him seeing us." She hadn't wanted to think about climbing down that rock face.

"We'll get down, and you'll be fine." Ben sounded completely confident. "I have a plan."

"What's that?"

He took her hand in his and twined their fingers together. "I've gotten a lot of people out of these mountains. Some of them were a lot higher than we are now. And I haven't lost one of them."

"I trust you, Ben," she interrupted. "That's not the issue. I believe that whatever you've decided will work. I just want to know what it is, then do it, as quickly as possible."

He looked at her for a moment, then bent to kiss her. "You really are remarkable, Janie." Their mouths clung together for a moment, then Ben pulled away. Her heart lifted when she felt his reluctance.

"All right, then, this is what we're going to do. You're going down first. I tried to think of a way to avoid that, but I don't think we have a choice. And once you're down, it will take me less than a minute to join you. So I think you'll be safe."

"Believe me, I'd rather go first than be stranded in this cave by myself," she said fervently. "I'm just afraid I'm going to freeze on you again. If I'm stuck on the cliff, I'll be a target. And so will you.''

Ben reached into his pack and pulled out a length of rope. "You're not going to have to worry about that. All you have to do is keep yourself from banging into the rock. I'm going to tie this rope around you and lower you down.''

She eyed the rope with trepidation. "Are you sure that rope will hold me?''

"It'll hold someone twice as big as you.''

He gathered their belongings quickly and replaced them in his backpack, then tied the rope around her waist. "There are other, fancier ways of doing this, but it's not that far to the bottom of the cliff. This will work just fine.''

Then he looped the rope around an outcropping of rock and pulled up the slack. "Are you ready?''

"As ready as I'll ever be." Janie moistened her lips and glanced at the edge of the cave. All she could see was the lake in the distance and the blue of the sky. "What do I do?''

"Go down facing the rock. Basically, you're going to slide down the cliff and use your hands and feet to keep from smashing into it. It'll take about twenty seconds and you'll be at the bottom. And don't look down.''

"Don't worry," she muttered. She looked around the cave, trying to make sure they had everything, until she realized she was stalling. "Okay, I'm ready.''

"Back out the door, then let yourself begin to slide. I won't let you fall.''

"I know you won't." She leaned over to kiss him again, then moved toward the entrance to the cave. When her feet dangled in the air, she took a deep breath and slid off the edge.

For one sickening moment, she felt herself falling. Then the rope caught and tightened around her waist. She was suspended in the air, and she scrambled for a place to put her feet.

As soon as she was braced against the rock, Ben released more of the rope and she slid a few inches down. "Are you all right?" His voice was barely above a whisper.

"I'm fine." She spoke equally softly, and he lowered her some more.

Her hands scraped against the rocks, and her boots scrabbled for a hold, then she slid some more. Before she realized it, she was on the ground.

The next instant, Ben appeared in the entrance to the cave and tossed the rope down, then he scrambled down the cliff face. He made it look easy as he practically leaped from one tiny crevice to another. As soon as he hit the ground, he pulled her toward a jumble of mesquite bushes and boulders, dragging her into a crack between two large rocks.

She opened her mouth to ask him something, but he held up his hand, demanding silence. The only sound was the whisper of the rope as Ben coiled it in his hands, then replaced it in his pack.

They sat wedged between the rocks for what felt like a long time. The sun crept higher in the sky, soaking into her and warming the dark flannel of her shirt. When she glanced over at Ben, she saw he wore a look of complete concentration.

Finally he bent closer to her. "I think it's safe to move now," he whispered. "I haven't heard a thing. My guess is that our stalker left when he realized we weren't coming back to the house."

"What are we going to do?" Janie stretched her legs, loosening her cramped muscles.

"We're going to circle around the lake and come out

behind the house. We should meet up with Dev at some point.''

"Do you think the killer is just waiting for us somewhere else?" Janie asked. "I can't believe he'd give up this easily.''

"He might be. But Dev or his men should find him, if he is.''

"Unless he finds us first," she muttered. "Why don't we just wait here and let the sheriff find him?''

"Anytime we're in one spot, we're vulnerable. I want to keep moving. And I'd rather not retrace our route from yesterday. He's probably already seen our tracks. So we'll just continue around the lake.''

"All right." She pushed herself away from the rock and crouched beside him. "Tell me what to do.''

He hesitated for a moment, then said, "Thank you for trusting me.''

"Always." She glanced around at the cliffs towering above them, listened to the quiet lapping of the lake against the rocks. "If anyone can get us out of this, you can.''

Heat filled his eyes for a moment, and he started to say something. Then he closed his mouth and nodded. "I'm going to go first. Stay as close to me as possible. And try to make as little noise as you can.''

They began walking through the scrub and the rock debris. Janie moved her feet carefully, trying not to kick any of the slabs of rock that had fallen from the cliffs. Every time her foot connected with a piece of debris, the sound echoed like a shot in the still air.

They had hiked for about fifteen minutes when Ben held up his hand once again, then led her behind a large rock. "Be as quiet as you can," he breathed into her ear. "I thought I heard something.''

She sat motionless behind the rock, beginning to sweat

in the flannel shirt. The sun was higher in the sky, and its heat reflected off the slope next to them and the boulders that tumbled crazily down to the lake. Ben crouched next to her, tension quivering off him. They sat still and quiet for a long time, then Ben nodded.

"I didn't hear anything else. We might as well keep going."

He stepped out from behind the boulder, and Janie moved close behind him. Suddenly a gunshot exploded into the air and a piece of rock flew past their heads.

Ben yanked Janie down and pulled her back behind the boulder. As soon as they were behind the rock, she reached for him.

"Are you all right?" she whispered frantically. "Are you hurt?"

"I'm fine." His voice was grim as he ran his hands over her. "How about you? Did that rock hit you?"

"No. I'm fine, too." Fear held her paralyzed. "How could he find us?"

"He did just what I expected him to do." Ben's voice was full of self-loathing. "He just anticipated what we would do and moved a little closer."

"Do you think he saw us climbing down from the cave?"

"It's possible. If he had, he could have watched us and saw what direction we were going, then picked his spot to wait."

"What do we do now?" Janie tried to keep the despair out of her voice.

"You're going to stay right here. I'm going to try and circle around, using the boulders for cover. I'll try and come up behind him."

"He has a gun, Ben! What do you think you can do?"

"Surprise him." Ben slipped a deadly looking knife out of his pack, then set the pack on the ground. "With any luck at all, he'll be watching for you and won't notice me.''

He leaned over and kissed her. She tasted his determination and strength, and it steadied her. ''Come back to me, Ben.''

''I will.'' He touched her face once, then slipped away.

Janie strained to listen, but Ben made no sound as he moved from boulder to boulder. She tried to watch for him, but could see nothing on the rocks above her but a quick flutter of shadows.

Praying for Ben's protection, she stared at the bleak cliffs above her as if by watching for Ben she could insure his safety. Her eyes began to water, but she refused to look away.

Suddenly she saw a flash of light to her right, and she eased around the rock until she had a clear view of the boulder field. The light flashed again, and the long barrel of a rifle appeared between two rocks.

She wanted to yell, but fear swallowed the sound in her throat. She watched, horrified, as the rifle moved slowly away from her, and she realized that the man holding the gun had seen Ben and was trying to get a clear shot at him.

She didn't even think as she jumped to her feet. ''You up there with the gun! What are you doing?''

The muzzle of the gun faltered, then swung down in her direction. The man holding the gun remained hidden as a gunshot exploded again. It struck the rock in front of her with a high-pitched whine and a slice of the rock flew into the air.

Janie's stomach clenched with fear and her whole body shook, but she forced herself to call out, ''You don't want him. He has nothing to do with you. I'm the one who can identify you.''

The only answer was another gunshot. But it was at her

again, not toward Ben, and Janie gathered herself to move. "Come down here and get me. You don't need to hurt any other innocent people."

She was being foolish, she knew. Clearly the man above her wouldn't hesitate to kill anyone, innocent or not. But she needed to keep him distracted. She stared up at the rocks again, but still couldn't see Ben.

The man above her didn't answer, didn't move. So she picked up a handful of pebbles and threw them as far as she could to her right, away from the direction Ben had gone.

Another gunshot split the silence of the mountains. Then she heard the man above her mutter a vicious curse. He fired two shots in the other direction, then she heard the rocks begin to slide. He was moving.

He was heading down the cliff, in her direction. Maybe he couldn't see Ben anymore! She prayed that was true as the murderer slid down the slope toward her. She risked a glance around the boulder and saw a dark-haired man far above her, moving carefully down the slope.

Without thinking she moved away from the boulder, heading up the hill in the opposite direction Ben had gone. Her only thought was to draw the murderer away from Ben. She scrambled from one boulder to another, using them for cover, grabbing at rocks, ripping her fingernails and scraping her palms. She refused to think about how high she was, refused to look down. All she could think about was luring the killer away from Ben.

He was gaining on her. He had spotted her moving from boulder to boulder and was getting closer. But he had apparently forgotten about Ben, and that was all that mattered.

Suddenly she heard a thud behind her, and she turned to look. Ben and the stranger were tangled together on the ground, and the killer was trying to turn his rifle around and point it at Ben.

Janie scrambled as fast as she could over the rocks, bouncing off one boulder, sliding partway down the cliff then lunging for another. By the time she reached the two men, Ben had managed to knock the rifle out of the other man's hand. When he saw her, he yelled, "Pick up the gun, Janie."

She reached for it tentatively, as if it were a snake that could bite her. When she had it in her hands, she carefully pointed it away from the two men.

Then all she could do was watch helplessly as they rolled around the rocks in a silent but frighteningly vicious fight. Both men were fighting for their lives. Janie picked up a rock, but she was afraid she'd hit Ben instead of the other man. So she circled around them, watching for an opening, waiting for a chance to use the rock.

She saw Ben's hand scrabbling on the ground, then his hand closed around a sharp piece of rock. He brought up his hand and hit the man twice in the side of the head. The man slowly crumpled to the ground, and Ben hit him once more before jumping to his feet and running over to her.

"Janie, are you all right?" he said.

"I'm fine," she said shakily. "Shouldn't we tie him up, or something?"

"Give me your shirt."

She pulled off the flannel shirt and handed it to him. In a moment he'd torn it into strips and tied the killer's hands and feet together. Then he turned to her again and pulled her into his arms.

"Oh, God, Janie. When I heard you yelling at the guy, I just about died. Why did you do it?"

"He had seen you, Ben. I saw a flash of metal, and saw that he was pointing the gun in your direction. I had to do something to distract him."

"You could have been killed." He held her tightly against him, as if he would never let her go.

"He *would* have killed you if I hadn't yelled. I didn't have a choice."

His arms tightened around her, and she melted into his embrace. They were both alive, and the man who had haunted her dreams for three years was no longer a threat.

"Janie, do you realize what you did?" There was awe in Ben's voice.

"I didn't do anything," she protested.

"You ran up that cliff without hesitating." His arms tightened. "Don't look down. Keep looking at me. How did you do it?"

"I couldn't think about the height," she said simply. "I didn't have a choice."

I would have done a lot more than run up a hill to save you, she added silently.

Ben held her for another moment, knowing he would relive the nightmare over and over again. He would never forget the sight of Janie, scrambling up the cliff. He had been frozen for a moment, knowing that at any moment she would remember where she was and freeze. And the man chasing her would catch her.

Finally, when he could bear to let her go, he moved away and cleared his throat. He had to get a grip on himself. "Let's get a look at your mystery man," he said. He rolled the man over with his boot, and saw a handsome, striking man.

He saw the bewilderment in Janie's face as she stared at him. "He looks familiar to me, but I'm not sure why. I have no idea who he is."

"We'll find out soon enough."

Ben reached for the man's pockets, but stopped when he heard a shout from below.

"You all right up there, Ben?"

It was Devlin, the sheriff. "We're both fine," he called down. "We've got a package for you, though. Something to keep you and the other deputies busy."

He waited, his arm around Janie, as Devlin scrambled up the slope. There were two men behind him. "What happened, Ben?"

"He must have seen us coming down the cliff this morning, because he was waiting for us as we walked back to the cabin. I tried to circle around and come up behind him, but apparently he saw me. Janie distracted him and I finally was able to grab him."

"Do you know the guy, Janie?" Devlin turned to her.

She shook her head. "He looks familiar, but I don't know who he is."

"We'll find that out." The sheriff looked behind him at his two deputies. "All right, get the cuffs on this character. And make sure he doesn't have any other weapons."

Ben watched as Dev and the other deputies secured the man, then searched him. Then they pulled him to his feet.

"He doesn't have any identification," Dev said grimly. He gave the man his Miranda warning, then started him walking with a hand on his back. "Let's go."

"No identification? I find that very interesting," Ben said.

The man glared at Devlin, but didn't say a thing. "Who are you?" Ben asked.

He didn't answer.

"What were you doing up here with a rifle?" he continued.

Ben didn't think he would answer, but after a long time he said, "I was hunting."

Ben started to ask him another question, but Janie stumbled next to him. He tightened his grip on her hand and looked over at her.

Her face was sheet white, and her eyes were dark pools of horror as she stared at the man in the handcuffs.

Chapter 15

"What's wrong?" he asked sharply.

"It's him," she whispered. "His voice. I recognize his voice."

The man in the handcuffs flinched, but Ben paid no attention. "Are you sure?"

"Absolutely. I didn't see his face, but I'll never forget that voice."

Ben nodded. "Dev will get his fingerprints when he gets him into the office, and we'll call the cops in Chicago, let them know what's going on. If he's ever been printed before, we'll know who he is real fast. Then we can figure out why he wanted to kill you."

"He wanted to kill me because I knew he was the other man in the greenhouse when my boss was killed." Her face was pale, but she stared at the man in the cuffs. "He was the one giving the orders."

They'd reached the path that led to the cabin, and they began walking more quickly. When they passed the cabin, Dev stopped them.

He ordered one of his deputies to get the evidence kit from his Blazer and secure the scene. He turned to look at the man in custody. "If nothing else, we have him for attempted murder. He's not going to be going anywhere for a long time. Except maybe into custody in Chicago."

Dev guided the suspect into the back seat of the truck, then put one hand on Ben's arm. "Why don't you follow us down to the house? Rafael heard what was going on, and he's scared."

"We'll be right behind you."

They rode back to the ranch in silence, but he held on to Janie's hand the whole way. She still looked white and shaken. The house was in sight when he said, "It's all over now. He's been caught, and you don't have to be afraid, ever again."

"It won't be over until he's in prison. He must be a powerful man, and they have a way of making things work to their advantage."

"Not here in Utah," he said, picking up her hand and kissing it. "If nothing else, he'll spend a long time in a Utah prison for attempted murder."

When they got to the ranch, Shea and Jesse and Rafael, along with Carly, were waiting for them on the porch. They all ran toward the cars.

"Ben?" Rafael's voice was thin with fear, and Ben reached down and swung him into his arms.

"Here I am, buddy. And here's Janie. We're both fine, and we caught the man who was scaring Janie." He swung Rafael around and pointed toward Devlin's car. "See? There he is. The sheriff is going to take him to jail."

Rafael clung to Ben as he studied the man who sat in the car. Gradually his arms loosened. "Did he shoot a gun at you?"

"Yeah, he did, but he didn't hit us. All he hit was a bunch of rocks."

"Did you shoot at him?"

"I didn't have a gun. So I hit him with a rock instead."

Rafael gave the man one last look, then he turned back at Ben. "You have blood on you. And so does Janie."

He reached up and touched a tender spot on his head. He'd hit a rock, he remembered, while he was rolling around with the suspect. "Yeah, but we're both tough. A little blood wasn't going to slow us down."

Janie came over and touched Rafael's arm. "I cut my hands on the rocks," she said, showing him her scratched and bloodied palms. "But I'm not really hurt."

"Is he really going to jail?" Rafael finally asked.

"Yep. The sheriff is going to lock him up. Would you like to go see for yourself, maybe tomorrow?"

Rafael nodded, then looked back at Ben. "Does this mean you don't have to go away again?"

A lump swelled in Ben's throat. "You bet. The next time we go away, you'll come with us. Okay?"

The boy looked from Ben to Janie, then began to smile. "Okay. Do you want to see what I taught Buster while you were gone?"

"I'd love to see what you taught Buster."

As Rafael raced away to get the dog, Janie moved closer and took his hand. "I think he's going to be fine." He heard the wonder in her voice.

"He just needed to know that we were all right, and that the man who wanted to hurt us was caught. I suspect that wasn't the case in San Rafael."

Before she could answer, Shea and Carly came running over to them. "Janie, Ben, are you all right?"

Ben watched as Janie reassured the two women, then Shea asked, "Who was it, anyway?"

"I don't know who he is, but he's involved in a murder in Chicago. It's a long story, which I'll tell you later."

They both looked over at the car, where the murderer

sat in the back seat, and Carly drew in a sharp breath. "I know who that is," she said.

"Who?" All three of them spoke at once.

"Let me get a closer look." She walked over to the truck and stared in the window. When she walked back to them, her face had a strange expression.

"That's Edward Turnbull. He's running for governor of Illinois."

"How did you know that?" Janie asked.

Carly's face turned pink. "I've always been a news junkie. And I have a good memory for faces. Turnbull has been in the news magazines a lot lately. He's running an aggressive campaign."

"I know that name," Janie said thoughtfully.

"Are you from Illinois originally?" Carly asked.

Janie glanced over at Ben, and he took her hand again. "It doesn't matter anymore, does it?"

"I guess it doesn't." She turned back to Carly. "Yes," she said, and she began to smile. "I'm from Illinois. Chicago, in fact."

"Then I'm not surprised he looked familiar. He was a Chicago alderman for a long time, then he decided he wanted to run for governor. Why on earth was a man who's running for a high political office chasing you through the mountains with a gun?"

"Because I was a witness to a murder he committed. Oh, he didn't actually pull the trigger, but he stood there and watched while someone else carried out his orders. No wonder he wanted me dead."

Carly looked stunned for a moment, then she slowly smiled. "Hot damn. I know what I'm going to be doing tonight. *Focus* is going to be eating out of my hand to get this story."

But suddenly her smile faded, and she turned white. Devlin leaped forward to wrap his arm around her and lead her into the house. Janie started to go after her, but Shea grinned at her.

"They're all right. They'll be back out in a minute. Carly's not going to let a little thing like morning sickness stop her from getting this story into *Focus*."

"Morning sickness?" Ben said blankly.

Shea's smile faded. "Shoot. I've spoiled their surprise. I forgot you were up at the cabin when Dev and Carly told us their news."

As soon as they reappeared, Janie hurried over to them, hugging Carly and asking her when the baby was due. Ben watched Carly beaming with happiness as she answered. He could barely force himself to look at Dev's sappy grin as he remembered the day when Amber had told him she was pregnant.

There had been no smiles that day. Amber had thrown only angry tears and ugly words at him, and he still remembered the shock of learning they would soon be parents.

His happiness couldn't dull Amber's resentment, and the eight months before Robbie's birth had passed far too quickly, their house tense with Amber's sullen misery. He would have given anything if Amber had been half as pleased as Carly about her impending motherhood. Ben turned away to look for Rafael, unable to join in the celebration.

A moment later Janie touched his arm. "I think we need to go home," she said quietly.

When he turned to look at her, he saw the understanding in her eyes. He wanted to pull her into his arms and kiss her, hold on to her forever, but instead he nodded. "I'll find Rafael. Dev can get our stuff from the cabin and bring it into town later."

Janie nodded. "I'll tell Shea and Devlin that we're leaving."

* * *

Janie felt like she'd fallen through the rabbit hole. During the next few days her life turned upside down with a speed that bewildered her. When she contacted the witness protection program, her contact told her that she was one of their successes. Since she was certain that the suspect in custody was the man who committed the murder, she had no further need for protection. The man on the phone had told her that he'd be in touch in a few days, but as far as he was concerned, she was back among the living. Just before he said goodbye, he gave her the address and phone number of her sister and niece and nephew.

As she stared at the phone with tears in her eyes, Ben moved to her side. "Why don't you call her?" he said quietly.

She turned to look at him. "I'm almost afraid to. I'm afraid that this is a dream, and that I'll wake up and realize that I still don't even know if they're alive."

He smiled, the first time she'd seen him smile since they'd returned from the Red Rock. "This isn't a dream, Janie. And if you still have any doubts, look out the front window." He gestured toward the street, where several members of the national media were camped out. "Give her a call."

Joy and hope tightened in her chest until she was afraid she would burst with happiness. She picked up the phone and dialed the number she'd written down. Her hand shook so badly that she had trouble punching in the last few numbers.

She could hardly breathe as she listened to the phone ring. Finally someone picked up the receiver. "Hello?"

It was her sister's voice. Janie's throat swelled and she had to swallow twice before she could say, "Amy? This is Mary Frances."

Over her sister's squeal she heard Ben leave the room.

She turned to look for him, but the back door closed quietly behind him. Then her sister started asking her questions, and she allowed herself to be swept into the conversation. But she wondered where Ben had gone, even as she caught up on three years worth of news about her sister and her family.

Ben didn't come back for three hours. Janie paced in the house, reluctant to leave and face the cameras that waited for her, but anxious to know where he'd gone. Finally the back door opened, and Ben walked in with Rafael, who'd gone out to the Red Rock with Devlin that morning.

"There you are," she said with relief.

Ben looked over at her. "You weren't worried, were you?"

"Not exactly. I just wondered where you'd gone."

"I picked Rafael up from Shea's and then took him down to the office." Ben looked over at the boy, and his expression softened. "I promised him he could see Turnbull, and so we went and took a look."

"Has he said anything yet?" Janie asked.

"Not a word. But we got the fingerprints back from Chicago, and they're a match. So there's no doubt that he's Edward Turnbull, candidate for governor. His lawyer is screaming about false arrest, but we've got an airtight case against him. I talked to the police in Chicago. Apparently there were some rumors going around that Turnbull had accepted a lot of bribes in his days as an alderman. Their guess is that when he decided to run for governor, he figured he'd have to eliminate anyone who'd given him a bribe. Your boss probably had to pay him off to get city business. And now that he was aiming for the big time, he didn't want to be susceptible to blackmail." His mouth tightened. "They told me there were a few more unsolved murders that were a lot like your boss's. They suspect Turnbull was behind those, too."

"So he won't be getting out of jail?"

"Turnbull won't be going anywhere for a long time."

"Now we can concentrate on more important things," she said.

Ben looked away. "Like the adoption hearing next week."

"That, too," she said. "But I was thinking about our marriage."

Ben glanced toward Rafael's room, where the boy had gone. "Maybe we shouldn't discuss that right now."

"Then when should we discuss it, Ben?"

He shrugged. "I think Rafael has enough to worry about right now. Why add in something else?"

"Our marriage has nothing to do with Rafael. They're separate issues," she said.

"Are they?" He watched her steadily, his face unreadable. "That wasn't our deal."

"Don't you think the deal has changed?" she demanded.

"Has it, Janie?"

An icy fist clutched at her chest, wiping away the joy that had bloomed there. "Don't you think it has?" Her voice was quiet.

He shrugged. "I don't know. Maybe now you don't want it to change." He shoved his hands into his pockets. "Are you going to go visit your sister?"

"I can't leave now. We have the custody hearing next week."

She thought he relaxed slightly. "Good," he muttered.

"Did you think I was going to renege on my part of the bargain?" Her voice rose.

"I didn't know what to think, Janie. You've just been

freed from the prison that your life has been for the past three years. I didn't know what you were going to do."

"I thought you knew me better than that." Shards of pain skewered her heart. "I can't believe you had to ask if I would be here."

He rubbed his hand over his face. "I just wanted to be sure," he muttered. "I know you want to see your sister."

"She's coming to Cameron to visit me. She'll be here in a couple of days." Janie stared at him, not sure what to say, feeling a chasm opening up between them. "Things were so different up at the cabin," she whispered. "Why has everything changed?"

"Your life has changed," he said, his voice harsh. "You need to keep your options open."

Her heart felt like it was crumbling into dust. "I see." She knew she should ask him if he wanted her to go, but she didn't have the courage for that. So she forced a smile on to her face and said, "I don't have time to worry about that right now. We have the custody hearing next week. That's all that's important right now."

She thought it was relief that eased the tightness on his face. "You're right. When we're done, that judge won't have a single doubt about where Rafael should be."

A week later as they stood together in court, watching the judge settle into his chair, Janie prayed that Ben's words were true. Even though the air in the courtroom was warm, she shivered. She knew her hands were trembling, and she laced her fingers together to stop the shaking.

Ben must have sensed her fear, because he reached over and took her hand. It was the first time he'd touched her all week, and she clung to him gratefully, even though she suspected it was only for show. He'd avoided her during the day, and come into their bed after he thought she was asleep at night. But today they had to present a united front.

After stating the facts of the case and giving a history of Ben's involvement with Rafael, the social worker for his case turned to them. "This is really a fairly simple proceeding. The judge needs to decide if you'll make good parents for Rafael. I've already given him my recommendation. Now it's your turn to tell him what you want him to know."

She and Ben had already decided that Ben would be the one to speak, since he had spent far more time with Rafael. Ben stepped forward in the new suit he'd bought for their wedding. He cleared his throat and said, "Thank you for the opportunity to address you, Your Honor."

He waited for a moment, then he said, "Rafael means more to me than anyone in the world, with the possible exception of my wife." He quickly told the story of how he'd met Rafael when he'd found him in the mountains, and how the boy had become attached to him. He told the judge honestly that he hadn't planned on adopting a child, but that he hadn't been able to resist Rafael.

"It didn't take me long to realize that Rafael needed me. For some reason, he trusted me. He felt safe with me. And he's becoming a vital part of the town of Cameron."

He described Rafael's success in school, all the new friends that he was making, the way the boy was opening up to the people around him. "I think that it would harm Rafael to be taken away from Janie and me and placed with another family. But that's not the main reason we want to adopt him."

Janie heard Ben swallow in the quiet courtroom. "Janie and I want to adopt him because we both love him. We can't imagine being a family without Rafael. The three of us *are* a family now, and if you took him away, you would destroy all of us." Ben turned to look at her. "Janie and

I married only recently, but I know she cares just as deeply for Rafael as I do. And Rafael loves her, too.''

The judge pushed his glasses up his nose. "I'm glad you brought that up, because I want to ask you about your marriage. The timing seemed suspicious. Did you marry only to provide the appearance of a stable home for the boy?''

"No, Your Honor." Ben's answer was instantaneous. "I know the timing seems very coincidental, but Janie and I have known each other for three years. It took me that long to convince her to marry me. She had reasons for not wanting to marry.''

"Hmm." The judge looked down his nose at her. "I've heard about your recent adventures. Is this the reason you didn't marry sooner, Mrs. Jackson?''

"Yes, it is, Your Honor. I didn't feel it was fair to put Ben in possible danger.''

"Yet you finally decided to marry, anyway?''

"Ben convinced me that the danger wasn't as acute as I'd feared. And he also felt that he could protect me, if the need arose.''

"Which he did.''

"Yes." She looked over at Ben, who had turned to look at her as she spoke. "He saved my life.''

She knew her feelings were written on her face as she remembered their stay in the mountains. They had faced danger, but their time together was unbearably precious to her, and she would never forget what they had shared. Ben's expression softened as he watched her, and she could see the matching flame leap in his eyes. Then the judge spoke again.

"Ahem. Yes. I don't think I have any more questions about your marriage." He turned back to Ben. "What do you plan to do with the boy?''

"We plan to love him," Ben said simply. "We plan to

raise him and guide him to adulthood, to the best of our ability. And we hope to eventually heal the pain inside of him.''

''He hasn't told you anything about what happened to him in San Rafael?''

''He hasn't told anyone. He hasn't even told us his real name.''

''But you think he will?''

''Yes, I do. He just needs time, and lots of love.''

The judge leaned back in his chair and studied Ben for a long moment, then turned his gaze on her. Janie wanted to shout at him, to tell him that no one could love Rafael as much as she and Ben did, but she bit her lip and returned his gaze as calmly as she could.

Finally he nodded. ''I already have the social worker's report. I'll have a recommendation for you in a week or so.'' He banged his gavel and walked out of the room.

She and Ben hurried from the courtroom. When they were outside, Ben slowed down and took a deep breath. ''I didn't know we'd have to wait a week.''

Janie took his hand. He didn't flinch away from her, and she held on tightly. ''He'll approve the adoption. How could he not?''

''Anything could happen.'' He scowled at her. ''Should we call your sister and make sure everything is all right?''

''Why don't we just go home? I'm sure they're fine. Rafael has been getting along great with Amy and her kids in the past few days.''

They got into the car for the hour-long drive back to Cameron, and neither of them said anything for a long time. Finally Ben said, ''You've been enjoying your sister's visit.'' His voice was neutral.

''Of course I have. I wasn't sure I'd ever see her again.'' Her voice softened. ''I can't believe how much her kids have grown. Beth was a baby when I left, and now she's in kindergarten. And Cal was a little boy. Now he's a year older than Rafael." She smiled as she thought of the two boys. "I never imagined I'd see them playing together."

"You and your sister talked a lot about the past. I didn't realize how much you missed being a landscape designer." Again, Ben's voice was carefully neutral.

"I miss growing the flowers, watching the seeds turn into plants. I miss getting my hands dirty and watching new life come from the soil. But I have big plans for landscaping the house."

She thought he tensed, but he didn't say anything for a few minutes. Finally he said, "Are you going back to Chicago with your sister?"

She swiveled around in her seat, astonished at the question. "Why would I do that?"

"That is your home," he said stiffly.

"Cameron is my home. It has been for the past three years. I have a business here, and I thought I had a family here. I have no desire to go back to Chicago. Why would you even think I did?"

"Because you can't be a landscape designer in Cameron. You can barely grow anything in our desert dirt."

"My life isn't about being a landscape designer anymore, Ben. I loved my job in Chicago, but my life has changed. And I have no intention of going back."

He was silent for a few moments. Then he said, "Then what are your plans?"

Janie's heart shriveled in her chest. "If you have to ask, then I guess it doesn't matter."

"What's that supposed to mean?"

Was he being deliberately obtuse? "I thought we had a real marriage, Ben. I thought everything changed up on the mountain." She stopped, racked by pain. "At least it did for me. I thought you lo…cared for me." She couldn't bring herself to say that she loved him. She was certain he didn't want to hear that.

"What happened between us up on the mountain was stress and fear." His voice was harsh, and she couldn't force herself to look at him. She didn't want to see what she feared would be in his face. "You can't make a dream grow from a moment of illusion."

It wasn't an illusion for me. She longed to say the words, but instead turned to look out the window. She didn't want him to see the tears that gathered in her eyes.

"How do you know it wasn't real?" she finally whispered.

He turned into their driveway and turned off the engine, but made no move to get out of the car. Instead, he turned to face her. "Fear does funny things to your emotions," he said. "It can make you believe all kinds of things that turn out not to be true. It distorts everything."

"What did it make you feel, Ben?" she asked.

He scowled at her. "It made me remember not to believe in illusions. Because they can be shattered in an instant."

He got out of the car and walked toward the house. Janie slowly followed him, her heart aching, wondering how to convince Ben that they had something worth believing in. Something worth fighting for.

Before they reached the door, Rafael came flying out of the house. Tears had left tracks down his face, and Janie saw the terror in his eyes.

They both ran toward him, but Ben reached him first. He swept the boy into his embrace, and Rafael's thin arms clung to his neck.

"What's wrong, buddy?" Ben's voice was low and soothing.

Sobs tore from Rafael's throat, harsh and primitive. It was the first time he had cried, she realized. His arms tightened around Ben's neck, and he buried his face in Ben's shoulder.

Ben shot her a worried look, and she wrapped her arms around Rafael, too. "Whatever it is, we can fix, Rafael," she said.

"No, you can't." He clung more tightly to Ben. "I can't live here anymore, can I?"

Chapter 16

Ben sat down heavily on the front porch, still holding tightly to Rafael. "What do you mean?" he whispered.

"The lady at the park told me," the boy hiccuped through his sobs. "She said you were talking to a man today about whether I could stay with you. That means that maybe I can't stay."

Ben had deliberately not said anything to Rafael about the adoption hearing. He'd known the boy would worry, and it wouldn't have changed anything. Now a murderous rage began to grow inside him at the unknown woman from the park.

The front door of the house banged again, and Janie's sister Amy came running out of the house. "Thank God you're back. I'm so sorry, Ben, Janie. That stupid woman told him before I could stop her."

Janie laid her hand on her sister's arm. "What exactly happened, Amy?"

"We were at the park. The kids were playing, and someone came up and started a conversation with me. I don't know who she is." She sighed. "I don't think she meant any harm. I think she was just trying to be nice to Rafael. When he came over to ask me when you'd be back, she said he must be very excited about what was happening today. When he asked her why, she said that when you got back, you'd know if the two of you could adopt Rafael."

The fear and worry that were never far from his mind when he thought about Rafael came surging back. Would he be able to reassure the boy? Would he say the right things? His failure to save Robbie's life was never far from his mind.

Slowly he eased Rafael away from his shoulder so he could look at him. "Are you afraid, Rafael?" he asked softly.

The boy nodded.

"I'm afraid, too. It's true that we went to a judge today and asked to adopt you. But the judge didn't give us an answer. It'll take a while before we know for sure." His arms tightened convulsively around the child. "But you won't be leaving, Rafael. You're my son. And you're staying with us."

Ben knew he was being rash. He knew he was taking a chance. But the lost, terrified look on Rafael's face was more than he could bear.

"What if the judge says I can't stay with you?"

"Then we'll talk to another judge. And if he says no, we'll talk to another one after that. We'll keep talking to judges until there aren't any left."

"And then what happens?"

"Then you'll be old enough to decide for yourself where you want to live."

"I want to live with you, Ben. And Janie."

He didn't dare look over at Janie. "Then that's where you'll stay."

Rafael's lip began to tremble. "That's not what the lady said."

"She didn't know what she was talking about." Ben hoped his voice was firm enough. "I do."

Rafael watched him for a moment, then nodded. "Okay." He sniffed once, then slid off Ben's lap. "I want to go play with Cal again."

"He's inside," Amy said, and held open the door. Rafael disappeared into the house.

The three adults were silent for a moment. Then Amy said, "I'll go keep an eye on the kids." She went inside, leaving him alone with Janie once more.

He didn't want to be alone with Janie. He was having a hard enough time staying away from her. If he spent any time alone with her, he was afraid he would get down on his knees and beg her to stay. And he owed her far too much to ask that of her.

A real marriage had never been part of their deal. Janie was free for the first time in three years, and he didn't have the right to ask her to stay with him and Rafael. No matter how much he wanted to ask.

Janie was grateful to him for helping her escape Turnbull, and the sex had been mind-blowing. But that was all it was, and she'd realize it in a few months. So it was better that he let her go now. The longer she stayed, the more his heart would ache when she left.

He ignored the voice inside him that mocked his words, that told him it didn't matter if Janie left now or in a month. She'd take his heart with her, no matter when she left.

Mary Frances. She hadn't even told him her real name. When he'd heard her talking to her sister, he'd felt like a knife had stabbed through his chest. Mary Frances wasn't anyone who would stay in Cameron, or with him. Mary Frances had better things to do with her life.

"What are we going to do about Rafael?" Janie asked quietly.

He glanced over at her, then quickly looked away. She looked as sick at heart as he felt. "Just what I told him. If the judge says we can't adopt him, we'll appeal. And we'll keep appealing until he's old enough to be allowed a say in where he lives. I'm not giving him up."

She sank down on the step next to him. "I was hoping you'd say that. But I don't think it will come to that. I think the judge will approve our petition."

"That's wishful thinking." He couldn't keep the harsh edge out of his voice. He couldn't bear to let the hope trickle into his heart.

"I don't think so." She turned to him and finally smiled. "I didn't say much at the hearing, but I watched the judge. He'll approve us."

"I'm glad you're so optimistic," he muttered.

"It was so clear how much you love him," she said gently. "No one could miss it. And I'm sure the social worker knows how attached Rafael is to you."

"Bad things happen, Janie," he whispered. "Sometimes for no reason at all. We both know that. I can't afford to hope."

"Then I'll do the hoping for both of us." She reached out to touch his arm, then pulled back her hand at the last minute. "Rafael belongs with you, Ben. And everyone, from the judge to the social worker, will see that."

"We'll find out in a week, won't we?"

She leaned against the house and gave him a serene smile. "In a week you'll find out that I was right." She stood up and said, "I'm going to check on Rafael. Why don't we take him on a picnic this afternoon?"

"What about your sister?"

"Amy will be fine by herself." Janie grinned suddenly, and his heart turned over in his chest. "She can go down to Heaven for dinner. I've got to drum up business somehow."

Rafael enjoyed the picnic, but it was hell for Ben. They went into the mountains, staying away from the Red Rock. There were too many memories there. Every time he watched Janie with Rafael, he wanted to beg her to stay. And every time she glanced over at him, he remembered everything they had shared the last time they were in the mountains.

Janie had said she wanted to stay, but he was afraid it was her gratitude speaking. And he would never keep her with him because of gratitude. So he watched her play with Rafael, watched her smile and laugh and run, and felt his heart contracting in his chest.

He had hungered for her before she'd been free, wanted her when she was still imprisoned in her fear and dread. Now she was a different woman, open and laughing, allowing herself to show the caring, loving side of her nature. And all the barriers in his heart tumbled to her feet.

The irony wasn't lost on him. When she'd been living in fear, she was bound to him with the chains of that fear. Now, when she was free to do whatever she wanted, she was also free to leave him. And he was powerless to stop her.

He wouldn't stop her, even if he could. He owed her too much. And he was too afraid that Janie's sense of obligation would keep her with him.

So he watched Janie and Rafael, refusing to listen to his heart. His heart told him they could be a family like this forever, but he was afraid to believe it. Afraid that if he reached out to grasp happiness, it would be snatched away from him.

"It's about time to head back to town," he finally said. "You have school tomorrow, buddy."

"Just a few more minutes?" Rafael pleaded.

The whine in Rafael's voice brought a smile to Janie's face, which she quickly hid. Ben felt his heart twist in his chest. Rafael was acting like a normal child in a normal family. How many times had Robbie begged for just a few more minutes? "Two minutes," he said. "Then we have to go."

A grin split Rafael's face, then he and Janie headed for the cliffs. As far as Ben could tell, he was reenacting the night that Ben had found him in the mountains. A night that had changed his life.

An hour later Rafael and Amy's kids were in bed and the three adults sat in the living room. Wordlessly, Ben thanked God for Amy's presence. It masked some of the tension that simmered between him and Janie. Then Amy turned to face Janie.

"The kids and I are going home tomorrow."

"It seems like you just got here," Janie protested.

Amy reached over and squeezed her hand. "I know. But now we can visit any time. You and Ben have to concentrate on Rafael. Whatever happens with the adoption hearing, it's going to be an emotional week for all of you. You need to be a family without worrying about guests."

"We'll come and visit you." Janie leaned forward. "Are you moving back to Chicago?"

Slowly Amy shook her head. "I don't think so. We all like St. Louis. We've made friends, and I like my job there." She flashed a smile. "And we're closer to Utah."

Her words shot a tiny pain through Ben's chest. Janie might not be in Utah for much longer. Then Amy spoke again.

"What about you? Are you going to open up a land-scape design business?"

Janie shook her head. "No, Heaven on Seventh is all I can handle." A wistful look crossed her face. "Although I may build a greenhouse one day."

"A greenhouse in the desert?" Amy laughed. "Isn't that like growing orchids in the Arctic?"

"Not at all. With a greenhouse, I could control the humidity and grow a lot of plants that wouldn't make it in Cameron." She shrugged. "But that's a long way off. I don't have the time or money right now."

Ben watched the disappointment flicker across Janie's face, then disappear. An idea slowly took hold, and he silently blessed Amy for her question.

Amy gave them a pointed look. "Are you two going to bed so I can get some sleep?" She gestured to the couch, which pulled out into a bed. "You're sitting on my bed."

Ben caught Janie's almost imperceptible stiffening, but he tried to ignore it. "We'll get out of your way, Amy." He searched for an excuse to leave the house until Janie was asleep, but couldn't find one. Devlin had given him the day off, and there was no excuse to go down to the office. And it was past closing time for Heaven on Seventh, so he couldn't make an excuse to close up Janie's restaurant, either.

Janie stood and looked over at him. "Ready, Ben?"

No, he wasn't ready. But he stood up anyway. "Good night, Amy."

"'Night, Ben." She looked over at Janie and grinned. "'Night, sis. Sleep tight."

"What did she mean by that smirk?" he demanded as soon as the bedroom door closed behind him and Janie.

She gave him a weary smile. "Don't pay any attention to Amy. She's hopelessly romantic. She's noticed that we've been avoiding going to bed at the same time, and she's trying to throw us together.''

"You go ahead and go to sleep. I'll read for a while," he said stiffly.

"Don't be ridiculous, Ben. It's not as if we haven't slept together before this. You're dead tired." She gave him a weary, defeated look. "Don't worry. I can control myself."

But could he? Ever since they'd come back from the mountains, he had avoided going to bed at the same time as Janie. He was afraid he'd reach for her, spinning one more tie that would bind her to him. And, God forbid, what if she got pregnant? He couldn't bear to picture Janie desperate and trapped in a pregnancy she didn't want.

"Go ahead and get ready for bed." He looked around for the book he'd been reading, desperate for any distraction. By the time he joined her, he hoped she'd be sound asleep.

He lingered as long as possible, then slipped into the bed as silently as he could. She was motionless on the far edge of the mattress, but she wasn't sleeping. Tension pulsed from her, rolling over him in waves. The air between them crackled with it.

He ached to pull her against him, to hold her tightly and feel her fall asleep in his arms. Hell, he ached to do a lot more than that. But he was determined to do the right thing by Janie, the honorable thing. And the right thing wasn't making love to her again. The right thing was giving her the space she needed to make a decision.

So he closed his eyes and tried to ignore the tension. But it was a long time before he finally relaxed into sleep.

The next morning, Janie woke stiff and uncomfortable. She'd clung to the edge of the bed, afraid to make any contact at all with Ben. She didn't want to feel him flinch away from her, like he'd done a couple of nights ago.

Amy and Beth and Cal were leaving today, she thought with a wisp of relief. As much as she loved her sister, she was glad they were leaving. She and Ben wouldn't be able to work anything out as long as they had guests staying in the house. And she didn't want anyone around when they heard the decision from the judge.

She managed to keep up a cheerful front until they waved goodbye to Amy as she drove off in her rental car. When the sedan disappeared around the corner, Janie slumped back against the railing of the porch.

"Thank goodness they're gone."

Ben spun around to stare at her. "I thought you were enjoying Amy's visit."

"I was. I *had* to see them. Until last week, I didn't even know if she and the kids were still alive. But now we need to be alone."

She felt Ben's sudden tension. "Why is that, Janie?"

"Because of Rafael, of course." She turned to stare at him. "Don't you think the next week is going to be hard for him?"

"Yeah," he muttered. "I didn't think you were talking about Rafael."

She took a deep breath. "Maybe we should talk about us. Rafael is in school, and they're not expecting me down at the restaurant. You're working the afternoon shift, so we have plenty of time to get things hashed out."

"Is that what you want to do, hash things out?"

"It would be better than the tension that's been sucking all the air out of the house," she retorted.

"Fine. What happens if the judge says we can't adopt Rafael?"

"Then we appeal, just like you said yesterday." Her answer was immediate.

"That means that you're stuck in this marriage for an indefinite length of time."

Janie's heart felt like it stopped for a moment, then it started again with a swift, painful surge. "Is that what you think? That I'm stuck in this marriage?"

"That was our deal," he answered, his voice stiff.

She should tell him how she felt. Now was the time to tell him that she wanted to stay in this marriage forever, that she wasn't looking for a way out. But she couldn't bring herself to say the words. She saw the fear on Ben's face, and she knew how he felt about being married again. She didn't want Ben to feel obligated to stay married. Because a marriage of obligation was the worst hell she could imagine.

She couldn't tell him that she loved him. She couldn't trap him like that. Ben was an honorable man. And he would do the honorable thing. He wouldn't divorce her, wouldn't leave her. And both of them would slowly wither and die. He would smother under the weight of her hopes. And she would shrivel into a bitter woman in a loveless, sterile marriage.

"I guess we need to wait until we find out what the judge has to say." But she knew what the judge was going to say. He was going to approve their petition to adopt Rafael. She had seen it in his eyes. "In the meantime, we need to make sure Rafael knows that we love him."

The coldness gradually faded from Ben's eyes. "That's not going to be hard."

"At least now you'll admit that you love him." She couldn't stop herself from pointing that out to him. She'd thought it was a good sign, when he'd talked about his love for Rafael at the hearing. But it didn't seem to have spilled over into the rest of Ben's life.

"He needs for me to love him. I saw that when we came

down the mountain after we caught Turnbull. He needed me then, and I realized that I needed him.''

"Thank goodness for that. I saw from the very beginning that you loved him.''

"You've seen a lot from the beginning, haven't you, Janie?" He finally looked at her, and she saw a spark of warmth in his eyes. He could afford it, she told herself harshly. She'd made it clear she wasn't going to press him to stay married to her.

"Yes. I may not have interacted with a lot of people in Cameron over the past three years, but I watched everything. It's amazing what you can learn by watching.''

"What are you going to do now?"

"You mean with the restaurant?"

He nodded.

"The same thing I've always done." She shrugged and looked out into the yard, then swallowed the lump in her throat. She had had such wonderful plans for landscaping the yard of this house. "The new cook Jim West is working out great, so I won't have to be there every minute that the restaurant is open. I'll have more free time. And now that I don't have to worry about Turnbull, I'll spend it getting to know my neighbors.''

"What about what your sister said about a landscape design business?"

She shrugged. "I'll see how Jim works out in the long-term. I still don't think I'll have the time to do both." When she'd told Amy she didn't have time for another business, she'd still been hoping that she'd have a family to care for. Now maybe she'd want another business to fill all the empty hours.

"Are you going to build a greenhouse?"

She forced a smile on to her face. "That was a pipe dream, Ben. I don't have the money for a greenhouse. And

I don't have the time to build one, either. Amy was right, I guess. A greenhouse in the desert would be foolish.''

He leaned against the railing and stared into the distance. ''How are we going to get through the next week?'' She saw the agony on his face and wasn't sure if he'd meant to speak out loud.

''Just like we've gotten through the past weeks.'' Her heart contracted as she saw his fear of losing Rafael. ''We stick to our schedule, work, help Rafael with his homework, and pretend like nothing is different. That's the best thing we can do for him.''

''Thank God for your strength, Janie.'' Again, she wasn't sure if she was supposed to hear his words.

''I'm drawing my strength from you. He's all you've cared about from the beginning. You've made huge sacrifices for him, in order to keep him. You don't know how that humbles me.''

''They weren't all sacrifices,'' he said, turning to her again.

The week flew by, and every day that passed ratcheted up Ben's fear and apprehension. Surely, if the answer was yes, they would have heard by now. He couldn't bear to say anything to Janie, but he saw his fear echoed in her eyes. By the time a week had passed, the tension in the house was at an almost unbearable level.

Ten days after the hearing, the doorbell rang just as they were finishing dinner. When he opened the door and saw Rafael's social worker, he froze. For a moment he wanted to slam the door closed, to lock it and pretend she wasn't there. He'd never had Janie's optimism that the court would approve their petition. But he couldn't delay the inevitable, so he opened the door and stepped aside so the social worker could enter.

Janie came into the room and saw the social worker.

Her face paled, but she said, "Let me take Rafael over to the neighbor's. I'll be right back."

Ben stiffly offered the woman coffee, and when she refused, they sat in a tense silence until Janie slipped into the room. She sat close to him on the couch, and he reached for her hand without thinking. She twined her fingers with his and held on. Her hand felt as cold as the lump in his chest.

Slowly the woman smiled. "Your petition to adopt the minor child known as Rafael, no last name, has been approved. There will be a six-month waiting period, and you'll be subject to random, unannounced home visits during that time, but that's a formality. We'll see you in court in six months for final approval."

Janie gripped Ben's hand tightly. Ben felt tears gathering in his throat and swallowed hard to dislodge them. Rafael was officially their child. No one could take him away. He was safe in Cameron.

The social worker stood up. "I imagine you'll want to tell your son as soon as possible, so I'll be on my way," she said briskly. Then she gave them a smile filled with genuine warmth. "I want you to know that I'm personally thrilled with the outcome of this case. The boy belongs with you."

She slipped out the door, and there was silence in the house for a long moment. Then Janie turned to him and wrapped her arms around him.

"You did it, Ben," she whispered. "You won. Rafael is yours now."

He tightened his arms around her. "*We* won, Janie. It wouldn't have happened without you. And he's not just mine. He's ours."

Chapter 17

Janie trembled in his arms for a moment, then she pulled away. Her eyes were glittering with unshed tears, but a smile trembled on her mouth. "I'll go get him so we can tell him the good news."

Moments later she was back with Rafael. The boy looked at him with uncertain eyes, and Janie urged him forward. "Ben has something he wants to tell you," she said gently.

Rafael stepped into the circle of his arm, and Ben swept him onto his lap. "We have good news, buddy. The judge said we can adopt you. So we're officially your parents now, and you're our son. You're never going to have to leave us."

Rafael smiled, his face radiant with joy. "Never, ever?" he whispered.

"Never. You can't get away now."

The boy threw his arms around Ben's neck and hugged him tightly. Ben buried his face in Rafael's hair and inhaled deeply, the familiar scent filling him with love. Rafael was already his son, but now it was official.

Rafael turned to Janie and hugged her, then he drew back and looked at them, a worried look on his face. "What do I call you now?" he asked.

"What do you want to call us, Rafael?" Janie asked gently.

"You're my parents now, aren't you?" he whispered.

"Absolutely." Ben tightened his arm around the boy.

"Then could I call you Mom and Dad?"

Ben was speechless for a moment as his throat tightened again. Finally he was able to say, "We would like that, son."

"And what will my name be?" the boy asked.

"Rafael Jackson. How do you like the sound of that?"

Rafael ducked his head and fiddled with a button on Ben's shirt. He didn't say anything for a long time. Finally he said, "I like that. But Rafael's not my real name."

Ben held his breath. "Do you want to tell us your real name, son?"

Rafael nodded, then took a trembling breath. "My real name is Alejandro Fuertes."

Janie slid closer and took Rafael's hand. "That's a lovely name. Do you want us to call you Alejandro?"

Rafael shook his head vigorously. "No. I want my name to be Rafael Jackson."

"Then that's what it'll be." Ben felt Rafael relax slightly in his lap. Pulling him closer, he said softly, "Do you want to tell us about what happened in San Rafael?"

For a moment the boy froze. Then slowly he nodded.

"You don't have to tell us, Rafael," Janie said. "It's not going to change anything."

"I want to." The boy's voice was barely above a whisper. "The soldiers came to my house. They asked my papa about my uncle, and they were yelling. Then they killed my mama and my papa and my sister. They were looking for me." Ben felt the boy's tears soaking into his shirt, and he smoothed one hand over his head.

"But you got away," he murmured.

"I hid. There was a place in the wall where my papa kept his money. It was very small, and I was almost too big to fit. But when she heard the soldiers coming, my mama pushed me into the space and told me to be very quiet. Mama hid my sister in a different place, but the soldiers found her."

Ben looked at Janie, horrified by the child's story. He saw sympathy and a fierce protectiveness in her eyes as she stroked the boy's hand. "You were very brave, Rafael."

"I stayed hidden for a long time." He began to cry again. "The leader of the soldiers was yelling at the other ones, telling them to find me. They were in my house for a long time, then they finally left. I was afraid to come out."

"Not only were you brave, you were smart." Ben kissed Rafael's tear-stained cheek. "How did you get to Cameron?"

"When I came out of the hiding place, I ran to my neighbor's house and told her what happened. She was afraid, too. But she told me I had to find a man named Miguel and how to find him. I was scared to go back into my house, but I was more scared to leave." He clutched at Ben's shirt. "I took my mama's shawl, and my sister's hair comb, and my papa's shaving mug. And I took a piece of the blanket that was on my bed. Then I looked for Miguel. It took a long time, but I found him. Miguel brought me to the house near Shea and Jesse."

"And now you're here with us. You'll be safe in Cameron, Rafael. No one will hurt you here."

"I know." The boy drooped against him, and Ben realized that telling his story had taken an emotional toll on him.

He leaned back and held the boy, murmuring to him and stroking his back until Rafael relaxed. He carried him into his bedroom and tucked him into his bed. When he returned to the living room, Janie's eyes still reflected her shock and horror at Rafael's story.

"Is he asleep?"

Ben nodded. "He didn't move when I put him to bed." He shoved his hands into his pockets. "What can we do?"

"We can't do anything about what happened in San Rafael. We can only thank God that he was smart enough to get out of the country." Janie looked thoughtful. "I think the leader of the rebels was named Fuertes. I wonder if Rafael's father was a relative. We can do some checking and find out. Rafael will probably want to know about his family when he gets older."

Ben nodded, still numbed by the horrors Rafael had confided. "I know a therapist in St. George. When he's ready, Rafael should probably see her."

"He'll need to talk to a therapist to work through his grief and his guilt," Janie agreed. "I'm glad you know someone."

He wanted to gather Janie close, to ease the pain in her eyes, but he didn't dare. He was afraid that one touch, one taste of her would shatter his self-control. He ached to hold her again, to feel her responsiveness when he kissed her.

So he stepped back and said gruffly, "It's been a long day. I'll go down to Heaven and make sure that Jim gets it closed. Go on to bed."

Janie watched him with sad resignation in her eyes. "Good night, Ben."

She turned and walked into their bedroom and quietly closed the door. He wanted to follow her, wanted to have the right to lay her down and make love to her all night.

But he couldn't.

He'd vowed to give her the space she needed to make a decision about her future. Now that Rafael's future was assured, Janie could decide what she wanted to do.

But there would be nothing wrong with giving her an incentive to stay in Cameron, he thought suddenly. He stood in the living room and thought about the idea that had just occurred to him. No, there would be nothing wrong with making Cameron a little more attractive to Janie.

He turned and hurried out of the house, but for the first time since he'd heard her identify herself as Mary Frances, some of the chill began to thaw.

Janie woke up the next morning to find that Ben had already disappeared. And he'd taken Rafael with him. On this bright and sunny Saturday, the quiet of the house grated on her nerves. She felt like an intruder wandering around the empty rooms. Ben had left a note, saying that he'd taken Rafael on an errand, and she wondered when they'd be back.

When she realized she was sitting at the kitchen table, holding the note and staring at nothing, she told herself sharply not to be an idiot. She got ready for work and went down to Heaven on Seventh.

Everybody, from the waitresses to her new cook, wanted to rehash the events that had taken place in the last couple of weeks. Her first instinct was to run and hide in the kitchen, but then she realized she never had to hide again. So instead she sat down with a mug of coffee and spent the morning talking to her neighbors.

By the time she got home, Ben and Rafael had returned. Rafael came bounding out of the house.

"Hi, Mom."

Her heart turned over in her chest and she hugged him tightly. "Hi, yourself. Where have you been?"

He gave her a wide grin, and she didn't see any of the shadows that had filled his eyes the night before. Was it really that easy to banish the ghosts? She didn't think so, but apparently Rafael had a good start.

"I can't tell you. Dad says it's a secret."

Dad. She swallowed once, hard, as Rafael grinned at her happily. Then Ben came out the door.

"How're you doing, Dad?" she asked him.

His eyes softened and lingered on Rafael. "Still having a hard time believing it's true." Then he looked at her. "Where did you go this morning?"

"Down to Heaven. I wanted to see how things were going."

"And is everything going smoothly?"

"Too smoothly," she said ruefully. "I'm not sure I need to go back."

"You're the heart of that restaurant, Janie. Things will start to fall apart without you."

"How about you?" she asked. "I asked Rafael where you were, and he said it was a secret." She couldn't quite hide the hurt in her voice.

He ruffled Rafael's hair. "I told him it was a surprise, not a secret."

"Oh." She wasn't sure what to say, but apparently there was some father-son bonding going on. So she plastered a smile on her face and said, "What are we going to do for the rest of the day?"

"Rafael and I have some plans, don't we, buddy?" Ben said.

Rafael nodded vigorously. "We have things to do."

"Okay," Janie said after a moment. "I guess I'll go back to the restaurant. It's about time I got back to work."

She hadn't been able to make her voice casual enough. Ben looked over at her. "Is something wrong?"

"Of course not." She swallowed. "You and Rafael need to spend some time together. Come on over to the restaurant for dinner."

"We'll see you there."

They went into the house together, giggling and whispering, and Janie felt like a door had just been shut in her face. She stared at the house for a moment, fighting the urge to run inside and break down the barriers that Ben had erected around his heart. But instead she turned and headed back to Heaven on Seventh. She wouldn't have a confrontation with Ben in front of Rafael.

There wasn't any time to talk to Ben during the next week, either. When he wasn't working, he was with Rafael. And when he wasn't working or with Rafael, he disappeared, sometimes for hours.

Her heart ached. He seemed to be doing everything he could to avoid her. They hadn't even had a real conversation since they'd found out they could adopt Rafael. Janie was beginning to think that she had been deceiving herself, that she hadn't seen caring and love in Ben's eyes. Maybe she should have believed him when he told her that theirs would never be more than a marriage of convenience.

Her pride urged her to leave, to wrap the remains of her dignity around her and move back to her own house. But she couldn't do that. Rafael's trust was too tentative, too new to do anything that might shatter it. She might not be a wife to Ben, but she could be a mother to Rafael.

She wasn't sure how long she could stay in the house, living with Ben, and not break. She needed to talk to him, to ask him point-blank what he wanted her to do, but he seemed to be avoiding her. He was certainly not giving her any opportunities for a frank discussion.

Finally, Saturday evening, she knew she couldn't take it any longer. She felt brittle, as if the slightest touch would shatter her. When Rafael went to bed, she and Ben were going to talk.

But when she got home from the restaurant, neither Ben nor Rafael was in the house. There was no note, nothing that would explain their absence. Desolate tears filled her eyes and swelled in her throat, and she buried her face in her hands and let herself cry.

After a long time her sobs trailed off and, drained and empty, she stumbled into her bedroom and curled up on top of the quilt. She would talk to Ben when he got home, she told herself, but the emotional storm had exhausted her. She fell into a restless sleep haunted by wrenching dreams.

When she woke the next morning, she found that Ben had tucked her into the bed and carefully covered her with the blankets. She rolled over, but his side of the bed was empty. Hurrying through the house, she found that Ben and Rafael had already left.

Instead of the tears of the night before, anger began to stir. Was Ben running away because he didn't have the nerve to face her and tell her how he felt? Was he trying to drive her away?

She stared out the window at the barren yard surrounding the house, the yard that she'd had such plans for. She'd had big plans for their marriage, too, she thought. She'd already given up on the yard. Was she going to give up on their marriage?

"No, I'm not."

Her words were startlingly loud in the empty house, but she didn't care. She moved closer to the window and looked at the red dirt that bordered the house, looked at the clumps of grass that clung to life in the yard. Ben might not want to admit that he felt anything for her, but she wasn't going to let him drive her away.

She would stay and fight for this marriage, fight for Ben's love. Because she did love him, and nothing would ever change that. She could retire in defeat to her own house and live out a sterile existence there, sharing custody of Rafael with Ben, or she could face down Ben's demons and help him drive them away.

Suddenly energized, she threw on some clothes and hurried down to Heaven on Seventh. After checking in with Phyllis and Jim, she hurried home, thinking about what she wanted to say to Ben. When she got there, she found him and Rafael waiting for her.

The boy was practically dancing from foot to foot. "We got a surprise for you," he yelled the minute she walked in the door.

She squatted down to face him. "What kind of surprise?"

"You have to come with us." Rafael beamed at her.

Slowly she stood up and looked at Ben. He watched her carefully, anxious anticipation in his eyes. And underneath it, she thought she saw hope. Her heart began to pound. "What's going on, Ben?"

"Just like Rafael said, it's a surprise. Can you come with us?"

Her heart thudded against her ribs as she nodded, her movements jerky and stiff. "I'm not going into the restaurant today."

Ben seemed to relax a little. "Good. Let's go, then."

They got into Ben's truck, Rafael squeezing into the middle of the bench seat in front. No one said anything as they drove out of town, but she could see that Rafael was bursting to tell her the surprise.

"Does this have anything to do with you two being gone for the last week?" Janie finally asked.

Rafael nodded vigorously. "We worked and worked. And now it's…"

Ben laid his hand on Rafael's leg and shot him a warning glance. "What did we talk about, buddy?"

"We can't blab." He subsided for a moment, then began bouncing on the seat again. "We're almost there," he squeaked.

"We're turning into the Red Rock," Janie said, realizing where they were.

"I needed some land for this surprise," Ben finally said. "Dev and Shea let me use the ranch."

Mystified, Janie watched as Ben drove away from the house and finally pulled into a tiny meadow. There, in the middle of the field, stood a small greenhouse.

"What's that?" she gasped.

Ben made no effort to get out of the truck. "It's for you," he said, watching her. "You said you wanted a greenhouse."

"Come and look, Mom." Rafael tugged at her hand, and she let him pull her out of the truck. She heard Ben right behind them.

Rafael opened the door carefully, and she followed him inside. The greenhouse wasn't big, but there were tables set up at the perfect working height, already filled with rich, black dirt. A watering can and tools were laid out neatly on a workbench.

She felt her eyes swimming with tears as she turned to Ben. "It's wonderful," she whispered. "Why did you do this?"

"I know how much you miss your plants. I wanted to give you something that you loved."

Rafael darted out the door and ran to roll in the leaves that had fallen from the trees. She didn't even glance at him. He would be safe in the tiny meadow. "The greenhouse is perfect. And I love it already."

She looked over at Ben and saw the uncertainty in his eyes, and she saw the hope again. And suddenly she understood.

Ben was a man who had been hurt before, a man who had his love for his family thrown back into his face. He'd vowed never to love again. The greenhouse was his way of saying that he loved her.

She turned to face him. Gathering her courage, she took his hands. "I love the greenhouse, Ben. There isn't anything I wanted more, except you. I love you, Ben. I've loved you for a long time. There will never be anyone but you. You didn't have to build this greenhouse for me. I was never going anywhere."

"You don't know what you're saying, Janie." He gripped her hands. "You have your life back now. You can do anything you want to do. I don't want to tie you down here in Cameron."

"Who says I'd be tied down?" She reached out and touched his cheek, loving the feel of his stubbly beard. "Cameron is my home. You and Rafael are my family. I love you."

He closed his eyes and reached for her. When he pulled her against him, the chill that had filled her for the past week slowly disappeared. "I don't deserve you, Janie. But I love you, too. I never thought I'd say that again. I didn't want to fall in love, but you're everything I want."

"I've wanted you ever since that night we spent together five months ago. But I was afraid for you, so I stayed away."

"And I was afraid of my feelings for you. I didn't want to need you. But I did."

He bent his head to kiss her, and passion flared between them. She hungered to taste him, to touch him, to join her body with his. His hands clenched on her hips, pulling her closer, and she arched into him. He trailed his mouth over her face and her neck, his hand trailing behind, as if he couldn't get enough of her.

He groaned and lifted his head. "I don't know if I can wait until tonight."

"Me, either." She kissed him again, pouring her heart and soul into the kiss, allowing herself to express all she felt for him. When he kissed her back with an almost desperate desire, she lost herself in his passion.

But Ben pulled away, leaning his forehead against hers. "Rafael is here," he gasped. "If I keep kissing you, I won't be able to stop."

The last shards of doubt disappeared, and she allowed herself to relax against him. "I've missed you so this past week. I wanted you so badly, and you seemed to be pushing me away."

"I was trying to give you time to make your decision. I didn't want to touch you, because I didn't want to influence your decision. And it was too hard not to touch you, so I stayed away." He smiled then, one of his rare smiles that made her quiver inside. "Rafael and I got this greenhouse built in record time."

"You didn't need to build a greenhouse for me." She touched his face. "All you needed to do was ask me to stay."

"I didn't want you to feel trapped. I didn't want you to stay out of obligation, or because of Rafael. I wanted you to stay for me."

"It's always been you, Ben. Couldn't you see that?"

"I was afraid to believe it. And after Turnbull was caught, I thought you'd want to go back to your old life."

"Why would you think that?"

"I overheard you on the phone when you called your sister. Your real name is Mary Frances, but you'd never told me that."

She remembered the phone call, and guilt slivered

through her. "I never told you because I didn't think it mattered. My name is Janie now. Mary Frances is gone. I'm Janie Jackson, and will be until the day I die." She touched his face again. "Is that why you didn't say anything?"

He nodded. "I saw how much you would be giving up to stay here in Cameron. Your family, your profession, your life and your friends in Chicago. I didn't have the right to ask you to stay."

"I'm not giving up anything," she said fiercely. "Everything I want is right here in Cameron, Utah. Don't you understand, Ben? Nothing is more important than how I feel about you. You are my family, and Rafael and any other children we might have. This is my home."

Ben shook his head, wonder in his eyes. "What did I ever do to deserve you?" he whispered. "What miracle brought you into my life?"

She wrapped her arms around him. "I never would have believed that something so wonderful could come out of such pain and ugliness. If it hadn't been for Turnbull, I never would have come to Cameron. I never would have met you."

Ben gave her another slow, tender smile. "I think I already knew, deep down, that I was crazy about you when I asked you to marry me. I knew there would be nothing convenient about marrying you, but I couldn't even imagine being married to anyone else."

"That's why I resisted so much. I knew my feelings for you would get in the way. I knew how hard it would be to keep my distance if we were actually married."

"Tell me again," he said. "I don't think I'll ever get tired of hearing it."

"I love you, Ben." She pressed a kiss against his mouth.

"And I love you. I intend to tell you that, every day of

our lives." He deepened the kiss until everything faded away. Only Ben existed, and nothing mattered but him.

"Can we go home? I'm getting hungry," Rafael's voice jerked her out of the trance.

Ben pressed another kiss on her mouth, then took her hand. "Sounds good to me, buddy. Let's all go home."

* * * * *

**Coming this September 1999
from SILHOUETTE BOOKS
and bestselling author**

RACHEL LEE

CONARD COUNTY:
Boots & Badges

Alicia Dreyfus—a desperate woman on the run—
is about to discover that she *can* come home
again...to Conard County. Along the way she
meets the man of her dreams—and brings together
three other couples, whose love blossoms beneath
the bold Wyoming sky.

Enjoy four complete, **brand-new** stories in one
extraordinary volume.

Available at your favorite retail outlet.

Look us up on-line at: http://www.romance.net   PSCCBB

If you enjoyed what you just read,
then we've got an offer you can't resist!

Take 2 bestselling love stories FREE!

Plus get a FREE surprise gift!

Clip this page and mail it to Silhouette Reader Service™

IN U.S.A.	IN CANADA
3010 Walden Ave.	P.O. Box 609
P.O. Box 1867	Fort Erie, Ontario
Buffalo, N.Y. 14240-1867	L2A 5X3

YES! Please send me 2 free Silhouette Intimate Moments® novels and my free surprise gift. Then send me 6 brand-new novels every month, which I will receive months before they're available in stores. In the U.S.A., bill me at the bargain price of $3.57 plus 25¢ delivery per book and applicable sales tax, if any*. In Canada, bill me at the bargain price of $3.96 plus 25¢ delivery per book and applicable taxes**. That's the complete price and a savings of over 10% off the cover prices—what a great deal! I understand that accepting the 2 free books and gift places me under no obligation ever to buy any books. I can always return a shipment and cancel at any time. Even if I never buy another book from Silhouette, the 2 free books and gift are mine to keep forever. So why not take us up on our invitation. You'll be glad you did!

245 SEN CNFF
345 SEN CNFG

Name	(PLEASE PRINT)	
Address	Apt.#	
City	State/Prov.	Zip/Postal Code

* Terms and prices subject to change without notice. Sales tax applicable in N.Y.
** Canadian residents will be charged applicable provincial taxes and GST.
All orders subject to approval. Offer limited to one per household.
® are registered trademarks of Harlequin Enterprises Limited.

INMOM99   ©1998 Harlequin Enterprises Limited

SILHOUETTE BOOKS
is proud to announce the arrival of

THE BABY OF THE MONTH CLUB:

the latest installment of author
Marie Ferrarella's
popular miniseries.

When pregnant Juliette St. Claire met Gabriel Saldana than she discovered he wasn't the struggling artist he claimed to be. An undercover agent, Gabriel had been sent to Juliette's gallery to nab his prime suspect: Juliette herself. But when he discovered her innocence, would he win back Juliette's heart and convince her that he was the daddy her baby needed?

Don't miss Juliette's induction into
THE BABY OF THE MONTH CLUB
in September 1999.
Available at your favorite retail outlet.

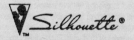

Look us up on-line at: http://www.romance.net   PSBOTMC

THE FORTUNES OF TEXAS

*Membership in this family has its privileges
...and its price.
But what a fortune can't buy,
a true-bred Texas love is sure to bring!*

Coming in October 1999...

The Baby Pursuit

by

LAURIE PAIGE

When the newest Fortune heir was kidnapped, the
prominent family turned to Devin Kincaid to find the
missing baby. The dedicated FBI agent never expected
his investigation might lead him to the altar with
society princess Vanessa Fortune....

THE FORTUNES OF TEXAS continues with
Expecting... In Texas by **Marie Ferrarella**,
available in November 1999 from
Silhouette Books.

Available at your favorite retail outlet.

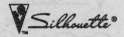

Of all the unforgettable families created by #1 *New York Times* bestselling author

NORA ROBERTS

the Donovans are the most extraordinary. For, along with their irresistible appeal, they've inherited some rather remarkable gifts from their Celtic ancestors.

Coming in November 1999

Enchanted

Available at your favorite retail outlet.

Silhouette®

Visit us at www.romance.net

SIMENCH